Three Days

Felicia Case &
Michael Wojciechowski

Black Rose Writing | Texas

The author grants the final approval for this literary material.

First printing

This is a work of fiction. Names, characters, businesses, places, events, and incidents are either the products of the author's imagination or used in a fictitious manner. Any resemblance to actual persons, living or dead, or actual events is purely coincidental.

ISBN: 978-1-68433-256-4
PUBLISHED BY BLACK ROSE WRITING
www.blackrosewriting.com

Printed in the United States of America
Suggested Retail Price (SRP) $18.95

Three Days is printed in Traditional Arabic

For: Colbyn, Aidan, Kessler, and Bohde

Author's remarks

The genesis of this story began in a frozen yogurt shop. The premise was simple: Felicia would write the odd-numbered chapters from Kadie's perspective, and I would write the even ones from Paul's. The next week Felicia wrote the first chapter and sent it to me. I loved it. I wrote the second chapter and sent it to her. She hated it. (She said Paul was too much like me.) After two more attempts, I got it right. This book is by her and for her. She is greatly missed.

Michael Wojciechowski, 2018

Three Days

Chapter 1

"Damn it," I said under my breath when I realized I wasn't going to have the comfort of a companionless flight. I was very much looking forward to reading my book. I did not want to engage in small talk with a stranger. But to my dismay, seconds before the plane door closed, a frenzied passenger rushed in and found his seat—right next to mine.

I intentionally paid him little attention. I needed to send a clear message right from the start: I am a nontalking flight companion. Sometimes it's just easier to be unfriendly than to find the energy to converse with others.

Besides, not being able to get my book read, and therefore not finding out who is responsible for the murder of Janie, a seemingly innocent suburban wife and mother, who may or may not have been having an affair with her best friend's husband—well, that was unacceptable.

So, I kept my nose in my book and tried my damnedest to *not* acknowledge the man invading my space. I did notice, however, his scent. It wasn't wholly unpleasant. This, unfortunately, *was* a little distracting, despite my resolve to not let him disturb me. At least he didn't stink. Yes, that *would* be worse. I smiled coyly and continued ignoring him.

During takeoff, I found myself staring at his shoes. They were stupid shoes. Neon green sneakers with bright blue shoelaces and the Nike swoosh emblazoned on the side. I assumed, when I glanced in his direction, that he was in his late thirties. Definitely not twenty. Yet, he was wearing some very loud-ass shoes with jeans and a hoodie. Maybe he was in college? A late bloomer? Maybe he lost his luggage and had to wear his younger brother's clothes? Or perhaps his wife packed his clothes, and she's stuck in whatever era neon green shoes were hip? But…I didn't notice a ring, not that I was looking for one. Agh! I shook my head; I was too busy *not* caring about him to care about him. I delved back into my book with renewed focus, annoyed that I'd let a forty-year-old man-child distract me so much.

Maybe he was colorblind? I read somewhere that about 8% of males are colorblind. He must be completely ignorant to the god-awful colors screaming from his feet. Yes, that must be it.

At least he smelled good....

Stop it, Kadie! I again snapped out of my senseless reverie as the pilot came over the speaker to announce that we were now at 35,000 feet and free to move about the cabin (aka—you can pee now). Thank you, Jesus! Not only did I need a distraction from the distraction sitting next to me, I did have to pee. Badly.

This was an inconvenience for a few reasons—the most obvious being the process of navigating my way to the back of the plane, where I would then drop my pants in a six-foot by two-foot wide bathroom closet and squat over the toilet and attempt desperately to keep my pants dry throughout the...elimination process. This is a very difficult feat. One of which I am not fond of. It's basically a port-a-potty blazing through the sky at 500 mph. Not the most stable, or comfortable, peeing situation. Yet, it was an all too often necessary evil for me because of my insatiable need for my first true love: coffee.

Strong and black with two sugars.

I wonder when they're coming by with the coffee?

As I unbuckled my seatbelt, while contemplating the Tyler Durden conundrum of offering my seatmate my ass or crotch while I wiggle my way into the aisle, the man surprised me by standing up to help me pass more comfortably. However, his chivalry only complicated things seeing how I opted for the "crotch" and thus, now that he was standing, we found ourselves face-to-face.

And WAY too close.

So close I could see the blond, day-old scruff on his cheeks close, and his holy-mother-of-god-GREEN-as-hell eyes! They were like a neon-green that matched his shoes, and somehow, they looked into my soul.

I was so startled by this new development that I let out a low grunt-moan thing. (Prior to this situation, I had no idea such noises lived inside of me.) To top it off, this curious noise came out a little louder than I'd have preferred. Well, I'd have *preferred* for it to have never come out at all. But it did, nevertheless, and now I had to pretend as if he hadn't heard it. But, of course, he had.

So here we were, standing close enough for our naughty parts to be touching (thank goodness for clothes), staring into one-another's eyes…and I'm moaning. I'm moaning! God!

"Sorry," he said through a half-grin.

"S'fine," I mumbled before gracelessly shuffling past him and into the aisle toward the potty-closet. It took every ounce of strength not to look back and see if he watched me as I walked toward the bathroom.

Chapter 2

"Just in time," the gate agent said as I handed her my boarding pass. She scanned my ticket and handed it back to me and told me to enjoy my flight. I nodded and made my way down the ramp, towing my carry-on.

I hate being the last one on a flight. The first-class passengers don't pay you much attention. They're too busy doing all the important things people in first-class do—like avoiding eye contact with us lowly serfs who must traverse past the first-class opulence on our way to our cramped coach quarters. The people in coach, my people, make me the most uncomfortable. They stare as I shuffle down the narrow aisle, cautious not to bump anyone with my carry-on. They shoot accusatory stares, asking with cold eyes what took me so long to board.

I kept my head low and muttered apologies as I made my way to my seat. The flight was full, and I thought for a moment that maybe my seat had been assigned to someone on the standby list. That's an encounter I did not want to have.

"Excuse me, sir/ma'am, it appears you're in my seat," I'd mumble apologetically. Then the dejection that would turn to anger as the passenger looked to the flight attendants hoping they had a hidden seat somewhere. No one needed to withstand the embarrassment of de-boarding under the gaze of 170 angry passengers. But luckily, my seat materialized just as I was going over my mental apology to the hypothetical traveler. There it waited. Ready and willing with upright rigidness to accept me into its uncomfortable bosom.

I looked at my seatmate briefly, and then I looked again. There, occupying the seat next to mine, sat a strikingly beautiful woman. She had dark skin and long dark hair that partly concealed her face. Sensing my approach, she glanced up at me and then promptly lowered her head when she caught me staring back at her. Her eyes were blue, sexy, but also cold and indifferent when they met mine for a brief appraisal. Her features were delicate, yet somehow sharpened and smooth at all the right places. She was innocent and seductive, and I sensed she knew she was both. I waited for her to look back at me, if only to take in her features again, but she kept her head lowered, making it clear that she wanted nothing to do with me. She shared the rest of the cabin's disdain for my tardiness. I sighed and began the clumsy process of stowing my bag in the overhead. I opened the small cubby and noticed a Victoria's Secret shopping bag crammed inside. I assumed it was the woman's. I took care not to hit the delicate bag with my own. If it was filled with lingerie and other sexual paraphernalia (which I had decided it was), I wanted to treat it as delicately as the woman to whom the items most certainly belonged. I managed to fit my bag into the compartment and then sat down. I glanced at the woman and followed her gaze all the way to the floor; her eyes were locked onto my shoes.

I was wearing my green Nike's with the blue logo. They were horrendously ugly (albeit comfortable) and did not match any items in my wardrobe. But I didn't care. I got them a month ago. I had taken my seven-year-old nephew, Holden, back-to-school shopping. Holden refused all clothes that were not outfitted with ninja turtles. Even the polo shirt with the small crocodile stitched on the chest did not meet his stringent amphibious standards.

"Crocodiles and turtles aren't the same thing," Holden argued.

"Yeah, but your mom wants you to have some nice clothes for school."

"These are nice," Holden said, holding up t-shirts featuring the awesomely mutated turtles. I didn't argue. It is impossible to win an argument with a seven-year-old. They don't hear logic and sound reasoning; they hear that they aren't getting their way, and therefore conclude that they need to "reason" louder and more vehemently, until they win. Nonetheless, I hid a couple polos in the stack of t-shirts that Holden had deemed appropriate for school and secretly bought them to satisfy his parents.

Not surprisingly, we couldn't find any shoes that fit Holden's strict criteria. He reluctantly settled on a pair of green Nikes. (He loved that the swoosh was blue because his favorite ninja turtle was Leonardo. Seriously, who thinks *Leonardo* is best?) He wasn't thrilled with the shoes until he noticed another pair just like his, only bigger. He insisted I get my own pair, so we could be "twinners."

"Dad wears boring shoes," Holden said. "I want a grownup to have cool shoes like me. Please, Uncle Paulie."

Of course, I caved. Holden could talk me into anything. I even let him call

11

me *Paulie*. I was Paul to everyone else.

Holden called every day after school for a week and asked me which shoes I was wearing. I learned the only acceptable answer was, "The green twinners." This put Holden into a fit of laughter that couldn't be contained.

I wore the shoes proudly every day since I bought them, but now, as I watched the woman next to me staring at my footwear, I wished I had dressed more my age: thirty-seven. I figured she thought I was another stereotypical millennial living in my parents' basement sleeping till noon, eating Hot Pockets, and wearing obtrusive name brand sneakers. I should have nudged her and said, "I wear them to make a seven-year-old happy. Stop judging."

I wanted to say something to her, but I wasn't sure what. If I thought too much about conversation starters, nothing ever sounded authentic, so I usually said nothing. I had to just wing it. Let spontaneity guide me. I opened my mouth to say something but paused when I noticed, resting on the woman's lap, my latest book staring back at me. Just below the title—*Trainride*—was my penname: Kurt McCarthy. Kurt as in Vonnegut and McCarthy as in Cormac. A penname was my idea. When I ran it by Zoe, my agent, she said, "I think it's stupid, but whatever…" and then commenced sending a text message. I liked my penname though. I liked it better than the books the pseudonym was given credit for writing.

The woman picked up her book, my book, and started reading. I saw she was in chapter nineteen, about seven pages from the big reveal. I wondered if she would approve of it. It had divided critics and readers alike, solidifying a solid three-out-of-five-star rating on Amazon and Goodreads. A few called it genius, some said great, most argued it was derivative. It appeared that one of the few things fans and critics agreed on was it wasn't nearly as good as my debut novel. That seemed to be the universal consensus: nothing I had written since my debut novel had been as good as my debut novel.

I decided it best to let the woman read rather than engage her in a conversation she probably didn't want to have. I spied her ring finger as she turned a page and noticed it wasn't weighed down by a commitment to someone else. If this were a novel or a movie, I'd take that as a sign. A sign for what, I wasn't sure. I'd read too many books (and written a few) to know that life, in all its beautiful chaos, should not be lived looking for signs and omens. I was sitting next to a beautiful woman simply because we both needed to go to

Chicago. I was doing a reading there—my first ever—from my latest novel.

I let the woman read and tried to put her out of my mind. I succeeded for about three minutes, and then she stood and motioned that she needed to use the lavatory. I stood to let her out. As she passed, our eyes locked, and I found myself staring stupidly at her with my mouth opened. I quickly closed it and offered an apology, but for what, I couldn't say.

"It's fine," she answered and hastily made her way to the bathroom. I watched her go, staring hypnotically at the curve of her body as she walked away. An older man across the aisle watched me watch her. He nodded approval and smiled. I was embarrassed.

"She's not with me," I explained.

"Not yet," he winked. "It's a long flight."

I leaned closer to the old man. "I don't usually get nervous around people, but this one frightens me. Not sure why."

"It's because you're drawn to her," he explained.

"Is that it?"

"Yep."

I nodded. "Any advice?"

"Women want to be the center of attention," he whispered. "The less you reveal about you, and the more you inquire about her, the better. You'll know she's worth pursuing if you care what she has to say, instead of just nodding at the appropriate moments in hopes of getting laid." The man's wife, seated next to him, hit him in the shoulder. He snickered and turned to her and kissed her on the cheek.

His advice was sage. I took my seat and started playing in my head the conversation we'd have once the woman returned.

Chapter 3

I returned to my seat, this time opting for the ass-angle to mask any residual embarrassment from earlier. As I scooted past, I caught him checking me out. I'd be lying if I said I wasn't flattered. He was easy on the eyes—I had, after all, recently gotten an up close and personal view, so I didn't mind if he was appreciating what he saw. If I can't secretly bask in those moments, then what's the point of all the dieting and exercise I've been doing?

I shifted into a comfortable position in my seat and resumed reading. I was almost finished with the novel, and I was anxious to see how it ended. For the most part, I enjoyed Kurt McCarthy, though this particular book had been unsatisfying. I was hoping for a substance-filled conclusion to help compensate for all the predictability and cheesy one-liners that had littered the rest of the book. But as the ending drew nearer, only disappointment appeared to be on the horizon.

Thirty minutes later I closed the book, still unsatisfied. I pondered the ending. It was *almost* great. McCarthy had been on the brink of achieving the highly sought-after combination of realistic, yet hopeful, conclusion to the complicated love story, but then he just…didn't. The story just fizzled out— like a potential orgasm. Almost there…so close…c'mon, you can see it…just…gotta…concentrate… Shit. It's gone.

And at that moment, I was almost just as disappointed.

I'd usually enjoyed reading Kurt McCarthy because he seemed to be able to find a palatable cocktail of both the real *and* fairytale. His books were often easy to get sucked into when I needed an escape, but also easy for me to move on from once I closed them—except his first novel. That one was definitely on my top ten list. But, his latest book seemed to be lacking more than his others when it came to anything genuine or poignant. It wasn't even in the same league as his debut novel.

I wondered who McCarthy was outside his writing. I pictured a middle-aged playboy driving a yellow sports car. I imagined his thick head of hair (plugs of course), phony smile, and overly tanned skin. He had to be a cliché—that's why he's so fond of using them in his books—so of course, he was also outfitted with facial scruff, tweed jacket, and jeans. I shook my head and scoffed inwardly as I mused at the ridiculousness of my daydreaming.

I retrieved my phone to shoot a quick text to my sister vis-à-vis my final opinion on the novel:

Finished *Trainride* just in time for tonight. Another success—I suppose? It's not as good as his others. Sorry, Sweetie, I know you won't agree with me, but I've never loved him the way you do. We'll talk more at the meeting. See you tonight.

"You're not supposed to text on flights."

What the fu—startled, I turned and looked at my flight companion. He spied me from the corner of his eyes. He pointed to my phone as if to clarify. "You're not supposed to text on planes," he stated again matter-of-factly.

"I *know*," I didn't even attempt to hide my irritation. "I just typed it, so I wouldn't forget. I'll send it when we land." Why was I explaining myself to this stranger?

"You're lying," he said.

"What?"

"You sent it. I saw you."

Wow. Maybe he was the undercover federal agent assigned to the flight. Would an agent wear such atrocious shoes? "So what?" I said. "Will the plane go down now?"

"How bad would you feel if it did?"

He seemed to be teasing me, but it was hard to tell because he refused to look directly at me. Was he being shy, flirty, or just a jerk? He was difficult to read. I scoffed and looked out the window and wondered if I was going to have to keep talking to him now. After a conversation starter of that nature with a stranger on an airplane, do you just regress to ignoring each other for the next ninety minutes? I rolled my eyes. This was why I avoid interacting with other humans. Too much responsibility.

"That text must have been important, huh?" he said with a lopsided half-smile.

I looked at him. *Was* he flirting or genuinely bothered I had sent a text? I wasn't sure.

"I had to tell my sister I finished the book she asked me to read," I explained, confused as to why I was allowing myself to be sucked into a conversation. I've always prided myself in being especially skilled at one-syllable, conversation-killer, responses when strangers attempt to initiate a conversation. One must nip that in the bud before strangers are encouraged to continue trying to converse. It is an art form, really, and I'm a pro.

"What book?"

I held it up. "*Trainride*. McCarthy's new one. You ever read him?"

"Sure," he said. "You like it?"

"Not so much."

"Why not?"

I paused, contemplating if I wanted to explain myself. He looked at me with smoldering eyes. If I were standing, my knees might have buckled. He appeared worth the effort it would take to talk with him.

"It was good enough," I said. "I enjoy his work, for the most part, but...I don't know...he seems to be going downhill. This book was...fine, I guess," I shrugged and ended my thought abruptly.

"What was wrong with it?" he asked.

"It dragged a bit in the middle. I had to push through some of it. And it was littered with clichés. It had glimpses of good writing. It was decent. I'd give it a mild recommendation."

"Well, that's generous of you," he said sharply. Was he being sarcastic? He faced forward again and began flipping through the Sky Mall magazine. I stared at him for a beat, unsure what caused his sudden change in demeanor. *Suite yourself, weirdo.* I discarded my annoyance and put my phone in my bag.

"What would you have done differently?" He closed his magazine and faced me again. Good Lord! He was pretty damn sensitive about my book critique. Had I found a McCarthy fan equal to my sister?

"Have you read this book?" I asked, referring to *Trainride*. He nodded. "Well, what did you think of it?" I asked.

"I want to hear from you first. What was wrong with it?"

I studied him for a moment. I wasn't sure how to answer, and I didn't care enough to think too hard about it. Was I supposed to take it seriously and have some kind of Narrative 101 debate in the middle of a flight? "I don't know…" I said. "Perhaps it was a little melodramatic. Superficial. It just felt…fake in some places."

"It *is* fake. It's fiction," he retorted.

"I know, but I want a story that still feels real…that feels…plausible. Some parts were way too cliché for my tastes." He contemplated what I'd said, and feeling the need to fill the silence, I again attempted to pacify him. "But to each his own. Most people love clichés. They eat 'em up."

"Which parts?"

"Huh?"

"Which parts did you feel were cliché?" he asked.

"Look, we don't need to get into his," I said. "Don't let me ruin it for you." He looked away for a few minutes, staring at the back of the seat in front of him. Was he pouting or just deep in thought? This had become one of my more interesting flight conversations. Though, admittedly, there weren't many others to compete for the top spot. He was peculiar. "It's a decent book. I…it was good enough, really," I offered, breaking the silence with the most genuine and humble expression I could muster.

"You're lying again," he said with a slight smile.

"Yeah, maybe I am," I said. I resigned from the conversation and returned to my previous, and more desirable, plan of passing the flight by self-entertainment. I pulled a magazine from my purse and was soon enveloped in an article about how to use lemon juice to remove stains. Who knew lemon juice was so versatile?

"So why are you headed to Chicago?"

I jumped slightly, startled. My seatmate must have forgiven me for my earlier McCarthy solecism and was ready to converse again.

"I'm heading *back*," I answered. "I live there." I offered a quick smile and returned to my magazine.

"Oh? What were you doing in Arizona?"

"Work?"

"What kind of work?"

I sighed. This was exactly the kind of conversation I didn't want to have.

"Interior design." I know my social cue was to ask him why he was going to Chicago and then feign interest in whatever answer he gave, but I just did not care. I turned the page in my magazine and pretended to read.

"I'm in Chicago for a few days. Three, to be exact. Would you like to go to dinner while I'm there?"

I turned slowly, mouth opened, to face him. "Are you serious?"

"Very."

I was looking straight at him now. He wore a stupid, albeit sexy-as-hell, grin mixed with his accompanying eyes and curly, slightly disheveled blond hair. It all made for a deadly combination that instantly made my pulse quicken. Then the grin dropped, and he was asking: "Sorry, I didn't even think to ask...are you in a relationship? I just saw that you weren't wearing a ring, so I assumed..." he stammered. Now *that* was adorable. I was drawn to him. I sat looking at him, way past the appropriate amount of time.

"You don't even know my name," I pointed out.

"Then tell me."

"No."

"Why?"

"How do I know you're not a rapist?" I questioned, quite fairly.

"You don't, but then again, you don't know that about most people, do you?"

I scoffed, closed my magazine, and then busied myself with my purse, pretending I was looking for something that was very important, like, essential to the continuation of humanity important. I was having a hard time knowing how to respond to this guy. (He'd be throwing me off my game, if I had one.)

He knew I was stalling. He waited patiently for me to rummage through my purse hoping to find my zombie-destroyer apparatus.

I gave up the facade and turned to him. "So, what are you thinking? We go to dinner, fall in love, have a three-day whirlwind romance? Then you head back to wherever you're from—"

"—Arizona."

"Right, Arizona, and I move on with my life, and we both live the rest of our lives with the sweet memory of that beautiful weekend spent with the would-be love of our lives that just didn't work out because..." I took a deep breath and laughed, "...insert your favorite clichéd reason here."

"What if that is *exactly* what happens?"

"Please."

He chuckled, "You've used that word a few times now."

"What word?"

"Cliché."

"So?"

"You have a distinct distaste for clichés. You know that everybody is a cliché on some level, don't you?" he challenged.

"What do you mean?"

"Everything has a cliché attached to it in some way. Being original is rare, maybe even impossible."

His look indicated he was waiting for me to respond. Probably assuming I had some gloves in my pocket I was going to get out and throw down. I didn't. With my award-winning poker face, I patiently waited for him to further enlighten me.

Sensing this, he continued, "And you know what? You're one of the biggest clichés I've ever met."

"What?"

"Yeah."

"How?"

"You're mad at the world. I can tell. And I bet you have a good reason too. What? Did some guy break your heart and now you hate every man because we're all the same? Is that how original you are? Hating an entire gender for all the clichéd reasons?"

I sensed he wanted me to respond to this. So I didn't.

"Naw," he shook his head, "I don't buy your facade. And you know what? Maybe your little scenario will happen. Maybe we *will* fall in love. Maybe we'll connect on some deep, transcendental level and remember this weekend for the rest of our lives. In fact," he snapped his fingers and pointed at me as if he'd just figured out what is black and blue and red all over, "neither one of us will ever be able to move on from it. Neither one of us will ever find love because we will spend the rest of our lives comparing every relationship to the happiness that we are about to experience. And for the rest of our lives, we will both be left wanting." He turned away from me and dramatically sighed. "Maybe you're right. Dinner is a bad idea. This could ruin us both."

I stared at him, mouth open again. (Disclaimer: I do that a lot—stare at people with a gaping mouth. Don't give him too much credit for achieving this effect on me. It's pretty much my go-to response to witnessing idiocy on any level.)

"That's one scenario at least," he continued. "But perhaps you'd have another outcome. Maybe you just meet someone new, someone that you enjoy and click with. Maybe you create some great memories that you'll look back on fondly." He smiled, and I noticed his perfect white teeth. I swear they actually twinkled. *Shit.* I'm a sucker for nice teeth. "Just have dinner with me. Free meal. You can't possibly have so much disdain for me, or all men, that you'd pass up free food."

I hesitated. I was tempted. But ultimately, I didn't see the point. "No," I said. "I'm sorry. It's just not a good idea. It's…pointless."

"Wow. Pointless?" He scoffed and shook his head. "Okay. Well, it was nice to know you, however brief," he said tightly and looked away.

"I'm sorry. That was the wrong word. I just…I can't go tonight. I already have plans." I wasn't lying. "This book," I patted McCarthy's book sitting on my lap. "McCarthy is doing a reading in Chicago tonight, and my sister is in love with him, so I agreed to go. She's totally smitten with the guy. Nobody knows much about him. He's very private. My sister is his biggest fan, and she's never even seen him. Not even a picture. She morphed into an excited puppy when she learned he was doing his first public reading in Chicago. So, it's not you. I have to go tonight. She would kill me if I backed out on her."

I looked at him, feeling I was talking too much, and wondered if he thought my ramblings were an attempt to compensate for the guilt of turning him down. Which it was, of course. "Personally, I'd rather spend the night in my tub with a cold drink. McCarthy's probably some seventy-year-old recluse that never showers or cuts his toenails." He chuckled at my astute analysis. "But regardless, my sister loves the guy, and I have to go with her. It is my sisterly duty."

"But you don't want to go to the reading?"

"Not particularly," I shrugged.

"Because of the clichés…?" he pressed, teasing.

"No. Well, yeah. Well, I don't know. Look, he's a decent author. Respectable. His first novel was impressive. It was, and I don't use this word lightly, brilliant. But he just doesn't rock my boat the way he does for Denise—

my sister."

"Hmmm…" he nodded.

"His writing can be weak. It's good in areas, but weak in more." Again, why was I explaining myself to this person, and more importantly, why was I enjoying our conversation?

"Weak?" he prodded quizzically.

"Yeah, maybe even spineless," I gave him an evil sideways grin. "Especially this last book."

"Wow! That's harsh."

"Every time that something, I don't know, deeper, profound even, was about to happen, or should have happened—it just didn't. There was potential for genuine human connection. Mess! I love mess! But it never came. Instead it was…insincere, and I hate that. Superficiality. Small talk. Fluff." I paused for a moment before continuing: "Maybe that's why Denise loves him so much; that's what she's comfortable with. The clean and tidy happily-ever-after. I guess most people prefer that." I sighed and then waved my hand as if to brush away an imaginary cobweb and continued, "In this book, McCarthy scurried past anything potentially *real* with these characters, into something more orderly. Something more palatable. Which is fine, I get it. That's easier. That's what's expected, and perhaps even what is desired by most. But for me," I shrugged, "that's boring. Cliché," I said, smiling. "I like messy. I like real. I like…fucked up." Realizing that I may have just exposed more about myself than I should, I forced a laugh to try and hide my sudden vulnerability.

"He hides from the messy, huh?"

"Yeah. He hides from the messy. I don't hold it against him, though. Most people do hide from getting too real. I guess my tastes are a little more perverse than most," I said. His eyes locked on mine.

"I think you should go to dinner with me," he said. "Worst case scenario it might get messy, but you love messy, so…what do you have to lose?"

He was a persistent little shit. I feared I was enjoying him more than I cared to admit.

After a minute's hesitation, I made a decision. "Look, we're having a book club meeting tonight," I confessed with my head down. "Yeah, I'm in a book club."

"Of course you are," he said.

"Whatever," I said. "Don't judge me."

"Too late."

"Well, we're meeting right before the reading tonight to discuss the book. That's why I was in such a rush to finish it." I hesitated, not sure why I was about to do what I was about to do. "You…should come. To the meeting, I mean. The reading is sold out. But you can come to the book club with me. You seem to have some strong opinions on the book," I mocked.

He hesitated—what was I thinking asking him to a book club meeting—and the fourteen-year-old girl inside me took over.

"But don't feel obligated. I mean, it's going to be totally lame. It's just my sister, two of her friends, and me." I was rambling. I needed to stop. "Never mind. It's silly. Forget I asked."

"I'd love to come," he said.

"Really?" I said surprised.

"Really," he laughed. "I have to be somewhere later, but I'll drop in. It'll be a learning experience, I'm sure."

He had to be somewhere later? But he wanted to get dinner with me a few minutes ago? Why did he ask me to dinner if he had someplace to be? I wanted to inquire but decided it wasn't my place.

"I'm Paul by the way," he said, holding out his hand. "Now we're not strangers anymore."

"I'm Kadie," I said, shaking his hand.

"Beautiful name for a beautiful woman."

"How many times have you used that line?"

"That was my first time."

"Well, it's stupid. Don't use it anymore." I know I sounded harsh, but he needed to know. He chuckled as the captain's voice came on instructing us to prepare for landing.

After the plane landed, I gathered my belongings and turned to find him standing with my Victoria Secret bag. I grabbed it, embarrassed. Why did I use a Victoria Secret bag for public travel? Flustered, I explained, "It's just crackers and some knick-knacks for the flight. It's not…" I trailed off. I was exasperated with my silly performance on the flight. I needed to be put in a padded room.

"That's too bad." He started down the aisle, and I followed. Once off the plane, he turned back to face me.

"Here," I said, handing him a business card with my sister's address scribbled on the back. "That's my sister's address. The meeting starts at five."

He studied the card. "I'm looking forward to it. I've never participated in a book club before. Unless you count my literature courses in college. They're just glorified, expensive book clubs."

"I can relate," I replied, remembering my own grueling college courses.

He motioned to the card, "I'll be there. Right at five. I'm very punctual," he said. We had stopped in the middle of the airport walkway. It was time to part ways. Surprisingly, I was feeling disappointed that our time was coming to an end, while at the same time eager to escape the mental fog clouding my brain.

"You're punctual, huh," I said. "Now I know something else about you, Paul, from Arizona, who is oddly defensive when it comes to Kurt McCarthy books, and is *not* a rapist…supposedly." I situated my bag and then started away. "And who has bad taste in shoes," I shot over my shoulder. I couldn't help it. "See you at five."

Chapter 4

The cab pulled to the curb two minutes before five. I studied the house, replete with standard Chicago architecture. I spotted someone standing at the front window looking through a crack in the curtain. Upon my inspection, it was pulled tight. I smiled, convinced Kadie was the woman behind the curtain.

Paying my fare, I stepped out from the cab when my phone buzzed with a new message. I started for the front door and retrieved my phone. I read the message and stopped. I stood halfway between the house and the street and glared down at the text.

`Hey babe ☺ Just thinking about you. Let me know when you get back from Chicago. We REALLY need to talk. I love you.`

It was from Lisa. She told me five weeks ago she never wanted to see me again. No explanation. No apology—heartfelt or otherwise. Just: "I don't love you anymore. Don't call. Don't text. Don't email. I never want to see you again."

The first week was the hardest. I stayed home and stared at my phone. She didn't call. She didn't come over. The second week was better. I started a new novel. I wrote seventy pages and then deleted the entire thing. It was crap—worse than the poetry I wrote in high school to try and funnel my adolescent angst—but at least I was writing. That was a step forward. By week three I had convinced myself that I just needed to get through week four. Four weeks. That was a month. Life would take on some level of semblance after a month. I was right. Life was easier after week four. Lisa was no more than an afterthought now. Today was the end of week five. I felt fine. I no longer had moments of sad reflection. I wasn't moving on; I had moved on. Lisa was a memory now. Someone I shared two years with, but now I was relieved to be free of her. I wasn't hurt when she ended things; I was shocked. The surprise of the action debilitated me more than the sadness. I was over the shock now, and no real sadness ever materialized. Now, with this text, I was just…confused.

"We REALLY need to talk," she wrote. Did "really" need to be in all caps? She loves me? Since when? Why? The breakup must be harder on her than she anticipated.

I deleted the message, pocketed the phone, and walked to the front door.

Kadie answered, gave me an obvious overview, stopped at my shoes, and asked why I changed. I changed because I didn't want to look like some yuppie hipster for my first public reading. That, and I was trying to impress Kadie. I mentioned neither of these.

"Well, I figured since I was walking into a shit-storm, I shouldn't wear my nice shoes," I said.

Kadie tried not to laugh, but my response was so awesome she couldn't help it. It sneaked up on her. She almost snorted but caught herself just in time and instead released some guttural howl that was beautiful in a special-needs sort of way.

Kadie composed herself and leaned into me and whispered, "I realized when I got here, and was grilled by my sister about who I'd invited to our sacred book club, that I don't even know what you do."

This sounded like a question, but it was more of a statement, so I just stared at Kadie dumbly. "So…what do you do?" Kadie officially asked. I continued my dumb stare. I should have thought this through better.

After a brief pause, I managed to say I was in sales.

"Sales?"

"Yep."

"What do you sell?"

"Paper." Great answer. Technically, I wasn't lying.

"You're a paper salesman?"

"Sure."

"In the digital age?"

"Yep."

"Well, I sure know how to pick them," Kadie mused.

"Has anyone ever told you it's nice to save your criticisms for someone when they can't hear them?"

"You need to hear this," Kadie said. "Your job is on the verge of being obsolete. Find a better one."

"I'm working on it."

"Who's this, Kadie?" A man rounded the corner and was standing in front of me with his hand outstretched. I took the offered hand because I always grab at things before thinking about what they might be. I even took candy from a stranger when I was a kid. It was a York Peppermint Patty. Disgusting. I would have rather been kidnapped.

"This is Paul," Kadie said, as I shook the stranger's hand. "He's a paper salesman from Arizona."

"Ah…paper," he said, refusing to release my hand. He smiled, and I noted a piece of beef jerky stuck between his teeth. "That's a…burgeoning enterprise."

"Don't encourage him," Kadie said. "I was just telling him he needs to find a new job."

He released my hand. "Kadie is brutally honest. You may want to pursue someone with a little more tact."

I smiled. "Who are you?" I asked.

"Oh, sorry," he said. "I'm Clay. Denise's husband. Kadie's brother-in-law." He pulled a plastic sandwich bag from his back pocket. Inside were strips of beef jerky. "Want some?" he asked. I shook my head. He reached into his sack and retrieved a strip. He pulled a chunk free with his teeth and chewed it with his mouth opened. "You here for the book club?"

"Yeah," I said.

"You a Kurt McCarthy fan?"

"He's all right," I said.

"Just 'all right'?" Kadie repeated. "You love him."

"I never said I loved him," I replied. My voice cracked, and I unintentionally sounded hurt, like a male preteen trying to convince his parents he didn't think girls were cute. Kadie laughed.

"Denise loves him," Clay interjected. "She's always saying how he's 'the truth'." Clay scoffed. "Rap music. Now that's the truth, you know what I mean?"

"Ah…I don't think so," I said, because I didn't. Kadie playfully hit me. I wasn't sure why.

"I've started three of his books," Clay continued, "but I've never finished one. I'd rather play Madden or GTA."

This wasn't surprising. Often I wondered how I, or any writer, made a living just by writing. We were in competition with better, more stimulating, products.

"You going to the reading, too?" Clay asked.

"No."

"Fifty bucks to listen to some guy read," Clay said. "Can you believe that?"

Honestly, I couldn't. "Crazy," I said.

"Kadie, is that him?" a voice shrieked from another room. I assumed I was 'him.'

"Yeah!" Kadie yelled back.

"Well, bring him in."

Kadie looked at me and smiled. "You ready to go into the lions' den?"

"Is it really going to be that bad?"

"Probably not for you," Kadie said. "I'm the outcast here. Everyone loved the book except me. Say Kurt McCarthy is a genius and you'll fit right in."

"Kurt McCarthy is a genius," I repeated robotically.

"Good luck," Clay said.

"You're not joining us?" I asked.

"Naw. Denise doesn't let me. She doesn't think I understand books too good."

I liked Denise already. "Well, it was nice meeting you, Clay." We shook hands again, and then he shuffled past me and into the living room. He sat down on the sofa and took up his X-box controller and headset.

Kadie watched him with mild curiosity. I watched Kadie watch Clay. I sensed he baffled her. She studied him a moment longer, shook her head, and gave up the internal struggle of making sense of Clay and his primitive instincts. She led me into the other room.

Right away I spotted the woman whom I assumed was Denise. She looked very similar to Kadie. She and her two other friends were already seated at the table. In front of each woman sat a glass of wine and a copy of my book. Denise's copy was noticeably worn. Colorful post-it notes stuck out from the pages, marking passages she felt needed marked. She even wore a Kurt McCarthy T-shirt. I had never seen it before. It was black, and on the front was a white outline of an unknown man's head. A silhouette. Underneath the mystery man it read: "Have you seen me?" On the back was my pen name. I'd never seen the shirt before. I'd wager it was for sale on my website. Zoe and my publicist were always putting products on my website. It was probably made in a Bangladesh sweatshop for a buck and sold on my website for forty. I should reimburse Denise.

Kadie introduced me to the group: her sister, Denise, and their childhood girlfriends, Samantha and Bridget. Samantha wore a sweater donning a cat eating a bowl of cherries. At the bottom, next to a pile of discarded pits it read: "Life's the Pits!" I wondered if owning bad shirts was a prerequisite for the club. Bridget was wearing some kind of white satin number that showed her black bra underneath. I believe it was meant to be sexy, but it reeked of insecurity. She was drunk or pretended to be. She laughed too hard at things that weren't funny and cried at the rest. She had lipstick on her teeth, and she wore too much perfume. "Embarrassment" by Calvin Klein.

These were my fans.

Denise paid me little attention. It was already five after the hour and she was ready to get started. I took one of the two remaining empty seats. Kadie went into the kitchen and returned a moment later with two glasses of wine. She gave one to me and then sat down. I wondered if Kadie recognized the irony of ridiculing clichés and then drinking wine at a book club meeting. I almost pointed it out, but nobody likes looking in a mirror when the reflection is unflattering. I don't care for wine, but I took a sip out of consideration of all things ridiculous. It tasted too sweet to be expensive. I suspected it came from a box.

"So, Paul," Denise said, "have you read *Trainride?*"

"Yeah, I have."

"And..." Denise wanted more.

"Um...I think his earlier stuff is better," I answered safely and honestly.

"Everyone thinks that, but I don't." Denise said. "All his works are brilliant. Some are just—what is it, Kadie—'less satisfying' than others?" She shot Kadie a look. Kadie smiled, tightlipped, and sipped her wine. "What else of McCarthy's have you read?" Denise asked.

I pretended to think for a moment. "I think I've read just about everything of his."

"Even his short story? 'Flannel Pajamas'?"

"Yeah," I said. "I read it in high school."

Bridget laughed, at God knows what.

"You know he wrote it in high school," Denise said. She seemed to know more about me than I did.

"Is that right?" I smiled.

"Denise worships Kurt McCarthy," Samantha said. Bridget laughed again. The room all looked at her, frightened by the sudden attention, she took a long drink.

"He's doing his first ever public reading tonight," Denise said. "We have tickets."

"I heard," I said.

"No one even knows what he looks like," Bridget explained.

"Kurt McCarthy isn't even his real name," Denise said.

"It's not?" Kadie asked. She seemed surprised and a little disappointed.

"No," Denise said. "It's a pen name."

"What's his real name?" Kadie asked.

"I don't know," Denise said. "He's never said. He's very secretive."

"Why Kurt McCarthy?" Kadie asked.

"What do you mean?" Denise asked.

"I mean just that—why? What's the significance with that name?"

"No one knows," Samantha said. "It's part of his mystique."

"There are theories," Denise said, "but he's never confirmed any of them."

"What are they?" I asked, my interest piqued.

"His father's name is Kurt, and he was blacklisted during the McCarthy hearings," Denise said. Bridget broke into hysterics. If this was a joke, no one else got it. "He came up with Kurt McCarthy to honor his father but also to remember his struggle," Denise explained.

My father's name is Howard. He was a plumber. The only thing he struggled with was being a Cubs' fan.

"So, he's one of those anguished artists, huh?" Kadie said. "Holed up in a cave somewhere removed from society. His only interactions are with the voices in his head." Kadie laughed at her observation. I thought it amusing, too. Caves terrify me. Bears live in caves.

"Kadie didn't like *Trainride*," Denise turned to me and said.

"That's not what I said."

"You said—"

"I said it was good enough," Kadie interrupted. "It's just...not amazing."

"I agree with Kadie," Samantha said. "I enjoyed *Trainride,* but I loved *Rearview Mirror* and *Boarded Window.*"

"I agree," Kadie said. "Nothing has been as great as *Boarded Window.* McCarthy seems to be faltering. *Rearview Mirror* wasn't too bad. *Pearl's Tool* was...a commendable effort. But *Trainride* was just too..."

"...clichéd?" I offered. Kadie turned to me and smiled.

"Yeah," she said. "Clichéd."

Bridget laughed. Wine spilled from her mouth. She wiped it away with her sleeve, leaving a red stain on the white satin.

"It wasn't clichéd," Denise said.

"Oh, come on, D," Kadie said. "He shows up at her doorstep in the rain. How many times has that been done?"

"It was romantic," Denise defended.

"It was crap," Kadie retorted. "It felt so forced. Sometimes I think McCarthy isn't even trying anymore. His characters used to be better, not so one-dimensional. I wonder if he's just writing for the paycheck now. Maybe that's why he's following the formula. There's no heart. His work now is generic and going downhill fast."

"You couldn't be more wrong," Denise countered. Truthfully, Kadie couldn't have been more right. I gritted my teeth.

"Maybe he's just old and tired and trying to make a little more money before he croaks," Kadie shrugged.

"He's only thirty-seven," Denise said.

"What?" Kadie asked surprised.

"Yeah," Samantha said. "He's thirty-seven. He published *Boarded Window* when he was twenty-four."

"I heard they're making that into a movie," Bridget said.

"Who said that?" I asked.

Bridget laughed, but when she sensed I expected an answer, she looked away and fell silent. For a moment I thought she might cry. She took another drink.

"I hope they don't butcher it the way they did with *Rearview Mirror,*" Samantha said. I winced at the memory of the film adaptation. Fans of my book said it was too complex a novel to be made into a movie. The movie critics and audiences agreed.

"Well, the movie is never as good as the book," Denise said.

"He's really only thirty-seven?" Kadie asked. She appeared to be grappling with my age. I wondered why it mattered so much.

"Why does that surprise you?" I asked.

"I don't know," Kadie said. "I just always assumed he was older."

"Maybe he's single," Bridget said. "Denise, wear your backless dress tonight."

Denise laughed. "He is one of my Five."

"Five?" I asked.

"Five men I'm allowed to sleep with without Clay getting mad."

"You've never even seen him," I said.

"I don't care," Denise said. She closed her eyes. "He could fuck me with his words."

Bridget spat wine across the table. Samantha's mouth dropped, while Kadie rolled her eyes and shook her head. I always knew words had power, but I never believed them capable of copulation. Denise kept her eyes closed, still lost in her fantasy. After a beat, she opened her eyes and scanned the table. "How romantic would that be?" she asked. "Meeting him at his own book reading. That's fairytale territory."

"It's almost as romantic as meeting someone on a plane," Samantha said. Kadie looked sharply at her. It was difficult to tell if she was being mocked or envied. I laughed to defuse the sudden tension, and because it was funny. Bridget looked at me, baffled that the conversation contained a joke and sad that she missed it.

"So funny," Kadie said. She looked at me and shook her head. Evidently, I had chosen the wrong side.

"It will be funny if things work out," I said. Then I winked. I don't know why. I had never winked at anyone before in my life. Winking is for philanthropists and pedophiles. All ambiguous gestures seem to be reserved for heroes or villains. The rest of us just hover awkwardly in the middle.

"Oh, God." Kadie rolled her eyes. "You sound like Gavin in this shitty book," she said, referring to the main character in *Trainride*.

"It's not shitty," Denise pouted.

"It wasn't until this moment," Kadie said. "But now I'm starting to see it for what it is. Just another by-the-book love story."

"Kadie doesn't believe in the notion of romance," Samantha leaned over and whispered to me loud enough for everyone to hear. Bridget leaned over too as if she had something to say. She realized she didn't, so she just giggled and sat back up.

"Is that right?" I asked. I looked at Kadie. "You don't believe in romance, huh?"

"I believe in romance, just not the kind in books and movies," Kadie said.

"She had her heart broken," Denise said by way of explanation. Bridget looked like she wanted to laugh, but instead she started to cry.

"That was over five years ago, Denise," Kadie said, "and nobody's heart was broken."

"Yeah? Tell Brock that. And why haven't you been with anyone since?" Denise replied.

"What happened?" I asked.

"Nothing," Kadie said, waving it off. She was noticeably annoyed.

"It doesn't sound like 'nothing'," I said, and realized I shouldn't have.

Kadie looked at me, straight in the eyes. "Well, you wouldn't know, would you?"

"I want to know…if you'll let me," I said. I kept my eyes locked on hers with the same intensity that she was looking at me. The women watched us, interested. No one spoke for a minute. The tension built and then Denise placed her hand over her sister's.

"Can we please talk about the book?" Denise said. She turned to me. "Paul, what did you think of it?"

I looked at Kadie for a moment longer and then answered Denise. "I agree. It's not his best work," I said. "It seemed…rushed. Maybe he was trying to meet a deadline or something."

"I don't think Kurt McCarthy abides by deadlines. He writes on his own terms," Denise argued for me. It was a sweet defense, albeit a false one. "What do you think, Paul?" she turned to me and asked.

"I hope he actually has the principles you seem to attribute to him," I said dispassionately.

"What would you ask him if you met him?" Denise said.

I gazed at Kadie and smiled. "I'd ask him if he believes in fate."

"Because of Gavin and Tracy?" Denise asked, referring to my book.

"Sure," I answered. I don't necessarily believe in fate, but I also don't discount there may be an order to the world too advanced for me to understand.

"What would you ask him, Denise?" Samantha asked.

"I'd ask why Tracy had to die," Denise said. Samantha and Bridget nodded in unison. Obviously, I had disappointed them by killing Tracy.

"What about you, Kadie?" Bridget asked. "What would you say to him?

"I'd ask him why he writes like a coward now."

Ouch! My mouth dropped. I looked at Kadie. She stared back at me. Something in, and behind, her eyes kept me trapped in her gaze. I was smitten. Suddenly, Bridget burst into a fit of laughter that she stifled with more wine.

Chapter 5

"Fate, huh?" I prodded as I walked Paul to the door. "You truly believe in fate? It's all in the stars? Planned out for us? We have no control or say?"

"I don't know. Maybe. What about you?"

"Not for a second. Fate is just a cop-out."

"Cop-out?" he asked skeptically.

"Sure. It's easy for people to believe in fate because then they don't have to put forth any effort," I explained.

He stopped and looked at me. "Okay," he said smiling. "I can't wait to hear your explanation. What do you have?"

"It's just people, you know. *I didn't get that job I wanted--oh well, I guess it wasn't meant for me. That just means there's something better out there waiting for me,*" I explained. "It's ridiculous. You didn't get the job because you weren't qualified. Or you showed up late. You had coffee on your tie. You needed to smile more, or you rubbed the interviewer the wrong way. Or you simply weren't what they were looking for." I scoffed, "But, rest assured, it's *not* because the stars know there's something better out there for you."

Paul appeared engaged, so I continued with more scenarios to further prove my point.

"*My relationships fail because I just haven't met my soul-mate yet,*" I mimicked. "No. All of your relationships failed because you're obnoxious, lazy, don't shower, a cheater, narcissistic, clingy, controlling, emotionally incapable, or...fill in the blank. People tell themselves stories about fate and stars so that life, and all its disappointments, are more easily digestible. They believe in fate, so they can get up each morning and face another lifeless day."

He stared at me with tender eyes that made me uncomfortable, and for some reason, defensive. "I sensed from the flight and the book club that you'd been hurt, but I had no idea it was this bad," he teased.

"That's not it," I said.

"Yeah, I think it is."

Naw," I waved him off. "I'm just a realist. I don't need to tell myself stories. I believe that people create their own fate. That we have control of our own stories. If I want something to happen, I make it happen."

"You believe it's that simple? That cut and dry?"

"Yes," I said, unwavering. "I won't sit back and hope for things to happen and then blame fate when it doesn't. When things don't go as planned, I'll own it. I'll think about what I could've done differently, where I messed up, and what I'll do next time. Not blame fate because it wasn't meant to be."

"Well, how is that working out for you?"

I studied him for a moment. "It's working just fine," I retorted. I tried to sound calm, but inside I burned, and I'm sure my face flushed. I was acting a little defensive and a lot stupid. "I'm just not naïve enough to live in some faux reality where things are how I want them, instead of how they really are," I explained coolly.

He nodded and said, "I'm starting to understand why you dislike McCarthy's books. You hate Romantic Idealism, and it's a key ingredient in his work."

"Yeah?" I scoffed. Then, feeling that perhaps I was coming off as a happiness-hater, I tried to soften things, "It's not that I don't believe in happiness or romance or even a healthy dose of idealism. I just…" I sighed heavily, not sure how to explain. "I need it to be real, I guess. Earned. Not a story I've created to pacify myself."

"Hmm," he murmured thoughtfully. "I think you're more of a romantic than you're willing to admit. A seed of romance has been planted inside you, and it's just waiting for you to bloom." He was teasing me, but I sensed that underneath his lighthearted tone was a measure of sincerity to his observation. It touched me.

I kept my eyes to the ground, not sure why I didn't want to look at him. We were both leaning against the porch and facing the street, waiting for his cab. We stood in the silence for a few minutes, but it wasn't awkward. It's rare, and refreshing, to find someone with whom you can stand silently with and not feel uncomfortable or the need to find something to say—even something senseless or superficial just to fill the empty space. After a few minutes, he looked at his watch. "You in a hurry?" I asked nonchalantly.

"I try not to be."

"What does that mean?" I asked.

"I'm not sure. I just seemed like a cool thing to say."

"It wasn't."

As if on cue, his cab pulled to the curb. Paul waved to the cab and then turned back to me. "Meet me for a drink later."

"I have the reading."

"After the reading."

"It'll be late."

"You have a curfew?"

I sighed. "I don't know…"

"Please."

I hesitated. Why was I so scared of this guy? "Look, I know I come across as…"

"Cold?"

I laughed and shook my head. "Sure, cold. But seriously, Paul, what's the point?"

"It's just a drink, Kadie."

"Yeah? And what's after?"

"I don't know. I'll tell you after the drink."

"You live in Arizona."

The cab honked. Paul turned to the cab, held up his hand, and turned back to me. "Take a chance on something."

"I don't take chances," I whispered. I kicked at the flaking porch paint and refused to meet his eyes. I had never been so intrigued by a man. He threw me completely off balance. I knew him for what? Seven hours? Why did he have such a hold on me? It didn't help either that I was extremely attracted to him. All these things seemed to be a dangerous concoction. Every time he looked at me with his bright green eyes, it was as if he saw something in me that was hidden to everyone else.

The cab honked again.

"You better get in before they take off." I nodded toward the taxi.

"Kadie—"

"It was good meeting you, Paul." I smiled at him. He looked as if he wanted to say something more, so I abruptly turned and went back into the house. It took everything I had not to go back outside and stop him from getting in the cab.

***

As we arrived at the book reading, a sense of dread welled-up inside me. How long could I pretend that I was enjoying myself? I wasn't sure if it was the encounter with Paul that had gotten to me, or if I was unhappy because I felt forced into coming to the reading. I think both were responsible for my sour disposition.

I didn't fit in with literary crowds. If I were honest with myself, I didn't fit in with my sister and her friends either. I love my sister dearly, but she is everything I am not. Sweet, friendly, outgoing…and borderline delusional. She is an avid believer in fate, happy endings, and everything else that she has been told she should believe in. I sometimes wondered if a part of her still believed in Santa Claus. She is naïve, and it drives me bonkers. Denise has never challenged herself to think outside the proverbial box. She's never thought about expanding her horizons regarding the plausible. She's just lived her whole life doing what she was told, making all the "right" choices.

Actually, maybe choices isn't the right word. They're more like steps. And she's followed the staircase that was put in front of her, one precise step at a time. She's a puppet. She's an adorable, likable, bubbly little puppet.

My thoughts amused me while I watched my sister bounce from person to person—chatting with them, helping them look for their seats, and laughing a little too hard when Samantha started down the wrong aisle. I sighed, jealous of her freedom. Life had to be easier when lived like Denise. Often, I've wondered how much easier my life would be if I had been able to just accept the stories that others did.

But it was too late for me. I knew those stories were nonsense. Life wasn't fair. It wasn't tidy. It sure as hell wasn't easy, and it never would be. Life is hard, and "Happily Ever Afters" don't exist. They were manufactured and marketed to keep the masses, people like my sister, dumb and happy. Watching my happy, naïve sister, I longed for the freedom of ignorance. Because once you know the aforementioned things, you can't un-know them. You become a 'realist' (i.e. a major buzz-kill).

And you can't go back.

I pulled off my sweater, took the seat next to my sister, and looked around. The auditorium was packed! I guess McCarthy *was* kind of a big deal. As I got situated, I noticed something fall out of my sweater pocket. A folded piece of paper. I picked it up and opened it.

844-555-1981 *Change your mind. Paul*

My thoughts returned to Paul and the different pretexts I gave him to avoid meeting him after the reading. I was sick of it all. Sick of feeling I needed to shield myself from…what? Getting hurt? Change? Something unpleasant? Something potentially not going my way?

What if I didn't have it all figured out?

What if I didn't know what the hell I was doing either?

My thoughts took a one-eighty. Maybe Denise is the one who has everything figured out? Maybe I should've gotten married and signed-up for the same white picket fence package she did. I almost did. Five years ago I was engaged to Brock, a handsome real estate agent. I would've acquired a nice home and maybe had a kid or two by now. I'd have stability, companionship, and maybe even happiness.

Brock was the recipient of his own rejected marriage proposal. It was textbook perfect, all the things that it was supposed to be, down to the big question carved out in the sandy beach. Brock was amazing. Probably still is. On paper, every box was checked. He had dark brown hair that contrasted with blue-grey eyes, ruggedly handsome, and handy in all the right ways. He could fix anything. Who turns that down? Oh—and he cooked, too. *Really* cooked. Rejecting him made me feel horrible, but his cooking might be what I missed most.

Shortly—a little too shortly, if you ask me—after I broke his perfect little heart, he met Isabelle. (I bet she preferred to be called "Izzy." She strikes me as the type.) Supposedly, it was true love. I was dubious about the whole thing considering his professed devotion towards me not even three months prior, but whatever. They had a whirlwind romance and eloped within six months of meeting.

I was shocked when I learned of his nuptials, and I had a brief "Oh shit!" moment. Had I blown it? Missed my opportunity? I could've been happy with Brock. Well, I could've been *content* with Brock. But when it came down to it. When all the checked boxes, the orgasmic meals, the strong jaw, and the fixed plumbing were stripped away—what was left was overwhelmingly barren. I wanted, needed, to love him more than I did. He never made my heart leap. I cared for him. In fact, I *did* love him. Just not enough for the man I was supposed to marry.

But what did I know?

I still thought about Brock (obviously) at random moments. I wondered if he was happy and if he ever thought about me. Did he have kids? It had been five years since I ended things. I have never been able to shake the insidious fear that maybe I screwed up, royally. I sometimes wondered if because of that idealistic hallucination of what I thought love should be, I was destined to spend my life alone.

Lonely.

Pretending everything is exactly how I'd planned it to be.

Poetic justice?

I wasn't alone because I hadn't found my soulmate yet, because our paths had yet to collide. I was alone because of choices that I'd made. Choices that were thought-out and pragmatic.

I was bound and determined NOT to turn into the woman who gets married too young, drops out of college to take care of babies, and ends up losing her identity in her husband and children. I avoided those pitfalls. I earned my degree, started my career, and then met Brock. The timing, on paper, was perfect. I'd met a wonderful, borderline-perfect man who loved me and wanted to spend his life with me. But I let that slip away because of some silly preconceived notions of love.

No higher power, or fate, was involved in the condition of my life. *I* had created my life, and I wasn't going to tell myself stories about fate having anything to do with it.

And yes, I was lonely.

This realization lit a fire in me. If I wanted to change my life, then I was the one who needed to change it. Fate wasn't going to jump down from the stars and fix anything. I wanted to see Paul again. To hell with the consequences.

I turned to Denise. "Denise, I have to go," I whispered as I started pulling on my sweater.

"What?" Jaw dropped and eyes wide, she was not pleased. "What do you mean you have to *go?*"

"I have to go. I…uh…I don't feel well. Stomach." I rubbed my stomach, proving I wasn't feeling well.

"Kadie!" I heard Denise's confused voice call after me as made my way toward the exit. It wasn't until I pushed through the auditorium's doors and into the lobby that I dared to look again at the paper I still had clutched in my hand. After another moment of hesitation, I threw caution to the wind, pulled out my phone, and dialed the number.

Chapter 6

Were these my people? The people filling the lecture hall? Tweed jackets. Mock turtlenecks. Scarves. Dark-rimmed glasses. Ponytails on men. Ponytails have only ever looked good on Steven Segal and Randall Hertzel.

I counted eleven berets. There may have been more. Probably were. I stopped at eleven because I realized *I* was being the stereotype that I scorned others for being. Is the guy that doesn't care about his appearance any better than the guy that does but pretends not to? Is wearing skinny corduroys and elbow-patch jackets worse than wearing green sneakers, even if it is to appease a child? Everyone is trying while pretending they're not.

My agent and publicist tricked me into the reading. For years they recited baseless rhetoric about my readers wanting to make a more personal connection. I didn't want my readers to know me, just my characters. I'm not worth knowing. Hence, the pen name. Kurt McCarthy had something to say, Paul Stevens didn't. I'm boring. Writers typically are—except Hemingway and Capote.

The advance money for *Trainride* was more than my other four books put together. Zoe, my agent, negotiated seven figures. I signed the contract without even reading it. Not because I was excited about the money, but because contracts are lengthy and confusing. I had a lawyer read my first one. He charged me a hundred bucks. He phoned me and said everything looked pretty standard and I should sign. I figured every subsequent contract would be the same, so I never consulted a lawyer again. I should have. Zoe was able to get me a higher sum due to two clauses: 1) a public speaking engagement, and 2) a deadline.

I wouldn't call myself an artist. Some writers are; I'm not. Writing for me basically involves slowing the hamsters in my head long enough to tell a story before they start up again. I don't try to pretend that what I do is important in the grand scheme of things. It's not. I can't cure any diseases; I can't even fix a fridge. If the apocalypse were approaching and only humanity's best could fit in the bomb shelter, I wouldn't get a seat. But one thing I can say unequivocally is this: Writers should *not* be given deadlines. A book is finished when it's finished. Deadlines are for people who will produce the same product no matter the timeframe. Justin Bieber can have deadlines; Jonathan Franzen shouldn't.

I knew my book wasn't what it should be. But I had a deadline. Zoe called me at 11:59 p.m. on August 31st. "Where's the manuscript?" she asked.

"I need more time."

"You have a deadline."

"I don't care."

She laughed.

"Seriously, I don't care."

She laughed harder. I started laughing, too. I wasn't sure why.

"I'll send it in the morning," I said. "It's not good. Just warning you."

"Can't be worse than your last one," she said. She meant it as a joke, but it stung because it *was* worse than my last one, and my last one wasn't good. I was becoming to books what M. Night Shyamalan was to movies.

I sent a very rough draft of *Trainride* to Zoe the next day—one day past my deadline. It wasn't good. I wanted to pretend otherwise, but I knew what it was. You know when your kid hands you some shitty macaroni art, but you hang the atrocity on your fridge anyway? That was *Trainride*. Shitty macaroni art trying to be better than it was. *Trainride* made it to the fridge because of my reputation. Sometimes all we are is what we were.

Trainride sold better than any of my other books. Go figure. I started to believe maybe it was better than I first thought. It wasn't. I had just momentarily forgotten how much the masses revere mediocrity. Sometimes if you don't take a moment for personal introspection, you start to believe popularity must equal quality. It's why Kanye West and Taylor Swift don't recognize their own unique ability to be average.

The critical reviews for *Trainride* were scathing, but the sales were not. I'd blown the literary world away with my debut novel, wrote a very respectable follow-up, and have been getting rich off a diminishing reputation ever since. I was losing the respect of my peers and the people that mattered, while gaining popularity with the masses. Fraud masquerading as art.

Zoe read the manuscript and then called to tell me it wasn't my best work, but it should still sell enough to warrant a hundred-dollar entrance fee.

"Fee for what?"

"For your reading."

"What reading?"

"The one you agreed to in your contract."

"What?"

"Read your contract."

I hung up and reviewed my contract. There it was on page seven. Funny how things are so much easier to see once they're pointed out to you. I called her back. She picked up on the first ring. Her voice had a lilt to it—happiness from my ignorance.

"I'm not doing a reading," I said.

"You have to."

"No, I don't."

"It's in your contract."

"You know how much I value my privacy."

"People want to see you, Paul...er...Kurt."

"I'm not doing it."

She laughed.

"The whole reason I have a pen name is so people won't know me."

"That's going to change."

"Zoe...please..."

"What's the big deal, Paul?"

"If people are focused on me, they lose focus of my work. It's like when a movie star does nudity in a film. The audience loses focus of the characters and instead think: 'hmmm...there's Angelina Jolie's tits.'"

Zoe laughed, but my argument wasn't convincing. "You should have read your contract," she said.

"I want a new agent."

Zoe laughed again. I felt like a kid who keeps trying to pitch his side of his story to his disbelieving parents, but no matter how much he tries, he isn't being heard. This was a fight I wasn't going to win.

"If I'm forced to do this, you can't charge $100. No one is worth that much."

"People will pay it."

"Is the fee already determined in my contract?"

"No."

Now I had some leverage. "I'll do it if a ticket isn't more than twenty bucks."

Zoe laughed. I enjoyed making Zoe laugh, but when she laughed at my demands, it upset me more than entertained me. This conversation was very upsetting.

"I'm serious."

"Seventy-five."

"Twenty bucks."

"Fifty, and you won't face any recourse for submitting your novel past your deadline."

"It was one day late."

"Doesn't matter. Legally, you broke your contract. I'm the only reason your publisher isn't suing."

"Are you serious?"

"Very."

I had lost my leverage. "Fine. Fifty dollars."

"Good," she said. "Do you still like me?"

"No."

"I think you like me more than you like yourself," she said. She was right.

"Zoe, was I foolish to think that all I would have to do as a writer is write?"

"Yes. You were."

I sighed and hung up the phone.

***

I was born and reared in a small Idaho town called River Rock. I received a partial scholarship to Boise State, and at the recommendation of my high school creative writing teacher, I studied English. I earned my bachelor's degree in three years and then enrolled in the university's graduate program shortly after. That wasn't my intention, but I met a girl, fell in love, and followed her right into the graduate program. Two years later I had an advanced degree and twenty-thousand dollars in student debt. Sierra, the aforementioned girl, took a teaching job at her high school alma mater in Boise. She said she could get me a job there too. I wanted out of Idaho. I had already decided that as soon as I was done with school, Idaho would become a distant memory. Taking a job teaching high school English felt like a step back, like planting my feet deeper into the place I wanted to escape. I told Sierra I wanted a life with her, but that it had to be somewhere new. She wanted to stay near her family. Brokenhearted and penniless, I moved the seventy-eight miles back home to try and reassemble my life; she started her teaching career that same fall. Several nights I hopped in my dad's pickup and started for Boise with an apology rattling around in my head to win back Sierra. I never made it to the city though. The drive always calmed me, and I'd eventually turn around.

An old high school friend landed me a job on the city's public works crew. I worked for three months, and then my father passed away after a brief and heartless battle with lung cancer. Later that year my mother died when she fell forty feet off the back of some bleachers at a high school football game.

After my mother's death, I quit showing up to my job at the public works department. I spent one afternoon in our attic and found an old typewriter that belonged to my grandfather. It didn't take me long to figure out the contraption. In an adjacent box, I found a stack of paper. I loaded a sheet of paper and started typing. Three months later my first novel was completed.

Boarded Window told the story of a boy growing up in River Rock, Idaho. It was honest and revealing, and I never thought about getting it published. It served as nothing more than a coping mechanism. Now that it was finished, I returned to work to learn I no longer had a job. I was numb to the news. When I asked why, my friend said, "You haven't been here for three months, Paul. What did you expect?" It was a fair question that I couldn't answer. I turned and walked away. It occurred to me then that I was nothing more than an unemployed orphan with a mounting stack of bank foreclosure notices made out to my parents and an unrepresented manuscript. I figured one problem might solve the other, so I started sending query letters to agents. Most went unanswered. A few had the compassion to reply with a generic rejection letter. And then I got lucky. An agent (Zoe) asked to represent me. She found a publisher willing to pay me a $1,000 advance and 15% of the royalties.

I opted for a penname so people wouldn't know I wrote *Boarded Window*. I wasn't embarrassed or anything, but it was a personal book, and if anyone from my hometown were to stumble upon it, they might have questions for me that I was unwilling to answer. I figured it would sell fifty copies (none of which would be in River Rock) and then find itself out of print within five years. But I had read enough rags to riches stories to know anything was possible. So, on the off chance that my expectations were skewed, I adopted my pen name. Kurt McCarthy allowed me to remain Paul Stevens. My success was beyond my imagination.

Shortly after *Boarded Window* was published, I took a job as a fry cook at a local diner where I frequently overheard people talking about this new book that told the story of a boy growing up in their hometown. The community wondered how an outsider knew so much about their small farming town less than a hundred miles outside of Boise. I even added to the mystery. No one was more vocal than me in trying to figure out how Kurt McCarthy pegged River Rock, Idaho so well. After the internet offered no clues to the identity of Kurt McCarthy, my friends and I looked through old high school yearbooks trying to figure out if the author could be someone we knew. Anyone that had moved away after high school was a suspect. We even contacted some and inquired if they were Kurt McCarthy. Our efforts went unrewarded. I was an English graduate from River Rock, and no one even thought to consider me as the clandestine author. Hiding in plain sight is the best way to stay concealed.

The book's royalties started to make my Idaho exodus a reality. When *Boarded Window* got nominated for the National Book of the Year (it lost), I packed a duffle, let the bank take my childhood home, and moved in with my older brother in Arizona. Six months later I had my own condo. Fifteen hundred square feet in a city that never saw temperatures below sixty. I put Idaho in the rearview mirror (hence the title of my second book) and haven't been back since.

I love writing because my stories and characters never have to be about me. Sure, elements of me transfer to my characters and stories, but I never have to be the center of attention, at least not publicly. And even when I am, like in my first novel, no one needs to know. I've never thirsted for fame. I've never sought shallow adoration. Those elements can effortlessly be attained through Facebook or Instagram pages. I've only ever wanted to write while maintaining as much anonymity and privacy as possible.

My thoughts drifted from Idaho to Kadie. I didn't really know her, but I missed her. She was rude. She was honest. She was beautiful. She hated my worst work and respected my best. She was someone worth falling in love with.

What would she think when she saw me walk onto the stage? Would she take back what she said earlier about my book? About me? Would she be upset that I never disclosed who I was? I didn't necessarily lie to her. Had she asked me if I were Kurt McCarthy, I would have told her the truth. It just never came up. Between criticizing my work and its asinine romanticism, I never found the right time to tell her I was the hack her sister plopped down good money to see. Once my identity was known, Kadie would likely demand a refund. With interest. I pictured her arguing her point. She made a good argument and punctuated it with just the right amount of vitriol. I smiled at the hypothetical, and then I spotted her.

She was following her sister down the aisle to their seats. She was four rows back, dead center. She'd have a perfect view. Her sister was giddy, as was Samantha. Bridget struggled to keep her balance, either from her inebriated state or her four-inch heels or both. Kadie looked…bored, like she would rather be anywhere else.

She had insisted on not seeing me again. Before I left her sister's house, I had written my number on a slip of paper and sneaked it into her sweater pocket. Now I had to wait for her to discover it and pray she'd call. I had my doubts, but I also had my hopes. In ten minutes, she would learn my true identity. If she wasn't too upset, she might call. I had to believe she wouldn't be too upset. Lois Lane didn't shut out Superman when she learned his true identity. Neither did Mary Jane with Spiderman. (Why was I comparing myself to superheroes?)

Frantically, Kadie stood. Something was wrong. Denise called after her, but Kadie didn't stop. She stepped into the aisle and bolted for the exit. I thought to go after her. I wanted to go after her. I stood paralyzed with indecisiveness. *Screw it. I'm going after her.* I took a step, almost emerging from behind the curtain when my phone rang.

"Hello?"

"Can I see you?" It was Kadie.

"When?"

"Right now."

I looked over the crowd. Near the stage was a group of people huddled around a selfie stick and smiling at the phone attached.

"Absolutely," I said.

So I left.

I walked out on 1,500…er…1,499 people. I knew Zoe would be pissed. So would my publicist. My publisher would probably sue. None of that mattered. Kadie had called, and I answered her call.

Like a superhero!

***

We met at The Bar on the Corner. Not a corner bar, but The Bar on the Corner. That's its name. What the name lacked in originality it made up for in all other areas. It was a quasi-restaurant/bar/brewpub hole-in-the-wall dive that Kadie often frequented. It was less than a mile from the reading hall. The place was small, dingy. It could seat thirty people if everyone held their breath. A piano sat jammed in the corner with a dirty beer mug on top for tips. The pianist played show tunes. He wore a t-shirt tuxedo with cut off pants and glasses with no lenses. Trying to be original in an unoriginal world. We ordered deep-dish pizza and Guinness. I loved everything about that place.

Kadie was sitting alone in the corner chewing her nails when I arrived. She spotted me standing in the doorway and waved and then embarrassingly lowered her arm and looked around anxiously. I made my way over and sat down across from her. She looked at me and offered a sad smile.

"What happened at the reading?" I asked, sliding into the opposite side of the booth.

"I didn't want to be there, so I left."

"Just like that?"

She reached into her pocket and pulled out my note. She dropped it on the table. "I saw this, and I had to get out of there."

She nervously tapped the table with her finger. I reached across the table and put my hand over hers. I had touched her hand before when I shook it on the plane, but this time it was different. My body, connected with hers, felt electrically charged. She looked at my hand on top of hers and then looked at me.

"You seem nervous," I said.

We stared at each other for a moment. Neither of us spoke because we knew the moment didn't require us to. She took her eyes from mine and looked back at my hand covering hers. I thought to move it, but I don't think she wanted me to. I know *I* didn't want to.

"All I know about you is you're overly sensitive about Kurt McCarthy books, and you're a paper salesman from Arizona."

"Yeah…so?"

"So…I don't care about paper nor McCarthy."

"Yeah…so?"

"So why can't I stop thinking about you?"

"Because I'm awesome."

She shook her head, but she did smile. "Be serious."

"What if we don't try and figure anything out right now and just go with it."

"What do you mean?"

"I mean I have two days left in Chicago. You can overanalyze everything and try to make sense of it all, or…you can just let yourself have a great weekend with a great guy."

"What makes you so great?"

"The person I'm sitting with right now."

Her face contorted, trying to decide if she wanted to laugh at my line or be touched by it. She looked away for a moment and whispered, "It's like you're reading this from a book or something."

The waitress arrived with our beers. I took a drink and savored the taste and took another. I put my glass on the table and felt my phone buzz. I knew it was Zoe, and I knew she would call at least twenty more times tonight. I pulled my phone from my pocket and forwarded her to my voice mailbox and then turned off the phone.

"Who's Zoe?" Kadie asked. She must have read the screen.

"No one," I said.

"Please don't tell me you're married or have a girlfriend. Don't make me a vacation tryst."

I tried, unsuccessfully, not to laugh. It was a fair question on Kadie's part, but the thought of being in a romantic relationship with Zoe was comical. She liked karaoke and owned DVD sets of every season of *Saved by the Bell*. She shaved one side of her head and bleached her bangs. She was a walking contradiction.

"I'm not married, and I don't have a girlfriend," I explained. "Zoe is a…coworker."

"Are you both here on business?"

"Yeah," I said. It was nice to not be completely lying.

"You're not worried why she's calling?"

"I know why she's calling, and I don't care."

"Why?"

"Why is she calling, or why don't I care?"

"Why is she calling?"

"Because I walked out of a business meeting."

"Why did you do that?"

"For the same reason you walked out of the reading." I took another drink. "I want to know everything about you," I said. "What's your story?"

Kadie smiled. "You first."

"What do you want to know?"

"Why aren't you married?"

"I've never met the right woman."

"You ever come close?"

"I came this close," I held my thumb and index finger about an inch apart, "to marrying my college sweetheart."

"What happened?"

"She never wanted to leave Idaho. That's where we grew up. As soon as I learned to walk, every step was meant to take me further from that place."

"So that's why you like McCarthy so much?"

"What do you mean?"

"His first book is about a kid growing up in Idaho who wants to leave."

"Yeah, McCarthy and I have a little bit in common."

"So what happened with the girl?"

"After college she took a teaching job in Idaho, and I left. I moved to Arizona and started selling paper."

"Do you miss her?" Kadie asked.

"No."

"Do you ever think about her?"

"Only when I'm asked about her."

"You can just move on that easy, huh?"

"It was years ago."

"Still."

"Do you ever feel that maybe you meet a person, and that person needs to be in your life just long enough until you can move on to something else?"

"Something else or someone else?" Kadie asked.

"Both, I guess."

"Sure."

"That's who Sierra was. She's a wonderful person, but after enough time passed, we realized we had nothing left to offer each other."

"So who came after Sierra?"

I took a drink and processed Kadie's question. I dated a few women after Sierra, but nothing ever materialized into anything serious. Some wanted to cultivate stronger relationships, but I'd never met anyone that I found more interesting than the book characters I was constantly constructing in my head. Calls and texts would go unreturned, parties and dinner dates unaccompanied. It wasn't my intention to be rude or insensitive. I was just distracted. My brother and his wife would have me over for dinner and spring a friend on me that they thought might balance me out. I'd feign interest, exchange numbers, but then I'd return to my isolated world where I didn't need to worry about the time or adhere to the social constraints required to date someone seriously.

Then I met Lisa. I had just finished my fourth novel and needed some repose. I was standing behind her at a bistro waiting to order my late morning coffee. She had a gift card that the cashier kept telling her had a zero balance. Lisa argued she had just received the card two days earlier as a birthday gift, so the cashier must be wrong. The cashier ran the card two more times to appease Lisa, but the result was the same. Things started to get awkward. I shuffled my feet and looked behind me. A line was forming. I smiled stupidly at the people behind me to let them know I wasn't the cause of the delay. Lisa didn't have her purse, only the malfunctioning card. I'm not sure what she expected the cashier to do with this information, so the cashier did nothing. They were at an impasse. I stepped forward and offered to buy the coffee. Lisa was adamant; my offer wasn't necessary because she had a gift card.

"I don't think you do," I said timidly.

Lisa gave me a quick overview, her piercing eyes burned into mine. "What do you hope to get out of buying me a cup of coffee?" she asked.

"I hope to get out of this uncomfortable moment," I answered. Evidently, people had been buying Lisa drinks for most of her life and they always expected something in return. She studied me, determined I didn't have a hidden agenda, and allowed me to buy her coffee. I paid the barista, and Lisa and I stood awkwardly off to the side to wait for our drinks. I pretended to be interested in a poster on the far wall. Lisa scrolled through her Instagram page. She bolted for the door after as soon as she got her coffee. She gave me a forced nod on her way out, grateful to exit the place. I gave her a head start and then followed her out the door to an empty table. Two minutes later she emerged from her car across the lot and made her way to me.

"I'm sorry," she said, avoiding making eye contact. "If you're here tomorrow, I'll…reimburse you."

I thought to tell her that wasn't necessary, but what I said instead was, "Okay." I didn't care to be reimbursed, but I was curious if she would actually show up the next day to do so. She nodded and turned back around and got in her car. True to her word, she was at the coffee shop the following day and bought me a cup. That's how we started.

We clicked early, and as is the case with so many other relationships, we hit all the high notes in the first couple of months of our relationship before realizing we had nothing in common. In the beginning, she was fun, engaging, and we shared a lot of the same interests. For our six–month anniversary, I gave her a copy of one of my books. She held it, scrutinized the cover, and then put in on the table, disappointed. She forced a smile and offered a half–hearted "thanks." I told her the book wasn't the gift; my secret was.

"Secret?" she asked.

"I'm the author," I said.

She didn't believe me at first. She thought, because I had told her, that I was a marketing executive with my brother. When I finally convinced her that I was Kurt McCarthy, her first question was how much I got paid for each book. I stared at her, dumbfounded. Of all the people, she was the one I confided in, and her biggest concern was a price tag. We weren't the same after that. In her eyes, I was a minor celebrity, and she wanted to cash in. She didn't care about Paul Stevens's character; she cared about Kurt McCarthy's social status and potential wealth. She questioned why I didn't buy a bigger house, go on tours, do readings. It baffled her why I wasn't more concerned with the money I wasn't making due to my reluctance to be more profitable. By the time she dumped me—just over five weeks ago—I had already checked out. I gave her two years of my life. Time spent that could not be recovered. It wasn't lost on me that she was my muse for *Trainride*—the worst book of my career.

I swallowed my beer and then told Kadie: "There was one woman. Lisa. I was with her for two years."

"What happened?"

"We…just didn't go well together."

"That's vague. Tell me more."

I exhaled and ran a hand through my hair. The thought of delving into whatever defined Lisa and I felt like a chore without a reprieve. How do you talk about someone that isn't worth talking about?

"Have you ever been with someone, and after, you wonder why you ever spent so much time with the person?" I asked.

"Sure."

"That was Lisa. One day in the next ten years or so I'll bump into her at the grocery store and struggle to remember her name."

"That's harsh," Kadie said.

"Yeah, but it hurts to think of how much time I wasted with her."

"What do you mean?"

"Life doesn't have a rewind button. We will never be as young as we are right now, at this moment. We're older now than we were three seconds ago when I fed you that pathetic line. We are on a one-way timeline, and things that have passed cannot be recovered. I'm not going to give my time to someone I don't feel something for again."

"So if time is so precious to you, why are you wasting some of it with me?" she asked.

"I don't feel I'm wasting it with you."

"Why? What's different?"

I thought for a moment, not wanting to butcher my answer. "When we made eye-contact on the flight as you were heading for the bathroom, did you feel something?" I asked. Kadie opened her mouth to answer, but before she said anything, I continued: "When I sat down five minutes ago and placed my hand over yours, did you feel something? Some kind of…connection?" This time I did wait for an answer.

"Yes," she whispered.

"That's what's different."

I sensed my answer moved Kadie. She looked deep into my eyes with a warmth that enticed me to lean across the table and kiss her. I chickened out though. I stayed as I was and just returned her stare with my own. I had set up the moment but failed to take advantage of it. Sometimes it seems people only do what they want in books and movies.

Chapter 7

"I need to…uh, go to the bathroom," I said, hurriedly. I needed to get away from Paul for a minute to gather my thoughts. Compose myself. Get my emotions back in check. I was falling for him. I had never experienced feelings so charged, so…alive. I paid attention to things about myself that I had previously ignored; I became self-conscious of my mannerisms in a hundred new ways.

I'd changed. He was changing me. In the twelve hours that he'd been in my life, I'd become a different woman. Not in a bad way. I was still me, just a different, maybe even better, version. A clearer, more distinct version. A version I liked more. It was as though a switch inside me needed to be flipped. A switch that had the power to complete the process of me becoming the person I was meant to be. And Paul had the power to flip the switch.

I took a slow, deep breath. Is that what love is? Bizarre, inexplicable feelings? I've read several books supporting that theory, I'd just never experienced it myself. In thirty-five years, I'd never had such an overpowering, debilitating, emotional reaction to someone. I needed to reel in my feelings. I despised losing control of my emotions; it was unnatural for me, and I was uncomfortable with it.

I stared at myself in the restaurant's bathroom mirror. Seeing, but not seeing, myself. I looked the same as I always had. Same brown hair. Same silly freckles and tanned skin. But I was different somehow. Something *had* changed. A stranger stared back at me. Who I thought I was had been disrupted. Why was my first reaction to fight the feelings I had towards Paul? I sighed and shrugged my shoulders helplessly. I took one last glance at myself and then returned to our table.

"Isn't this place great," I said when I returned, hoping to diffuse any residual atmospheric intensity that lingered prior to my bathroom escape. "The ambiance is great, and so is the food."

"I like it."

"Yeah, me too. I prefer this kind of place over hoity-toity restaurants." I poked my nose up with my finger, to show him what 'hoity-toity' meant, just in case he needed a visual to go along with the description. "My ex was that way. Not snobby, but he was raised with money, and it's hard to hide that. He *knew* his wines. He loved high-end restaurants."

"Tell me about him. Your ex."

Uh-oh. The ex story. "Not much to tell. It ended a while ago. He's married now, I think. Probably has a couple kids and the whole white picket fence scenario."

"How very cliché," Paul said, mocking me. I resisted the urge to poke my tongue out at him. I can't even remember the last time I had the urge to poke my tongue out at someone. Probably sixth grade. Brian Anderson. He kept kicking at the back of my chair, and every time I told him to stop, he'd wink at me like he was some eleven-year-old porn star.

"Yeah. Cliché. No wonder we broke up," I zinged back.

He chuckled and asked, "Really though, what happened between you two?"

"Oh…" I sighed, not knowing how to explain it. I never do. It could have worked. It *should* have worked. "Something was just missing, I guess…." I trailed off. I wasn't sure if he wanted more of an explanation than that. Seeing him stare at me answered my uncertainty. "We were together for three years, and it was…good. Then he proposed, and I just couldn't say yes. I have a hard time understanding it myself, much less trying to explain it to others. I just…didn't love him the right way."

"What's the 'right' way?"

"I wasn't…passionate about him. About us," I said.

"Passion," he said in a tone that was so sincere that my heart nearly stopped. "That's a big deal."

I looked down, worried that my expression may express my heartfelt understanding. I cleared my throat, "I was naïve. That's all fairytale nonsense."

"Fairytales again, huh? Fate. You don't believe that kind of dogma, do you?" He paused, then added, "Now I'm starting to see why."

Snapping up my head, I looked right at him. What did he mean by that? "Well, do tell," I purred back.

"Because you're a reformed romantic." He looked very proud of himself.

"A what?"

"Well, you *used* to believe in fate, and true love, and happily ever after, didn't you? Once upon a time, there lived a little twelve-year-old Kadie that dreamed of princes on white horses and happily-ever-afters. But it's not working out the way you imagined, is it? Those ideas, you've given up on them, and the easiest way to do that is to hate them. So, you've become a *realist*. You've decided all those ideals that have let you down are bullshit." He was looking at me so deeply. Talking so authentically. He wasn't mocking me. He was just being…real.

"So, what do you believe?" I almost whispered.

"I believe in letting life happen."

"Maybe I used to," I murmured, when I was able to reply. It's not like I even had a story about my heart being broken to explain my reasoning for rejecting any romantic ideals. I suppose I had allowed them to fade as maturity, and wisdom, set in. Then one day, they were gone. I don't even know for sure when it happened. I just realized one day that I no longer believed in shallow romantic rhetoric. So, what was I now? A realist or a cynic? I wasn't sure if I wanted to be either.

We worked on our pizza with slow determination, before setting out to meander the streets of Chicago. Neither of us wanted the night to end.

So we just kept walking.

And talking.

And sometimes not talking.

At some point, he grabbed my hand. Holding his hand while we walked the Chicago streets felt natural. His hands were big, calloused, and warm and enveloped mine in just the right way.

He told me about his brother in Arizona and his nephew, Holden. He explained the story behind his horrible neon-green Nikes. I thought it endearing and found myself softening toward the hideous shoes. As the night came to an end, and exhaustion began conquering our elevated dopamine levels, he turned to me. "Well, any suggestions where one might stay if he needed to make a last-minute hotel reservation?" he asked.

"You don't already have a hotel?"

"Well, I *did*. But that got tricky when I walked out on my meeting earlier tonight," he explained. "Zoe has probably left me thirty messages by now. She will be at my hotel. So…I need to be at *another* hotel for the night…or for the rest of the weekend. Maybe even the rest my life," he chuckled.

"I see…" I said. I had a major devil on one shoulder, angel on the other dilemma going on. I threw caution to the wind and went with my gut, or devil, or heart—who knows. "You can stay at my place. I mean, if you want. You don't have to."

"Really?"

"Yeah."

"Okay. Now we're getting somewhere!" He clapped his hands. Then he noticed my hesitant expression. "No funny business. I promise." He held his hand up with the Scout's Honor sign. I laughed and pulled him in the direction of my car, which was still parked near the auditorium. The reading had ended hours ago, so Denise and her entourage would be long gone by now.

I raised an eyebrow at him. "Just so you know, you're sleeping on the couch. And it's not a comfortable couch, I'm warning you now."

"Deal."

Being an interior designer, my income depended heavily on sales and the current economy. When people didn't want to, or could afford to, spend money on frivolous expenses, one of the first dispensable luxuries was hiring an interior designer. I'd always done well. I'd started to make a respectable name for myself. But I live modestly, fearful of the day that people realize that it's monstrously cheaper to decorate one's own home than it is to hire someone to take on the tedious task. Needless to say, I've prioritized my safety net, and I live quite frugally. My home does not exemplify the life of luxury that most of my clients have.

Not unlike the conundrum of the male gynecologist.

Gynecologists spend all day, every day, looking at hoo-haws, right? One must wonder if by the time they get home, are they even impressed by—or even interested in—their own wife's hoo-haw? Or are they sick of hoo-haws and would prefer a hoo-haw break? So after prodding around in hoo-haws all day, and supposedly being well-versed in hoo-haw needs, their own wife's poor hoo-haw is shamefully neglected.

Same concept with my house. For being an interior designer, my poor home is neglected and barren. By the time I get done with decorating, tending to, and making endless decisions about other people's homes all day, I return to mine and just need a break from it all. I have nothing on my walls except paint. I have very little that shows any kind of personality. My home is small (I prefer the term *cozy*), clean, and simple. And I love it. However, every once in a while, when I have people over, I feel a little self-conscious about it. Not enough to do anything about it, mind you. It's often just a fleeting emotion that I'm able to disregard.

I flipped on the lights as I pushed open my front door. "Home sweet home."

He looked around, appearing pretty impartial to my décor, or lack thereof. For some reason, I was certain his place was decorated in a similar fashion. "This place is nice. It's very 'Kadie'."

I wondered what that meant, but I let it pass. "There's the couch." I motioned toward the oldest piece of furniture in the room. Orange, tan, with brown stripes. It was an eyesore. I got it my first year of college, and for some oddly nostalgic reason, I hadn't been able to part with it yet. One day. "It's old and uncomfortable. You won't be able to stretch out, and you will wake up sore in places you didn't know you could be sore in." I looked at him and then rubbed my hands together. "So I'll go grab you some blankets!"

"Perfect," he said.

I found him cautiously sitting in the middle of the couch when I returned carrying an armful of blankets. He was softly bouncing, testing the aged springs. His face doing little to hide his concern. I tried not to laugh. He looked up at me as I walked in. "This should do it," I said, dropping the blankets next to him on the couch.

"Much obliged," he mumbled, still distracted by the angry springs that were grating into his backside. "I noticed your book collection," he said nodding towards my oversized bookshelves tucked neatly in the corner.

I wandered over to them and lovingly ran my fingers along their spines. He walked up behind me and spied my collection from over my shoulder. "What do you think?" I inquired.

"I think it's interesting how critical you are of clichés when you have every Jane Austen novel in your collection." He picked one out and thumbed through it. "Pretty worn," he said, smiling. "They've been read multiple times, haven't they? This one has water damage. Is that from crying or did you drop it in the tub?" He put the book back and grabbed another one.

As he thumbed through the second book, thoroughly enjoying his current upper hand, my heart swelled with love for the books. He was right. I was the stereotypical woman who has read every Jane Austen book—about five times. I loved them. I grabbed the book from him and put it carefully back on the shelf.

"What do you know about Jane Austen?" I asked defensively. "They're not all just romance and gush. They're also about strong women. Women that are ahead of their time. Just like she was. She was very intelligent and independent, a rare thing in those days. Not to mention she was a brilliant author, not just a gushy romance novelist."

"If you say so." He started looking around. "I'm just wondering where your cat is. She's probably called Elizabeth or Emma or..."

"...Elinor Dashwood?"

"Yeah."

"I don't have a cat. Just pet rocks."

"So which one is your favorite?" he asked, nodding towards the books.

I pointed to *Pride and Prejudice* with a shy smile. I knew what was coming.

"Of course it is."

I laughed. "Okay, okay. It may be a little bit cliché, but I'm not going to dismiss its greatness just because it makes me a... *teeny* bit of a cliché."

"How big of you." He followed my finger to *Pride and Prejudice* on the shelf and pulled it out. "So what makes this so great?"

I answered, "Elizabeth," without any hesitation

"I should have known."

"You've read it?"

"I've seen the movie."

"The book is better."

"Books always are. What's so great about Elizabeth?"

"She's not afraid to be different, even if that means she lives her life alone. And not because she was unconcerned to being alone or standing out. She *wanted* love and companionship, but not if it cost her even the slightest bit of her dignity. She stayed true to herself *despite* being afraid. That's courage." I nodded for emphasis and took the book, thumbing through it carefully. "She was willing to sacrifice a life with the man she loved, if having that life meant betraying herself. And she wouldn't do it."

"Would you?"

"Would I what?"

"Resign yourself to a life with the man you love at the expense of betraying yourself?"

"What do you think?" I asked.

He thought about my question longer than I expected. I appreciated that. He didn't just placate me with superficial responses. He was thinking about what I asked. He thought enough of me to give a response that was sincere. "I don't think you would. And you shouldn't. No man is worth that kind of betrayal."

I stared at him, willing myself not to cry. Instead, I placed the book in his hands. "Here. Take it. Read it."

He gasped. "What?" he mocked. "You sure you can part with it?"

"If you don't enjoy it, this won't work."

"What is 'this'?" he asked.

"I'll tell you after you read the book," I teased. "You can get started tonight because you won't get a wink of sleep on that godforsaken couch."

He laughed, and I started away, but he took my hand and pulled me back into him. He pulled me close, still holding onto my hand while his other, still holding the book, slid around my waist. I took in how tall he was. Not *too* tall, but tall enough that I'd have to stand on my toes in order to kiss him…which I desperately wanted to do at the moment. He looked down at me, his face just a breath away. The way he was looking at me, so intensely, somehow seemed more intimate than a kiss.

Our bodies were pressed together, and then he had both arms around me. I allowed myself to sink into him. He was warm, strong, natural. It was intoxicating. I gave in to the feeling. I shed the reticence that I had trained myself to adhere to. It was liberating to just allow myself to so freely want, and need, and feel. I stood enveloped in his arms, breathing him, taking in his scent—and free falling into an irreversible desire for him.

I whispered, "Are you going to kiss me?"

"Yes," he whispered back.

But he didn't. Not right away. Instead, he kept staring at me, appraising me. It was impossible to discern what was going on behind his eyes. He lifted his arm and tucked a strand of my hair behind my ear and then allowed his finger to trace my jawline. What did he see? I had to bite my tongue to keep from asking, which also helped curb the scream of frustrated desire that was caught in my throat. *Kiss me, dammit!*

Then he did.

***

I lay in my bed, wide-awake, wondering if Paul was doing the same on my couch. I still tasted him, smelt him, felt his hands on me. The remnants of our long, evocative kiss engrained on my lips.

I wanted more. But it wasn't just about sex or physical desire. Yes, I was most definitely interested in having sex, but it was more about being *near* him, partaking of him—in any way. I hadn't even known him twenty-four hours yet, and already he had become a part of my chemical makeup. I wondered if without him, would my corporeal body stop functioning? Would it collapse lifeless to the ground? How had I lived thirty-five years without him?

This was insane! I screamed inwardly and ran my hands through my hair. I was acting crazy! But even as I berated myself and questioned my lucidity, I knew that I wasn't crazy.

I caressed my stomach, my hips, my arms, and thought about his hands on each. His lips on mine. His breath on my neck. Then… Stop! Time to snap out of this. I grabbed the pillow and shoved my face into it and groaned.

I just needed to fall asleep! *Go to sleep, Kadie!*

But I knew that pleading with myself was fruitless. I needed Paul. I wanted Paul. I flung off my covers, walked to my door, and opened it quietly. I stopped and listened for a minute and, after hearing nothing, opened the door wider. My heart pounded as I tip-toed down the hallway.

When I reached the living room, he was lying still on the couch, breathing slowly and rhythmically, as if he were asleep. I stood watching his shoulder rise and fall with the rhythm of his breathing, looking at his disheveled hair and the blanket pulled tight around him. I decided not to disturb him. When I turned to tip-toe back to my bedroom, I heard him say, "Where are you going?"

"Ah, I… uhh…" Oh god! I had no idea what I was planning to say to him.

"Yes?" He turned and looked at me.

"Do you maybe, well, I just know that couch is awful and, well, I guess if you wanted to come in here with me…I guess, that'd be okay."

"You sure?" But even as he asked the question, he was rolling off the couch and stretching out the stiffness that had already set in.

"Sure. I mean, just to…you know. It's just more comfortable…I feel bad, I guess." I was rambling about things that didn't need rambling about. I needed to stop talking. I sighed heavily, showing my frustration and embarrassment, and turned toward my room, waving for him to follow.

I fluffed my pillow and was slinking into my bed while on the opposite side he arranged his own pillow and blanket that he had carried from the sofa. I was taken aback with how routine everything felt. In a good way. It was comfortable, natural.

I pulled my comforter over me and watched as he climbed into my bed. I couldn't shake the conflicting combination of how everything seemed so normal yet surreal. He slid in close to me and put his arms around me. Everything fit. His body was warm and strong. I felt safe. I felt…home. The late hour hit me. I pulled him close, allowed the newfound comfort and fatigue to take over, and fell into a deep, dreamless sleep.

Chapter 8

Kadie talked in her sleep most of the night. Well, maybe talking isn't the most accurate word; she mumbled. Nothing was coherent. Just mad ramblings of a woman sleeping too soundly to give her thoughts any semblance of clarity.

Unlike Kadie, I slept horribly. My mind raced. I was in bed with a beautiful woman that I had met sixteen hours earlier. I was reeling. I was thriving. I was…living. Who sleeps under those conditions? Kadie evidently. She rarely stirred. For most of the night, she had her back to me, and my arm cradled her body, spooning. She slept, and I tried to keep my erection from probing her while the wisps of her hair kept tickling my face. Spooning is a conundrum. Do you let the person go so you can sleep comfortably, or keep holding them for the greater pay-off of being closer to them? It was a good problem to have, but a problem nonetheless; I chose the latter.

As the sun started to peak through the bedroom window, I quietly got out of bed and went to the bathroom. With my phone, I pulled up the Yahoo News thread. The top headlines consisted of greedy politicians and greedier athletes— all wanting more than they were entitled to. Normal everyday occurrences. Further down were some videos from everyday people that had garnered enough attention to go viral. (A star athlete took a special-needs student to prom. A fat woman was fat-shamed for being fat. A cheating husband had to stand on the street corner with a sign that read "I cheated on my spouse. Honk if you hate cheaters.") I kept scrolling until I found what I was looking for. It was near the bottom of the page. The headline read: "Enigmatic Author Stands up 1500 Fans." I tapped the headline, and the story filled my screen. I read.

Evidently, I came down with a serious case of pneumonia that prevented me from attending the reading. I chuckled. The fabrication reeked of Zoe. I was a little surprised and a lot disappointed. (I thought I'd get a harsher diagnosis. Anal fissures or some unknown venereal disease.) Pneumonia was safe. Just deadly enough to keep me from performing, but also not too severe that if I had felt up for it, I could have made a last-minute decision to do the reading. The fans were dejected, and a representative for McCarthy—Zoe, presumably—promised the date would be rescheduled. At the end of the article was a picture of the packed hall. With my thumb and forefinger, I enlarged the pic. I spotted Kadie's empty chair in the middle of the auditorium. Denise sat to the left; she looked as if she were crying.

I closed the article and shut my eyes. I counted to ten, trying to ready myself for what awaited me. I needed to face the music. I went into my voice mailbox and began listening to the messages. Zoe left nineteen. At first, she sounded worried, then upset, then pissed, then apologetic for being pissed and finally, downright irate. Interspersed with Zoe's messages was one from Lisa. She had read the article and wanted to know if I was okay. I deleted her message and turned off my phone. Then I snuck back into bed.

I draped my arm over Kadie's body and pulled her closer to me. She stirred and rolled over and faced me. She opened her eyes and smiled when she saw me staring back at her.

"I thought you'd sneak out in the middle of the night?" she said.

"Was I supposed to?"

She yawned. "Yeah, but I'm glad you didn't."

"I only sneak out if I get laid," I said.

Kadie laughed. "I figured. That's why I didn't put out."

I leaned in and kissed her on the forehead. "What's the plan for today?" I asked.

She wrapped her arms around my neck. "Let's go get breakfast."

We went to a diner about a mile from Kadie's place. It was small, intimate, and every employee knew Kadie. Everyone greeted her warmly, with innocent inquiries about her life; I was given curious stares, with silent judgments concerning my relationship with Kadie. I was an outsider, like an outlaw that enters a saloon in a foreign town right before starting a shootout.

We settled into a booth and Kadie explained that she had been frequenting the mom and pop diner since high school. No other guys, save for Brock, had ever previously been invited to the diner. "It may take a few more visits before the regulars acclimate to your presence," she said. I was touched Kadie thought enough of me to let me infiltrate one of her routine destinations.

When strangers spend the night together, an inherent awkwardness often accommodates the next morning (assuming one doesn't slip out in the middle of the night in order to avoid this scene). The high from the previous night has dissipated, the alcohol buzz—if there was one—has waned. You're left with just yourself and the stranger, and you wake in an unflattering state. Makeup is smeared, hair is disarrayed, breath is unpleasant, body parts are unencumbered and given liberty to hang freely. It's weird. The next morning should be spent alone and reserved for personal introspection so you can tally the previous night. What was said, what was done, what worked, what didn't, and whether the person is worth reconnecting with.

Kadie and I had no discomfort. Waking up with her and going to breakfast felt as natural as any other routine task. Our conversations didn't stall; our desires didn't halt. I was completely present with Kadie, taking all of her in. She took her coffee black with two sugars. She ordered a veggie omelet. I ordered a western and a scone. When my scone arrived, she picked it up and took a bite. She didn't ask, and I didn't care. I liked how familiar we already were. When she bit into the fried bread, powdered sugar got on her nose. I didn't tell her. She kept on talking as one would who didn't have powdered sugar on her nose. God, she was beautiful.

It wasn't until my fake paper salesman career was broached that I had to be more mindful of what I was saying. Lying is an exercise that needs all faculties at peak attention to function. I was tired of keeping up the façade. I figured the easiest way out of my lie was just to squash it, so I told her I got fired.

"They fired you?" Kadie asked incredulously.

"Yes," I said. "They fired me. Walking out of the convention last night was the last straw. Zoe left me a message and said I was done."

"Convention?"

"Yeah."

"You said it was a meeting."

I blanched, trying to recall what I had said. "Did I? What's the difference?"

"Convention sounds more...I don't know. Professional?"

"Well, whatever you want to call it, I left it, and now I don't have a job."

Kadie looked at me for a moment. I shifted in my seat. "You don't seem to be too upset about it," she said.

"I'm not."

"Well, good," she smiled. "I did you a favor."

"You have no idea."

I lamented that I was still, on some level, keeping up the paper salesman ruse, but what was I supposed to do? Come clean? I was afraid to tell Kadie who I was. I was afraid she'd end things if she knew the truth. I wondered which would hurt more: the lie or what I lied about. I didn't want to find out. I just wanted to keep watching her talk with powdered sugar on the tip of her nose. Besides, everyone lies when they're getting to know someone they want to impress. When people go out for the first time, they always pretend they enjoy hiking, traveling, and reading. It's after you feel you've won over the person that you begin to reveal that hiking is hard, traveling is expensive and scary, and reading is a horrible alternative to television and video games.

"So, what are you going to do for work?" she asked.

"I haven't given it much thought."

"Do you have a degree?"

"Yeah."

"In what?"

I almost said business but opted for the truth. "English."

"You majored in English, and you haven't read *Pride and Prejudice*?"

"My emphasis was American lit," I explained. She rolled her eyes.

"English Majors aren't in high demand," she said.

"Yeah, I know."

"Why did you choose English? There's no money in that."

"Yeah, that's what I've been told."

"You should have listened."

"I never heard it until right now."

"How have you functioned without me for all these years?"

"I don't know. I think I need to move here just to be closer to you," I teased.

She smiled. "I'd say that's a good idea," she said. It was hard to tell if this was just banter or a thoughtful reply. Maybe it was both.

"Maybe I can work with you," I said. "Can you teach me how to strategically place couches to ensure the greatest return of Feng Shui?"

"Don't belittle what I do."

"I'm not. Interior designing is a serious matter. Without interior decorators, people wouldn't know that rugs go on the floor."

"Yes, rugs go on floors, and heads—as in your case—go up asses."

I laughed. "That's beautiful."

"I think you're mistaking my insults for flirting."

"I am."

"You shouldn't."

"Why?"

"Because I hate you."

"You're supposed to," I said. "In every great love story, the woman hates the guy in the beginning."

"This isn't a love story."

"Yes, it is," I said. I looked at my watch. "Happy twenty-four-hour anniversary."

"Has it been twenty-four hours?"

"And four minutes."

"Wow. Seems longer than that." She smiled and then leaned across the table and gave me a sugary kiss on the mouth.

***

If you reflect on your life, you probably have a handful of memories that stand out. The rest is just white noise. It's waking up, going to work, coming home, eating dinner, and going to sleep so you can do the whole thing over again the next day. If you're a kid, substitute work for school and it's the same concept. Life is a routine. It's uneventful and tedious. It's the constant drudgery that helps you recall when something spectacular occurs and reminds you that life is, in fact, worth living. You remember events that break the routine. Vacations. Holidays. Deaths. Your first dates are cataloged, but never your tenth, eleventh, twentieth, hundredth. Same with kisses and sex. The firsts stand out, while everything else gets lost in the shuffle.

Kadie was an anomaly in my life of redundancy. She was the blip on my radar telling me to pay attention because my life was about to change. I took it for granted. How was I to know the three days in Chicago were the only three days we'd get together? I remember so much, and because I still think of her every day, the memories still make me ache with what almost was.

I could give a detailed description of how her hand felt when I touched it in the bar. I could identify her perfume if given one hundred different choices in a department store. She preferred cinnamon gum (her first flaw), and eighties butt–rock (her second). She wore mint lip balm that contrasted surprisingly well with her cinnamon gum. Somehow, she made the conflicting flavors work, filling me with a desire to always have her lips on mine. Her style was practical, yet sexy. Her demeanor abrasive, yet somehow inviting. She didn't pander; she sought. She didn't reveal; she hinted. She drove me crazy in every imaginable way.

But even with what I retained, I still had so much to learn. Had I known three days were all I'd get, I would have paid better attention to the little things. I would have asked why she chose a Salvador Dali print as the lone picture that decorated her living room. Why she kept such an uncomfortable couch. If anyone ever told her she mumbles when she sleeps. Why she had so many Grisham novels. (Did she think he was a better author than me?) I wanted to know these things, but everything was impossible to learn in just three days. I thought I'd have the rest of my life with Kadie Park to learn everything about her.

As our weekend together drew to a close, I started to panic. It occurred to me that my flight to Arizona was in a few hours. We hadn't even discussed if, and when, we would see each other again. It was one of those things that sat on the horizon, glaringly obvious, but was avoided because neither of us knew how to address it. I didn't have any answers. All I knew was I wasn't ready to leave yet, and I wasn't sure if I'd ever be able to. My impending departure weighed on her mind too. Which is why I already had my answer when she asked me to miss my flight.

"Miss your flight," she said suddenly and without provocation.

"Okay," I said, and I meant it.

She jumped into my arms. I spun her around twice, stopped, and kissed her. We were on the street. People watched and scoffed at the ridiculous display they were forced to witness. (Is there anything more appalling than two people in love who have no qualms in expressing it?) I put her back on her feet, kissed her again, but when I pulled away, she was no longer smiling. Her chin was quivering.

"What is it?" I asked.

"I have to go to Vegas," she said.

My heart broke. "When?"

"I fly out early Tuesday."

"What for?"

"Work."

"When will you be back?"

"Two weeks."

"Two weeks?"

"Yeah."

"So, then, I'll come back in two weeks?"

"Is that what you want? Don't say it unless it's what you want."

"Yes, it's what I want."

She smiled.

So we made plans for me to return to Chicago in two weeks. I would stay for however long she would have me. She asked about money—a fair question since I had just "lost" my job. I told her I had enough. She laughed and said everything sounded too good to be true.

We had our last dinner at a quaint restaurant overlooking the lake. We were both quiet, reflecting on our sadness without speaking of it. She stared out the window and watched the moon dance on the water. I stared at her and contemplated how long the next two weeks were going to feel.

The waiter came with the check; I handed him my credit card, and he left to run it. Kadie's eyes watered. I didn't know how to fix her hurt, so I looked away and pretended not to notice. The restaurant had a patio that extended over the lake. It was empty. I stood and took Kadie by the hand and led her outside. The night was cool but comfortable. I turned to Kadie and took her in my arms. She rested her head on my chest. Navy Pier was in the distance, and we could hear a soft melody coming from it. It took me a moment to recognize the song was "Wonderful Tonight." We gently swayed to the music. I held her tight and thanked her for the best weekend of my life. She held me tighter and told me I'd better be back in two weeks. I wish that music had never stopped.

At the airport, Kadie laid out her stringent, nonsensical rules for the interim. No texts, phone calls or emails. No contact with each other for the two weeks that we would be apart.

"Why?" I asked, trying hard to understand.

"To give you a chance to reconsider," Kadie said.

"Reconsider what?"

"Whether you want to do this. Whatever 'this' is."

"I do."

"You think you do because I'm here right now. But take the next two weeks. Think about this, about us. Think about what we're doing here. The distance between us. Can this really work?"

"It can. It will."

She smiled. "I hope so. But in two weeks, if you don't feel for me what you feel right now, then you can just walk away. No explanation, no apologies. Just goodbye. You go live your life, and I'll live mine."

"And what if I don't want to say goodbye?" I asked.

"Then we do everything we can to make this work."

"I want that now. I don't need two weeks."

"Neither do I," she said.

"Then why risk it?"

"Because that's the hand life has dealt us."

"Let's change it."

"How?"

I thought for a moment. "Let me come to Vegas with you."

"I'll be working."

"I don't care. Just let me come. I'll stay out of your way."

She contemplated this for a moment, but ultimately decided against it.

"Look," she said, "I know what I feel right now. It's a new feeling, and it's scaring the hell out of me."

"Kadie…"

"But it's a good scare. The kind that doesn't frighten but excites. Let's take these two weeks to re-evaluate everything. Let the dust settle for a moment. And if you feel then how you feel now, I'll pick you up at the airport."

I looked at her for a moment and nodded. I agreed because it was what she wanted. That would become my life: doing whatever she asked.

Kadie's Las Vegas trip was for a high-end client who had just built a 6,000-square foot home right outside the city. The client requested Kadie's services. She offered to fly Kadie to the desert with a blank check to decorate her house however Kadie saw fit. It was a two-week job.

How was I supposed to pass two weeks without her? Sure, she was absent for the first thirty-seven years of my life, but now that I knew she existed, how was I supposed to go on without her? I could always try and write—writing had always been more comforting to me than human interaction—but I doubted I had the necessary concentration skills now that Kadie was in my life.

I just had to make it two weeks and then I'd be back. I resolved to tell Kadie I was Kurt McCarthy when I returned. And love or hate him, McCarthy's subpar writing was at least successful enough to give me the freedom to stay in Chicago, assuming she wanted me to stay. She would be incredulous, and maybe a little upset, but in the end, she would love the added element of surprise and irony it gave to our love story. Ours would be the story people talked about at dinner parties and other social gatherings. Boy meets girl, girl unknowingly tells boy he's a horrible author, boy tells girl he loves her, girl forgives boy for being a horrible author. It was beautiful. It was funny. It was something worth believing in. All I had to do was wait two weeks to make it a reality. No one told me that an entire lifetime can be re-written in just two weeks.

Chapter 9

I woke Monday feeling empty. The left side of my bed now had a proprietor, and he was missing.

I loved my king size bed. It's one of my few prized possessions. Even though I'm a fairly docile sleeper, I've always enjoyed a vast sleeping space. Small beds make me feel confined; I need space to roam if ever the craving hit. I suppose I mused about how this irrational need for a king size bed may be a metaphor for my philosophy on life, specifically with relationships. I was always hesitant to get serious about anybody during my college and early career years. I was worried about being confined, especially if the need to "roam" ever came over me.

Perhaps I assumed committed relationships inevitably created walls, and limits, in life. I know this fear played a role as to why I was always reluctant to fully commit to Brock. As much as I cared for him, I think on some level I feared he'd…suffocate me. Whenever I imagined a future with him, I knew exactly what it entailed. Some find comfort in that kind of stability and constancy, but it made me panic. It sucked the life from me. I needed options. I craved a particular level of the unknown. I didn't want 100% certainty of what we'd be doing from one decade to the next.

The feeling of infinite possibilities is exciting and liberating; it's a feeling that I always needed alive somewhere inside of me.

Brock stifled that feeling. Paul amplified it.

Paul wouldn't hold me back, make me feel trapped. He did the opposite. He stoked the flame of potentials. He broadened possibilities. I imagined a life with Paul that had no limits. I laid in bed thinking about all the things I wanted to experience, and now, with Paul, they took on more potential. Things that I'd always dreamt about doing now were more clear and vibrant.

I stretched and thought about getting up. I needed coffee but getting out of bed seemed too taxing. As I lay there, my mind wandered to Paul's hands and how his touch brought me to life. I couldn't help but smile.

I thought about Saturday night, our last night together. After dinner at a charming restaurant overlooking the lake—a place that I had never even heard of that he had managed to find and book a last-minute reservation—he took me in his arms on the restaurant's balcony, and we slow danced to the hypnotizing music that somehow drowned out the noises of the city.

It was a sweet moment. My eyes watered at the memory. When we left the restaurant, we took our time walking back to my place, hand in hand. We were both trying to make the night last longer, knowing what the next day held. When we arrived, we settled together on my horrible couch and watched TV. He held me close and kissed my temple, and when I looked up at him, he kissed me again so tenderly that it hurt.

The kiss became deeper, and soon what was once sweet and tender, turned into an intense desire. I wanted him. He reciprocated my desire when his kisses became more passionate, and his hands began to caress my neck before moving down my back.

He ran his hand along the curve of my thigh and pulled me closer to him. I could feel his want; he could feel mine. He pulled off my shirt and kissed my neck, right along the curve of my collarbone; it blushed under his touch. Then his kisses trailed lower while he gently removed my bra. I loved the feel of his hands on me. My skin burned, and his touch left a trail of fire. I moaned with delight. His touch drove me mad with desire. He lifted me, carrying me as a lover should. I was straddling him and kissing him and ready to have him while he carried me to my bed. He lay me down lightly, and I reached for him and pulled him to me.

I stripped him of his burdensome shirt. He had a great body, just the right level of muscular, and I allowed myself a moment to take him in. His blond and boyishly-disheveled hair made me smile, but the very un-boyishly desire burning in his eyes made my blood boil.

I felt alive.

I wanted him in every way. I pulled him back down on me and kissed him passionately. My body screamed. I was ravenous, mad with desire.

Sex with Brock had been so-so. Not bad, but not amazing. It lacked passion, spontaneity, love. We went through the motions. I was able to have sex when I wanted it and managed to climax if I focused long enough on something other than what I was engaged in. But if either one of us was too tired, it wasn't a loss. In fact, more and more I started preferring sleep to sex. It wasn't the typical long-term relationship sex story where it was great at the beginning, but then the passion waned. The passion was never there. It's not that I wasn't attracted to Brock; he was handsome enough. But we just never…connected. I never craved him, ever. That's where the problem metastasized. I *wanted* to crave someone. I craved Paul.

Paul pulled off my jeans and threw them on the floor. He ran his hand down my stomach, taking me in with hungry eyes. I moaned with delight. He felt how much I wanted him. But then, as I started on his zipper—my need for him was overwhelming and I was yearning to feel him inside me—he unexpectedly stopped me.

"What's going on? Paul…? What is it?" I whispered.

He sat up and looked at me. "If we do this, it has to be something you want."

"I do."

"I don't want you to think this is all I'm after."

"Wh–what do you mean?"

"I'm falling in love with you, Kadie. I want to make love to you, but I need to know that this is what you want. I need to know that I'm going to see you again after tonight."

I was stunned into a silence. What man halts sex? Should I feel touched or rejected? Initially, I felt the latter, but the more I processed his words, the more I understood. As badly as we both wanted each other at the moment, perhaps rushing into sex would somehow cheapen what was happening between us. He was willing to wait, making it—sex—something more…significant. Not just another notch on his bedpost.

My eyes watered, and my throat thickened. His words touched me. As much as I thought it impossible, I fell harder for him.

"I get it," I finally managed to say. "I…feel the same. I do. Let's wait."

"Come here," he said, opening his arms for me. I fell into him and found my place just below his chin.

I fell asleep in his arms, his face nuzzled against me. I've never enjoyed cuddling; it's too confining, but I loved being in Paul's arms. It was a reprieve.

With that night's memory lingering, I needed a distraction. I got out of bed and padded into the kitchen and started my coffee. Looking at the clock, I decided that it wasn't too early to call Denise. I had been putting her off since Friday. Responding to her inquiring texts, some of them quite malignant, with lame and concise excuses. I was in an intoxicated stupor called *falling in love* and reluctant to let anything disturb the short time I had with Paul. But now it was time to face the firing squad. I grabbed my phone and dialed.

"What the hell is going on with you?" was the answer that accosted me in lieu of the standard "hello?"

"I'm sorry, Denise. Just let me explain."

"You're damn straight you're going to *explain*!" she retorted, but I knew her act was just that—an act. I'd be forgiven. I always was.

So, I told her about Paul. About the whirlwind weekend and how much, and how fast, I'd fallen for him. I explained that he was the reason I had skipped out on the reading. I described the brief time we spent together: the walks, the slow dance, our *not* having sex, his willingness to miss his flight and stay in Chicago, and our plan to see one another again in two weeks. I imagined her on the other end listening with her gaping mouth. I was a stranger to her.

"Holy shit, Kadie."

"I know. Denise…it's like…a fairytale." Even as I said the words, I knew how dumb I sounded. I didn't care.

"Ohmygod. Seriously, who are you and what have you done with my sister?" I detected her smile through her criticism.

"Denise…I'm so happy right now." I choked back emotion.

"Oh, sweetie, I'm so happy right now, too." Denise always supported me with anything. Her love was unconditional. "So, have you heard from him since he left?"

"Well…no. It's forbidden," I said biting my bottom lip. I knew Denise was not going to approve of the rules I had laid out for the next two weeks.

"What do you mean 'It's forbidden'?" Her words were soaked in disapproval.

I sighed. How do I explain something, especially when I didn't fully understand my reasoning behind it either? The logic, although sound, was also somehow asinine. Classic right-brain vs. left-brain scenario. "It has all happened so fast. I think…I *believe* that we should take this time to think about what's happening here. After knowing each other for only three days, we were both ready to commit. To jump all in. Sure, it feels wonderful and intoxicating, but I need to be *somewhat* pragmatic about this, Denise." I realized how nonsensical my rationale sounded when said aloud. But still, I held my ground. I needed to know that I had used *some* logic in all of this. Not just my heart and hormones.

"Oh, posh to your 'pragmatic' little approaches, Kadie! Just jump in! Get dirty for once. What has living such a tidy little life gotten you? Are you happy?"

I looked at my feet, feeling embarrassed and self-conscious.

"This two-week rule is stupid. You need to call him. You need to talk every day. Fall more in love. Ride this train, Kadie! Don't stand at the station and risk letting it pass because you're worried about a little dust."

My whole life I'd been cautious and rational. About everything. I was tired of it. What *had* it gotten me? I couldn't say I was miserable, but I'd not been happy either. Something had been missing. And now that I'd found the missing piece, I was willing to let it possibly slip away? She was right. I was stupid.

"Okay. You're right. I'll call him," I said.

But I waited to call him. I packed for my trip, and the process took some of the wind from my sails. My heart slowed, and I started to think. So, I waited, the romantic side of me arguing with the pragmatic side. At what point do you just succumb to the human in you? That entity living inside that *feels* and *wants* and *desires*. What happens if you let that take over? The thought excited and scared me. I yearned for that freedom but questioned if I had the capacity to let go in such a way. I feared that letting go would be akin to handing over my power, making myself completely vulnerable.

For days I carried on with the angel vs. devil warzone inside me. Though which side was the angel and which was the devil, I wasn't sure.

It was Friday when I decided it was time to call Paul.

I was well into my job in Vegas, and it was moving along nicely. I was worried about a Persian rug, the final touch to an already superfluous remodel job, arriving before I was set to return home. Besides the rug, everything else was going smoothly. I estimated I'd be done in less than a week. That put me a few days ahead of schedule.

My mind reeled with indecisiveness. I could call Paul and ask him to come to Vegas on Friday and spend the weekend with me. Or I could even tell him to come now. We could spend our evenings together.

I was aching to see him.

But if I called him, I was breaking my rule. Stupid as it was, that was a big deal to me. I'd be sending him a message. I'd be opening myself up to him.

But it was time for me to take a risk. It was time to allow myself to be vulnerable and not in control of everything. Maybe it was time I believed in fate and fairy tales and all that silly stuff that seemed to make others so happy. All I knew at that moment was that the thought of calling Paul—hearing his voice, telling him how I felt, betting on us—made me happy. And in an instant, my life was a scene from every bad romance movie I'd spent my entire adult life ridiculing. I wanted my own silly, stupid love story. I needed to call Paul and tell him what I wanted. Tell him that I can't imagine a future anymore without him in it. That I want him to come to Vegas.

Once I realized what I wanted to do, I no longer wanted to wait one more minute for it, or for him.

I was heading to my hotel as I swung wildly to the right to pull off the road, not even taking the time to signal to the other drivers. I made my way into a gas station, many middle fingers and cuss words later, and scavenged my purse for my phone.

"Dammit!" I screamed, as my search failed to produce what I was after. "Where the fu…"

Found it. I needed a smaller purse.

I pulled up Paul's number, paused for a moment, took a breath, and hit dial.

"Paul!" I almost squealed when I heard his voice on the other end.

"Kadie?" he said. He sounded confused. Of course, he was confused. After all, I was breaking my rule.

"Yeah, it's me." I realized that I should have taken the time to gather my thoughts. This wasn't *When Harry Met Sally*. I didn't have a script memorized, no flawless monologue was preordained for this scene. This was real life. I suddenly realized how unprepared I was to lay my heart on the line. How does one do this? What words does one use? Why aren't there *premade* scripts for these types of moments?

The words to use. How small they are. Words. Yet, how much power they hold. Words were about to be said that would start my life—a life that a week ago I had no idea I so desperately wanted.

"Paul, I…come to Vegas. I was wrong. The stupid "no contact" rule. It's so dumb…that rule. And me, I guess. I don't know what I was thinking. Well,

I do, but I was wrong. I miss you… I think…I think I love you. I want…I *need* to see you." I was rambling and didn't know how to stop. Too many words were running from my brain to my mouth, and I couldn't halt their escape. "You said you wanted to come here to be with me, so…come. I want you." I stopped abruptly.

Enough words now.

"Oh, Kadie…you don't know how badly…" he paused. "What you said just now, all of it. It means…everything…" he paused again. What was happening? "Kadie…I can't…" A defeated sigh crept through the phone and grasped my throat in a death-grip.

"Paul?" My heart stopped, and my breath escaped me. My face, hands, legs, my entire body, went numb. I started shaking. What had I done? *Stupid!*

"Kadie, let me explain," he started.

I gulped for air. Everything was spinning. I knew better. How had I allowed this to happen? *Shit, Kadie! How could you be so stupid? Pathetic!*

"No…please don't," I cut him off. I didn't want to hear what he had to say. It would undo everything. It would break me. I was holding my breath. Trying to think beyond the pounding in my temples and the tightness in my chest.

He sighed heavily into the phone. "Something has happened…"

"Nope," I managed to utter before he said another word. "Stop. No need to explain anything, remember?" I had no idea how I was talking. I was not corporeal. My body numbed. The loss was starting on the outside and working its way in. "You get an easy out. I told you that if you had a change of heart during this time apart, you get to just walk away. No explanation, no apologies. Just goodbye." I paused and fought the invading sobs. *Don't let him fucking hear you cry!* "You go and live your life, and I'll go live mine, remember? And I meant it." I needed to get off the phone. A guttural scream was working its way up from my core. My head spun.

"Kadie…no. Please let me explain," he stammered.

"No. Please. I can't…" For some reason, I knew that whatever he was about to say would not dull the pain, but rather intensify it. He didn't want to be with me. He didn't want to come. He was playing his "pass" card. That was all that mattered. "It was a beautiful weekend, Paul. Let's just appreciate it for what it was and leave it at that."

"What was it then?" he asked.

"A beautiful three days. A momentary escape from reality." It was taking all of my effort to even whisper the words: "A fairytale." A small sob escaped me. "Fairytales aren't real, remember? They're cliché."

"Kadie…"

And then I hung up my phone and sobbed.

Chapter 10

Zoe was sitting in my kitchen when I got home. I didn't ask how she got in; I never lock my door unless I'm home. I'm fine with intruders if I'm absent. I live modestly. Any burglars would be disappointed if they went to the effort to rob me. The little I do have is insured, so why lock my house? I'd rather come home to a ransacked condo than a locked door whose key is on the inside. Have you ever locked yourself out of your own car or home? You feel ridiculous. It's a risk I don't take.

When my first novel was optioned for a movie, the studio sent me a $5,000 bottle of scotch. I'd have rather gotten a panini press or some disposable razors. Something useful instead of a pretentious status marker. Scotch is for men who close seven-figure real estate deals and think *The Wolf of Wall Street* is a documentary. I never opened the bottle. I put it in my fridge behind some expired mustard. Zoe found it, and as the unforgiving Arizona sun shot through my kitchen window and shone onto the bottle, it appeared that she was halfway through it.

I dropped my bag on the kitchen floor and sat down across from her. She refused to acknowledge me. She stared past me at something in the distance. She looked as if she had been crying, but it could have just been the scotch. I wondered how long she had been there.

I sent query letters to over two-hundred agents trying to get *Boarded Window* published. Some sent rejection letters, but most didn't even extend that courtesy. At the time, Zoe was an intern for one of the most prestigious literary agencies in New York. One day her boss called from Europe and said she needed some contact information from her address book. She'd left her book in the top drawer of her desk, and she needed Zoe to find it. Zoe retrieved the book, read her boss the requested information, and then hung up. She sat at her boss's desk for a moment imagining how she would run the agency. She gave imaginary demands to imaginary staffers and had hypothetical conversations about which writers to represent and which were beneath the agency. She enjoyed pretending to be someone she wasn't.

She found my query letter in her boss's trash bin. Spotted it when she spat out her gum and it ricocheted off the side of the can. Zoe pulled the letter from the trash and read it. She contacted me and asked for the first fifty pages of my manuscript. I sent it, and a week later she asked for the rest. She read it and then convinced her boss to do the same. She did. I got published, and Zoe got promoted.

I owe my career to Zoe. She said yes when everyone else said no. And now that she was sitting in my kitchen pretending I didn't exist, I felt, for the first time, sorry for leaving the reading. I knew from her voice messages that she was pissed, but it never occurred to me that she may be hurt also. I can handle anger, but sadness, well, that just makes me sad.

"I'm sorry," I whispered.

She didn't react. I thought to repeat my apology a little louder, but I knew she heard me the first time. She would speak when she was ready. Part of my punishment was waiting her out. I had walked out on her, too. Now I had to allow her to set the rules of whatever game we were playing. Fortunately for me, she didn't make me suffer too long. She wanted answers.

"What happened?" she asked.

"Evidently, I got pneumonia." I laughed at my own joke to try and ease the tension. It didn't work.

Zoe looked at me. Her haphazardly applied mascara stood in clumps at the corners of her eyes. She was not amused. "Your publisher wants to sue," she said.

"Sue? On what grounds?"

"Breach of contract."

Silence.

"I talked them out of it."

"How?"

"Well, your most loyal fans hate you. They're pissed you stood them up. But your little stunt seems to have generated an even more mysterious persona than you've already established. The public is intrigued. Your books are selling better now than they ever have." She scoffed and shook her head, baffled by the irony.

"Well, that's something, huh?"

"It's the best accidental marketing procedure they've ever seen," she said. "If you promise to do another reading, they won't sue."

"When?"

"They haven't set a date, but I'm sure it will be before the end of the year."

"Do I have to?"

Zoe shot me a look. I lowered my head. "Okay," I said.

Zoe took another drink. She looked at me, her eyes cold, and shook her head. "You're an asshole, Paul. Or Kurt. Or whoever the hell you are or pretend to be. I'm the one who had to go out on that stage and face your mob."

"I know," I said. "I'm sorry."

"Some threw books at me. Hardback books, Paul. Books. Not tomatoes or heads of lettuce. Books!"

I stifled a laugh, swallowed hard, and apologized again. She took another drink. "You're not supposed to refrigerate scotch, you dumb-shit," she said. She finished her drink, winced as it went down. "So, what happened, and if you say pneumonia, I'll break this bottle over your head."

"I met someone."

"What?" Zoe said. She was incredulous.

"On the flight to Chicago," I explained. "She was reading *Trainride,* and I asked what she thought. She was unimpressed, I got a little defensive, and then she invited me to her book club. She thought...she thinks I'm a sellout." I paused for a moment. Zoe wasn't following.

"What the hell are you talking about?" she asked.

"Her name's Kadie," I said, as if knowing her name would somehow make clear all the things that weren't.

"Kadie? Who the hell is Kadie?"

"The girl on the plane," I said, frustrated that Zoe wasn't following. "She called right before I was supposed to go on stage. She was there actually, at the reading. I was watching her from backstage. Right before I went on, she got up and left. She called me, and I met her for dinner."

"Wait. You left all those people, all your fans, to go have dinner with some woman you met on the plane?"

"Yeah."

"It wasn't stagefright or nerves or some sudden sickness or something like that? It was for a woman?"

"Yeah."

Zoe stared hard at me for a full minute. I'm not sure if what I said was harder to process because of the alcohol or if she just needed the silence because what I told her, sober or not, didn't make sense. The wheels turned in her head. I had no idea what she was about to say, but I was terrified of what it might be. She wanted to speak, opened her mouth to do so, but instead of saying anything, she grabbed the scotch and poured herself another drink. Her hand shook either from frustration or anger or both. She downed her drink and slammed her glass on the table.

"What the hell, Paul!" she yelled.

I lowered my head. I was like a child being reprimanded for skipping a chore or getting caught looking at his mom's tampon box. "I love her," I said, hoping my admission somehow justified my actions.

"You love her?" Zoe repeated trying to suppress a laugh. "You don't know her."

"We spent the entire weekend together."

Zoe shook her head and ran a frustrated hand through her hair. "Jesus, Paul, you don't love this woman. You're still on the rebound from Lisa."

"I haven't even thought about Lisa. This has nothing to do with her."

"Okay," Zoe said. She put her hands up in surrender. "I don't care. But what do you want me to tell your publisher, because I sure as hell won't tell them you skipped out on the reading to be with some woman."

Love is a foolish enterprise to the people uninvolved. It's a feeling that has been marketed and pitched as universal, but it isn't. It can't be. If it were, then all anyone ever had to say about anything was, *I'm in love,* and all other outside priorities and responsibilities would become obsolete. But I couldn't convey to Zoe what I'd experienced in the past three days. She didn't know my heart stopped every time Kadie's lips were on mine. She had no idea of the fortitude I displayed when I refrained from making love to Kadie. Zoe couldn't comprehend that, as we sat at my kitchen table, my heart leapt and broke every second because I still smelled Kadie's perfume on my clothes. It was impossible to relay those things to Zoe because they didn't involve her. She would not understand. Kadie was mine. She was for me. Trying to help a third party comprehend the exhilaration and excitement that accompanies meeting the person you're supposed to be with is a futile endeavor. They can't relate. They can empathize, maybe, if they too know what it means to love someone. But even that love is faulty because love's power is always only reserved for the people involved. If Zoe felt a fraction for anyone what I felt for Kadie, then she would *listen* when I told her I was in love, instead of hearing it and dismissing me. She laughed at my confession because she had no frame of reference.

"What should I tell your publisher, Paul?" Zoe asked.

"Tell them…I don't care what you tell them," I said.

Zoe sighed and shook her head. She was softening. "This woman, she's from Chicago?"

"Yeah."

"How you going to make that work?"

"I'm going back in two weeks."

"Yeah? You gonna move out there?"

"I don't know. If I need to. I can work anywhere."

"You sound like a character in a book."

"I know," I said. I wasn't going to try and make her see things from my perspective. "I am sorry, Zoe."

"Well, I hope she's worth it."

"She is."

Zoe studied me for a moment. I think she was now sensing my sincerity. She scoffed. "I have to use your bathroom." She struggled to her feet. "I don't know if it's you or the scotch, but I think I'm going to throw up." She started down the hall, keeping to the wall for balance, and then stopped and turned back to me. "You said she was unimpressed with your book?"

"Yeah. She enjoyed my first, respected my second, but thinks my writing is cowardly now. She called me a sellout."

"What did she say when you told her you're Kurt McCarthy?"

"She doesn't know."

Zoe nodded. "That makes sense. If she knew who you were, she wouldn't like you." She turned back and resumed her clumsy trek to the bathroom.

I stood and went into my kitchen to make coffee. Dirty dishes cluttered the sink. Dried pasta sauce and hardened spaghetti noodles were stuck to plates. Coffee rings lined the bottoms of mugs that were tossed into my sink. My house was spotless prior to my trip. I'd rather come home to a robbery than discarded food stuck to cutlery. Was this some cruel trick Zoe played for retribution? If so, finding a new agent had just become priority number one. I doused the plates with dish soap and turned on the hot water so they could soak. I shut off the water and then noticed Lisa standing in the kitchen. She entered undetected. She smiled. I tried, and failed, to remember the last time she seemed happy to see me.

"What are you doing here?" I asked.

"I've been staying here," she said.

That explained the dishes. Lisa was worse than a college roommate. "This place is filthy," I said.

"I wasn't expecting you until later this afternoon. I was going to clean them."

I didn't try to mask my anger. "Yeah, I bet."

"I'm sorry."

"You're not welcomed here."

"Are you sick?"

"What?"

"Don't you have pneumonia?"

"No, that was a lie."

"Why?"

"Something Zoe made up to cover for me."

"Cover for what?"

"Why are you here, Lisa?"

Her smile disappeared. She went to the table and sat down. She put her hands in her lap and lowered her head. I think she began to cry, but I couldn't tell, and I didn't investigate because I didn't care. I waited for her to explain herself. When she lifted her head and looked at me again, her eyes were red, and tears hung on the corners.

"Did you get my messages?" she asked.

"Yeah."

"You never texted me back."

"I had no reason to. We're over."

"I need to tell you something."

She wanted me to ask what it was, but I was completely disinterested so I stayed silent. She began crying again. I made for an exit when she said: "I'm pregnant, Paul."

The words floated from her lips, hovered in the air for a moment, before making their way into my ears. I heard them, but I didn't understand them. I stared at Lisa dumbly, thinking that if I didn't react, then maybe what she had just said couldn't possibly be true. I would have likely stared at her for the rest of my life had it not been for Zoe materializing from the hallway. She cut into the silence, "I guess now isn't a good time to tell her about Kadie, huh?"

I turned and looked at Zoe. She smiled, pleased to be a bystander as Lisa draped a millstone over my head. The weight forced my chin to my chest. I inhaled deeply; Kadie's scent was no longer on my shirt.

***

Pregnant.

Shit.

Shit!

SHIT!

It was after midnight. I paced my living room while Lisa slept in my bed. She'd moved herself in while I was in Chicago. As I thought I was starting a new life, she was here, re-planting herself in this one. I hadn't slept in days.

I wanted to call Kadie, but she forbade it. Even if she hadn't, what would I say? *Ah…you know that woman I was seeing? Turns out I got her pregnant before we broke up. Do you still want me to come to Chicago?*

I kept weighing my options. Abortion was off the table. Not for political reasons. That had nothing to do with it. Abortion was off the table because Lisa said it was. She wanted the baby, and even if I didn't, I respected that she did.

Adoption wasn't an option either. Again, not because I'm opposed to it, I just couldn't go through with it. Not with my kid. If I had a hand in creating a kid, I wanted to influence his/her upbringing.

Keep it. This was the most realistic option. The problem wasn't necessarily the child; it was the mother. The child tethered me to Lisa for life. I was a ship destined for Chicago; Lisa was the anchor keeping me from it.

Lisa and I had sex once in the past three months. We were at a friend's party. I stood in the corner talking with a proctologist. He was a small, bespectacled man with a nasally voice and nervous demeanor. More importantly though, he had stories worth listening to. Lisa stood in another corner talking with a guy I'd never seen before. She kept touching his arm when she spoke and laughing a little too loudly at jokes I knew weren't funny.

She was drunk. She was too happy not to be. From across the room, I spied another woman approach Lisa and the mysterious man. She looked upset. She whispered something to the man. He looked at Lisa, said something, and then walked away with the other woman. Lisa was left alone with just her overdone makeup and half-empty wine glass. She swallowed the rest of her drink and put her empty glass on a nearby shelf and scanned the room. She spotted me and made a beeline in my direction. The proctologist was almost to the climax of a story involving a banana and a gnome lawn ornament, when Lisa arrived and kissed me hard, jamming her sour tongue in my mouth. She released me and looked over her shoulder. The mysterious man stared back at us. He shook his head and turned back toward the woman who had led him away a moment earlier. Lisa looked back at me and said, "Let's get out of here."

"But I haven't heard the rest of Dr. Dover's story," I protested.

"Now, Paul," she said. She grabbed my hand and pulled me from the room.

We went back to my place and had passionless, three-minute sex. Once we finished, she rolled off me and checked her phone. I went to the bathroom and took a shower. That was about eight weeks ago.

Now, as I returned from my failed Chicago unveiling, Lisa wanted to give us another chance. She threw me every laughable romantic cliché about love and redemption and soul mates. I listened passively, while silently cursing defective IUD's. After she finished her litany of reasons why we should try again to make us work, she asked what I was thinking. I told her the truth.

"I don't love you."

She remained silent for a full minute. "You did once."

"Not how you think."

"Paul, we're going to have a baby together."

"And I will provide for this baby and be a constant presence in its…" I stumbled, "…his…her…life. But I can't be with you, Lisa. I don't feel anything for you."

"Nothing?"

"I don't know," I said. "Maybe resentment?"

I didn't intend for my comment to sting, but I knew that it had. "What happened to us?" she asked.

"Things changed after I told you who I was, and I learned who you were."

Ever since I told Lisa I was Kurt McCarthy, our relationship transitioned from getting to know each other, to her trying to exploit my potential fame. She wanted to meet celebrities and attend extravagant parties. She yearned for the hedonism that accompanied movie premiers and suites at the most expensive hotels in the world. When I told her that wasn't my life, she countered and said it could be if I made more of an effort.

When *Boarded Window* was optioned for a movie, I visited the set once (to appease Lisa) and skipped the premier (to appease myself). She was thrilled with the former and dejected by the latter. I received invites to social gatherings from people in show business. Inquiries about future projects, screenplay adaptations, offers to meet producers and directors at studios or other opulent environments. I told Zoe to handle everything. All I wanted was to write. Nothing else mattered. My idea of a good time was pizza and beer at a local hole-in-the-wall and slow dancing on a deserted patio. The idea of glad-handing the Hollywood glitterati exhausted me.

My indifference to the possibility of a life marketed through social media and TMZ sightings puzzled Lisa. I stood on the threshold of being someone to everyone, she told me. I told her I just wanted to be someone to someone. For a moment I thought that maybe Lisa was that someone. I was wrong.

Things went from bad to worse when I forbade her to disclose who I was to her family and friends. I even had Zoe write-up a fake confidentiality agreement that I forced Lisa to sign. Under the faux conditions of the contract, if Lisa disclosed my identity, she was liable for any future book sales under my pen name. She was confused about what that meant. Zoe looked at her coldly and explained: "If you tell anyone about Paul, you'd be on the hook for millions of dollars." Lisa frowned, and Zoe continued: "Keep your mouth shut if you know what's good for you, Lisa," Zoe said. She relished playing the villain.

Lisa wept at the threat. I left the room, went into the bathroom, and turned on the faucet full-blast to muffle my laughter.

I know I should have ended things with Lisa over a year ago. I can't defend why I didn't. It was apathy mostly. She didn't get in the way of my writing, and if I ever had any rare moments of loneliness, she was there. She let me live my life and focus on my novels unencumbered by the normal relationship obligations often meted out by girlfriends. She fulfilled my occasional physical needs and was absent enough to allow me to pursue my intellectual ones. As I admit these things now, I realize just how much of a bastard I was. I'm embarrassed to reflect on what my life was for the last two years. My redemption came in the form of Kadie. Karma came in the form of Lisa's pregnancy.

***

"You should know something," I said to Lisa. We were driving to a doctor's appointment. "I met someone in Chicago."

Lisa stared out the window. The past few days had been hard for us. I asked her to leave. She cried and said she had nowhere else to go. I told her to go home. She couldn't because she lost her job—let go because of cutbacks. Then she lost her apartment. She had no family—at least none that she spoke to—and she didn't want to impose on her friends. That only left me, the father of her child. It seemed that the right thing to do was to let her stay.

The following days were filled with awkward silences. She stayed in my bedroom, and I slept on the sofa. I tried to reject the probability that I'd need to convert the spare bedroom—my office—into my baby's room. It was either that or buy a bigger house. That wasn't practical. I'd forfeit my office. Fatherhood was killing me.

"Who is she?" Lisa asked.

"I met her on the plane. We spent the weekend together."

"Is that who Zoe was talking about the day you got home?"

"Yeah."

"What's her name?"

"Does it matter?"

Lisa thought for a moment. Decided her name didn't matter. "Did you sleep with her?"

"Does that matter?"

"Yes."

"No," I whispered, "I didn't sleep with her."

"Did you want to?"

People are always preoccupied with the notion of sex. I didn't sleep with Kadie, but what I did experience with her was more intimate than sex. I couldn't explain that to Lisa, though. Humans are too linear to think in terms of connectedness with another person, so instead they opt for the simple questions that they associate with romance: *Did you have sex? No. Well, did you want to?* What single man wouldn't want to sleep with an attractive woman? It was a stupid question, so I left it unanswered.

"I'm going back to see her," I said.

"When?"

"In a couple days."

"Does she know about us?"

"Us?" I asked incredulously. "She knows we broke up."

"Does she know I'm pregnant?"

"No."

"Why haven't you told her?"

"I haven't talked to her since I got home."

Lisa opened her mouth to say something else but decided against it. She put her hand on the window and spread her fingers on the glass. Outside the world passed in a series of colors and objects that wouldn't take shape.

***

I couldn't see the baby. It was just a dark screen with shades of grey that moved when the doctor slid the transducer over Lisa's shiny belly. I thought maybe Lisa was mistaken. That maybe she took a faulty pregnancy test and was duped into believing she was pregnant. But then I heard the heart beating. Like a hollow metronome, my child's heart filled the room. It beckoned me. I moved toward the monitor, and my child came into focus. It was a speck, but it was unmistakably there, and it was alive.

Some switch inside of me was flipped. I was going to be a father.

Lisa gasped and cried. I went to her and took her hand. She leaned into me and cried into my chest.

"I can't do this alone, Paul," Lisa sobbed.

My baby's heartbeat, steady and healthy, still filled the room. "You don't have to," I said, and I meant it.

Life is a series of choices. My choices, intentional or not, had led me to that examination room holding the mother of my child. My choices propelled me into a life I never intended, but I had to now live nonetheless. I would do what I needed to give my child the best possible life. I kissed the top of Lisa's head and tried not to cry.

Five minutes later, while waiting in the lobby for Lisa, my phone rang. The number looked familiar, but it didn't have a contact name attached to it. I should have just let it go to voicemail. I should have entered Kadie's name into my phone after she called me the night of my reading. I should have done anything besides answer it. But that's what I did. I answered it, and it was Kadie. I was caught off guard. Had I known she intended to break her own rule and call me, I would have been better prepared. Maybe even compose a few notes and be ready with an explanation.

"Paul," she said, "I…come to Vegas. I was wrong. The stupid 'no contact' rule. It's so dumb…that rule. And me, I guess. I don't know what I was thinking… Well, I do, but I was wrong. I miss you… I think…I think I love you. I want…*need* to see you." She paused for a moment. I knew I needed to say something, but my thoughts were scattered, so I stayed silent. "You said you wanted to come here to be with me," she continued, "So…come. I want you."

My mind raced. Lisa emerged from the bathroom. She spotted me standing dumbly in the center of the lobby with my phone to my ear. She smiled and started toward me. I began to sweat. Kadie wanted to see me. Could I go to Vegas tomorrow? No, I couldn't. Lisa had an appointment with a prenatal nutritionist tomorrow. She had asked me earlier to take her. "Of course," I told her. I was the father. It was my job to take her.

"Oh, Kadie," I managed to say. My heart raced almost as much as it ached. "You don't know how badly…what you said just now, all of it. It means…everything." I closed my eyes. I thought of Kadie and Chicago and the life that seemed so close a week ago.

"Kadie…I…can't," I whispered, but I knew she heard me clearly. I sensed something snap on the other end of the line. I couldn't see her; I didn't need to. I knew she was thrown off, hurt. The vibrations of her pain permeated through the phone. I wanted to explain. I wanted to tell her the truth about everything. That I was Kurt McCarthy, that I know I should have told her sooner, and I was sorry for the deception. But most importantly, that I was going to be a father. I had new obligations in Arizona that needed my attention, but I'd still come to Chicago if she'd allow it. We'd figure out everything, figure out a way to make things work.

But none of that was said. The words escaped me, and even if I found them,

Kadie refused to hear them. She cut me off before I could say anything else.

Lisa reached me and looked at me curiously, wondering why my face was flushed. I asked Kadie to wait a minute so I could clear my head, but she said there was no use. She hung up. She was gone. Out of my life as quickly as she had entered it.

"Who was that?" Lisa asked. I ignored her and looked at my phone. My hand shook. I retrieved Kadie's received call and called back the number. It rang once and went to voicemail.

"No," I panicked.

"Who was that?" Lisa asked again.

"Can you give me a minute, please. I need to make a call."

"Is that the woman you met in Chicago?"

"Lisa, please. Just give me a minute."

Hurt, Lisa started toward the exit while I called Kadie back. It went straight to her voicemail again. "Kadie, please give me a chance to explain…I…something happened here, and I have to stay here for…for…I don't know how long. It's my ex. She…she needs me for…I…don't know what to say or how to say it. I don't want to talk to your voicemail. Please call me. I want to see you again. I want to explain what's happening. Please, call me back. Please." I breathed into the phone a moment longer trying to think of something better to say before I hung up. I was at a loss. I ended the call and looked at my phone and waited for her to call back. But she never did. And she never would.

"Paul, are you coming?"

I turned. Lisa stood at the lobby's entrance. I looked at my phone again. My broken reflection in the dark screen stared back at me. I put the phone in my pocket and felt something inside. I pulled it out. It was a picture of the ultrasound. I looked at Lisa, perplexed. She smiled. "I slipped it into your pocket," she explained. I looked back at the photo. I saw my child, alive in the dark shadows surrounding the grainy picture. How was something unrecognizable so beautiful? I was so entranced with the picture that I didn't even realize that Lisa had linked her arm through mine, girlfriend style, as she led me out of the hospital.

Chapter 11

Life continued after my phone call with Paul, as life always does. It's funny. Life has moments where you should have the choice to continue carrying on with all of life's silliness or just be done. I'm not necessarily talking about suicide, but more of a waving of the white flag. You should be able to say, "Okay life. I've given it my best. This isn't working out so well, and I'm tired. Can I just be done now?"

It's a perfectly sound and compassionate option. Shouldn't a person be able to plead mercy? Shouldn't emotional injury be enough to eradicate you the same way physical injury can? It seems almost cruel that the system is not set up this way. Instead, we survive emotional death, and are forced to continue trudging through the remaining hollowed-out and painfully cavernous life day after goddamn day. A life that incessantly echoes at us of what should have been.

It's erroneous, it's unfair, and it pissed me off.

The body should be allowed to just shut down. I truly do not understand how it continues to work. How your heart continues to pump blood; your lungs continue to breathe air; your intestines still digest food; your nerves continue, persistently, to send messages to your brain.

You need food.

You need sleep.

You should get up now.

It's time to pee.

How the hell does your body just keep on carrying on when you are so obviously damaged?

I. Did. Not. Understand.

And to hell with God, or whomever is in charge of this life for making it this way. When one is *physically* injured beyond repair, the standard and compassionate result is death. That is how it should be.

Similarly, when one is *emotionally* damaged beyond repair, why isn't there a similar sympathetic result? Your body should be able to follow suit—to allow the damage to take over and shut down.

You should be able to wave the mercy flag.

***

"Kadie, answer your phone!" Denise's voice demanded. Again. "I'm tired of talking to your voicemail. What's going on? Why are you avoiding me? I'm coming over later, and I'm breaking in, okay?" A long paused followed. "Kadie," speaking softer now, "I…please talk to me. This isn't healthy… I… I love you, sweetie. I'm here. Call me back."

Click.

I listened to the message with complete apathy. One of the few I'd even taken the time to listen to in the last week. I wasn't going to call her back, and I didn't care that my actions were hurting her, either. I cared about nothing.

Paul had also tried calling me several times since our conversation. The one message I forced myself to listen to, was him stammering on about his ex. Nice, Paul, that's much better. I'm happy to know now that you've "passed" on me, and you're back with your ex. That definitely alleviates the pain. I rolled over and screamed into my pillow.

I hated myself. I hated everything about what I was doing. I was watching myself and hating myself. Disgusting and pathetic. I'd become everything that I'd always hated, thought I was better than, scoffed at. I was a silly, broken-hearted woman. A goddamn cliché.

Everything—all my beliefs, my plans, what I knew, my heart—was fragmented now, and I didn't care enough to even try and figure out how to piece things back together. I just wanted to lie in bed and stop existing. Stop hurting. I prayed for spiritual and corporeal dissipation.

Paul kept calling. Kept texting. I needed him to stop. I ignored his pleas to explain himself. Why he changed his mind wasn't important, all that mattered was that he'd changed it. Any explanations, no matter how sincere, would just cause more pain.

More hurt.

Please, Paul, I begged. *Just…no more.*

His voice wounded me. I had to remove it from my brain. After his first voicemail message, he left several more. I deleted them before I was tempted to listen to them. I refused to hear his patronizing "reasons" for not choosing me, not choosing us. He hadn't earned the privilege to hurt me anymore than he already had. The reasons were irrelevant; his choice spoke his true feelings.

That's what mattered. The choice. And he'd made it.

As much as I pleaded with myself not to, I kept reminiscing on our time together. Those three days. How much of it was *real.* Genuine. I was lost. At the time, it had all been so perfect. So right. Was it all in my head? Was I such an inane and delusional woman? None of it made sense. He loved me. He *told* me. He *saw* me. *Me.* I don't let anyone do that. We danced. Our souls became interlaced. It was REAL! I know it was just three days, but the time seems so trivial. We connected in such an indelible and complete way it might as well have been three years or thirty.

It seemed unrealistic to fall for someone the way that I fell for Paul in such a short time. But I did. It happened. My life had been knocked off its tracks. I couldn't go back and put everything back where it was before I'd met him and then pretend those three days never happened. If my heart and brain and being had an 'off' switch, I would have flipped it. Just turn off all feelings and functions and robotically get through the remaining days.

Somehow, I managed to finish the job in Las Vegas and find my way home. God only knows how. But the second I walked in the door, I collapsed. Physically, mentally, emotionally—I was done for. For the last week, I'd zombied my way through life, not leaving my house once.

I pictured Paul's face, his eyes looking at me so intensely. That look, his look, now fused into my brain. I'd give anything to somehow erase that weekend from my memory, to return to who I was before Paul. I was fine. I was competent. I was… mobile. I was blissfully unaware of all the things my life was lacking.

I wanted to go back to being unaware of what I was missing out on. Peaceful, heavenly ignorance. I wanted to go back to not knowing, needing, wanting Paul. That was the only way to feel whole again.

It was Saturday, I think.

I knew I had until Monday to get myself together. That gave me two more days to figure out how to face the world again. I had no idea how I was going to make that happen. I had given myself a week to fall apart, the whole time assuming that when the week was over, I'd be able to brush it off and be on my way. Well, the week was almost over, and I wasn't close to brushing anything off. Where to start remained a mystery. Nothing made sense anymore. My life—the life that I'd worked so hard to make a certain way, that I thought I loved—seemed…wrong now. Everything that was so strategically placed before was now it the wrong spot. Nothing fit anymore.

I sighed and rolled over and contemplated my current physical state. I hadn't eaten much more than toast, chips, and outdated popsicles for the week. I hadn't even been able to bring myself to lacing up my running shoes and hitting the pavement, one of my favorite pastimes. Eating, walking, showering, brushing my teeth—anything that involved getting out of my bed—seemed exhausting. Therefore, I dismissed most tasks that accommodate being a functioning adult. Consequently, my hair was greasy, my belly starving, and my breath wretched.

I stared at the ceiling for another thirty minutes and fell asleep while trying to find the energy to get out of bed and take a shower.

***

A horrible pounding woke me with a start. I was disoriented. It took a couple minutes before the fog cleared and I realized someone was pounding at my front door.

I looked at the clock. 11:37. I had no idea if that was A.M. or P.M. I took in, once again, my current physical state. The pounding subsided for a beat, and I began drifting back to sleep, and then it started again with new determination. Reluctantly, I got out of bed and padded down the hall to the front door. I opened it and was immediately accosted by my sister.

"Okay, girl, I don't care what…" Denise said, barging past me. Then she stopped short when she saw me, her eyes wide, full of shock and dismay, and her mouth dropped. I hung my head. This is what I'd become.

"Good Lord, Kadie! What the hell happened to you?" She was carrying two bags. I spotted the local bakery's logo on them, and my stomach turned at the sight. She dropped the bags to the floor and approached me. Her face softened, "Kadie, what's going on? Talk to me. Please."

I opened my mouth to speak, but I couldn't. I tried again, but all that came out were angry sobs. I tried explaining things to her, but my words—or more accurately, my sad ramblings—weren't coherent. She took me in her arms, despite my wretched state, and let me cry. Thank God for Denise.

Forty-five minutes later, after a much-needed shower, we sat at my kitchen table eating the rolls Denise had brought. It was nice to eat real food. My body needed the sustenance, and my stomach sang Denise's praises.

As I started on my fourth roll, I appraised Denise. She was easy on the eyes. We had similar features, obviously sisters, but hers were so much more...delicate. She had long legs and tiny wrists. Her dark bob trimmed her face perfectly, always. And it damn-well should, she paid a high price for it every three weeks. Her skin was naturally dark, similar to mine, but without the freckles. And also unlike mine, her eyes were bright and inquisitive—while mine were dark and introspective, always cautious. Her features complemented each other beautifully.

"I'm sure you don't want to talk about it, but I'm not leaving until you do," Denise said. She was right. I had no desire to talk about Paul and what had happened, but I knew she wouldn't leave until I explained things. At least she had the decency to let me eat first.

So, I explained everything. Every detail, every moment. I relived them in the retelling, and by the end, I wanted to return to my bed, and fall into a sleep far away from my current reality.

"Don't you want to know what happened?" Denise asked. "Why he had a sudden change of heart?"

"No. I don't want to know. I don't think it will make anything better. Or easier," I replied, numbly.

"But what if it does, Kadie? Isn't it worth finding out? One minute he's over-the-moon in love with you, and then next...he just can't come?" She scoffed and shook her head. "That doesn't make any sense. Which means he must have a good reason, Kadie. He has to."

"Just because I want something, doesn't make it so."

"What do you mean?"

I sighed, "Of course I want there to be a good explanation for his change of heart. But what if there isn't? I can't hear him say, 'I reconnected with my ex, and I was mistaken. You were just a random weekend tryst, and I'm not in love with you; I'm still in love with her.' That's a *very* possible scenario, Denise! And no, I don't want to hear that. I asked him to come to Vegas; he said no. Nothing else matters. People always want a chance to explain. You know why? To make themselves feel better. Not me. I'm not giving him that chance."

"But surely the real reason can't be worse than any story you're concocting on your own. You're just causing yourself unneeded pain and misery by not talking to him or allowing him to explain." Her eyes oozed confusion. This is where we were two very different people. Denise had spent most her life staring at me confused.

I shook my head. "No. I don't want to know." I looked down for a beat and then back up at her. "I can't believe I let a man affect me this way. This isn't me." A tear slid down my cheek. "I have always worked so hard to be…sane. Pragmatic. A realist." Denise handed me a tissue. "I watched friend after friend have their hearts trampled by some dumbass shmuck or get stuck in a loveless marriage where they became numb or robotic in order to survive. I was always conscious to avoid those relationship traps." I exhaled sharply. "I promised to never be *that* woman." I threw my hands up in surrender. "Well shit! Fail."

"No way. Not a *fail*," Denise argued vehemently. "Win!" she exclaimed, smiling.

"Win? Ha! C'mon, Denise. Don't patronize me. I'm the furthest thing from a winner. Did you smell me an hour ago?"

"You've *loved*, Kadie! You've loved real, and you've loved hard! Even if it was short lived. Do you know how many people never get to experience that? Sure, it's painful now, but that just means you're alive! You're living your life. You're having experiences that will make you better, stronger." Her bright eyes were full of excitement and hope. My heart panged with resentment. How was it that she always found the silver lining?

"Bullshit," I spat back. "I don't want *these* feelings! This *experience*! This is *horrible*! I would give anything to take it all back!" I stood from the table and started pacing. "I think I knew this a long time ago," I said mostly to myself.

"Knew what?" Denise asked.

"That I wasn't cut out for this!" I almost screamed, crying again. "I don't have the strength for these types of *experiences*! That's why I consciously, and maybe even subconsciously, avoid them!"

"Oh, Kadie…" Her eyes were full of pity and sorrow.

"See!" I pointed at her. "I'm a pitiful sob story now! You feel bad for me! I'm a pathetic mess! Crying over some guy that made me fall in love with him!

He made me believe in fairytales! I knew him for THREE days, and he undid thirty-five years' worth of work!" I collapsed on the chair.

Silence filled the room. I wait for Denise's rebuttal, but it never came. I looked at her. She looked past me, lost in her own thoughts. She waited another beat before she spoke again. "Then stop," she said.

"What?"

"Then just stop," she said, her eyes narrowed on me. "Stop being broken. You were broken for a little while, sure. But enough is enough. Stop now."

I stared at her, open-mouthed, tears wet on my face.

She continued: "He didn't *make* you do anything, Kadie. You know that. You're too smart to let anyone have that much control over you. You wanted to fall in love. You wanted this experience. I don't care what you say now. This happened because you wanted it, and you allowed it. I'll never understand how your brain works, Kadie. Why you fight so hard to keep a safe distance from...any kind of human connection. But you still crave it, or you'd never let this happen. And you know it!"

"Denise..."

"You're still in control of your life. You were still in control the weekend you spent with Paul. You've given yourself this time to be broken because you wanted it. Now if you want to be done, then be done, or put yourself back together and get on with it. Your self-pity is pathetic."

"But..." I started, but I had no argument. He logic was too sound.

"Put yourself together," she went on, "and then, a year from now, maybe two or three or twenty, you can come to me and tell me that you're still pissed that you fell in love and got your heart broken. Tell me that you still regret falling in love with Paul." She got up and started pulling on her sweater. "Because I'll bet you a bottle of Pinot Noir that you won't. Once you heal, once the wounds close, you'll be grateful that you got to experience such a raw and profound love."

I scoffed. "Seriously? You're giving me the whole 'It's better to have loved and lost than to never have loved at all' routine?"

"Yes, I am because it's true!" she spat back at me. "I've been searching my entire life for what you got to experience in one weekend. So, screw you and your self-loathing. Count yourself lucky."

"You?" I asked incredulously. "What about Clay? You're crazy about

Clay."

Denise exhaled heavily. "Clay is a kind man, and I'm lucky to have him. But I can't remember the last time my heart skipped a beat when he entered the room."

We sat silently for a few minutes. Denise had revealed things that I had been oblivious to. She was more conscious about things than I gave her credit for. She struggled, too. My happy-go-lucky, bubbly sister that saw the good in everyone and the silver-lining in every situation, had struggles that she hid so well that even I—in all my self-proclaimed astuteness—was completely unaware of. My heart became overwhelmed with love and tenderness towards her. Everyone was left wanting on some level. That's just life, I guess.

"It's time for me to be done with all this self-pity, isn't it?" I said to the floor.

Denise approached me and put her hand on my chin and forced me to look at her. "I don't envy your pain, but I do envy that you're not so numb as to be immune to it. You know why I love Kurt McCarthy so much? He gives me hope."

"Hope? Hope for what?"

"For you."

"I don't…I don't understand."

"'Your scars aren't imperfections; they're proof that you lived while everyone else existed.'"

"Who said that?"

"Who do you think?"

Denise kissed my forehead and walked out the door.

***

"I have a proposition for you," Cheryl Jackson said the moment I answered my cell. No 'Hello' or 'How are you?' or even an inquiry if she were actually speaking with me. She just blurted out, "I have a proposition for you." That was Cheryl. No nonsense. No small talk.

"Okay," I said. "What is it?"

"I don't want to talk over the phone. Can you fly back so we can sit down and talk?"

"You want me to come to Vegas?"

"Yes."

"Are you...dissatisfied with my work?" I asked. Cheryl was my Las Vegas client. She was a beautiful, powerful woman who exuded authority and demanded respect. I liked her almost as much as I envied her.

"Not at all. Quite the opposite."

"Well, I have a couple projects I need to finish up this week." ...because they should have been done last week, but I decided instead to take a sabbatical. I kept that part to myself. "I could come this weekend."

"Great. Let me transfer you to Lynn, and he'll work out the details. I'm excited about this. Talk soon, dear." And before I could say another word, I was talking to her assistant and booking a flight back to Vegas.

I hung up the phone, unsure about what had just happened. I think I may have just agreed to something...but had no idea what.

Cheryl Jackson came from a powerful family. She was the Assistant CEO of a string of hotels, not just in Las Vegas, but nationwide, including Chicago. A year earlier I had remodeled an addition to her Chicago hotel, not knowing that she was the owner. I learned in Vegas she had personally picked me for her Las Vegas renovation because of my work in Chicago. It felt great to be appreciated. She was extremely successful with everything she touched.

Four days later I was sitting across from Cheryl in her massive, overbearing office. I did not like being in her office. It had the tendency of making one feel quite small. It was decorated very strategically to create that effect, I presumed, down to the shag rug and massive oak desk she sat behind.

She was a beautiful woman, a powerful kind of beautiful, a Miranda Priestly kind, but with a more exotic look. She had jet-black, silk hair that hung straight down the middle of her back. I assumed she paid whatever it cost to keep it looking that way. Her high cheekbones and strong, pale skin did well at hiding her fifty-four years. Most believed her to be in her early-forties. I'd never seen her *not* wearing stilettos. They accentuated her toned calves and clicked when she walked, announcing her arrival everywhere. One pair I'd recognized as Manolo Blahnik's, which for her was on par to me buying a pair of clearance tennis shoes. She always preferred form-fitting dresses, as she should because she pulled them off amazingly well. She carried herself with the confidence of a woman who knew how much power she had, and that she earned everything and was handed nothing. All she needed was herself. She invited people into her life only if she wanted them. Those she viewed with indifference were dismissed without hesitation. Simple as that.

I looked up to women like Cheryl. I knew that I would never be a skin-tight dress with stiletto heels type of woman. I preferred a more comfortable—yet still stylish—look. I was drawn to attire that said both "look at me" and "I don't care."

But I respected women who knew their power, had confidence, and bowed to no one. I sought that. I wanted that level of self-confidence. For the most part, I did a pretty good job at faking it.

"Kadie, I'll get right to the point," Cheryl said the moment I sat down. Did she ever *not* get right to the point? "I need someone to head up my décor department. Someone good, someone who understands style and the connotations that are attached to specific themes and motifs. Someone competent. From what I've seen, you're all those things. The position is yours if you want it. I'd need you to start right away." She swiveled to the side and looked at me through her dark hair. "We're in a decorating rut. Everything needs revamped, like yesterday." She turned in her chair and looked out her office window—the kind that takes up the whole wall and overlooks the city, symbolizing her authority.

After a moment, I managed to mutter, "Oh, wow...." Even though her offer was what I'd been praying for, I never imagined it would be so...substantial.

Cheryl, taking my reaction as hesitation, clasped her hands together and looked at me. "Look, I understand this is a lot to ask. You'd have to quit your current job. You'd be traveling the world. It's a big decision. I get that. Your pay, of course, will reflect your competence and dedication. I can give you a week to think things over. After that, I—"

"Yes," I said, cutting her off. I needed Cheryl to know that I had no doubts. I wanted the job. I deserved the job.

She looked surprised for half a second, before offering a knowing smile. "Well, it's settled then."

She reached across her desk and firmly shook my hand. I smiled and realized it was possible to find life after Paul.

Chapter 12

I woke with a start. Lisa sat on the edge of the couch staring hypnotically at the TV. Her presence startled me.

"Jesus!" I shrieked. I sat up, catching my breath. "What are you doing out here?" I asked. For the past week, Lisa had slept in the bedroom, and I stayed on the sofa. My question was left unanswered. She kept her eyes locked on the TV, entranced by an episode of *Sex and the City*.

In the time since I'd returned from Chicago, Lisa and I had fallen into a routine. She spent her days in my bedroom watching shows on her tablet, and I spent mine on the couch watching different shows on the TV. She'd emerge every few hours, go into the kitchen, open the fridge, and frown at my lack of options. She would audibly groan and look at me. These weren't the most subtle hints, so they were easy to detect.

"Are you hungry?" I'd ask.

"Yeah."

"What would you like?"

"I don't care," she'd say, but this was never the truth.

Chinese?"

"No."

"Pizza?"

"No."

It wasn't until the fifth or sixth option that I recommended something she wanted. This was our life now. Take-out food and superficial conversations.

I'd spent the past two days clutching my phone, willing it to vibrate with a call from Kadie. It never did. My calls to her went unanswered. My voicemails filled her mailbox, but I don't know if she even acknowledged them. Same with my texts. Both said the same thing: "Kadie, please let me explain."

I got up from the sofa, went into the kitchen, and poured a glass of water. Stuck to my fridge, under a rainbow equality-for-all magnet, was the ultrasound picture of my baby. I pulled the picture out from the magnet and looked at it. Nothing about it had changed in the last couple hours since I'd last studied it. I stuck it back on the fridge and returned to the sofa.

"What are you doing up?" I asked.

Lisa took the remote and muted the TV. She stared at the screen for a moment longer, watched as the silent actors mouthed their lines, and then buried her face in her hands. Her body shook with the intensity of her sobbing. I sat up and asked what was wrong. She lifted her head and looked at me with desperate red eyes.

"Marry me," she said.

I didn't mean to laugh, and I tried to mask it with a cough, but she didn't buy the pretense. My ridicule didn't appear to hurt Lisa any more than she already was. She stared back at me and waited for an answer. I thought my derision was enough of an answer. I guess I was wrong.

"No," I said.

"Why?"

I ignored her follow-up question; I was thinking of Kadie.

"We're just like Carrie and Big, Paul. Don't you see that?"

"Who?"

She pointed at the TV. "Carrie and Big. They had their pitfalls, but they figured out a way to get back to each other."

"Lisa, I don't…" but I abandoned the thought unfinished. It depressed me that the mother of my child was heeding relationship insight from *Sex and the City*.

"Do you love me?" Lisa asked.

Love. It was such a simple word, yet I had no idea how to clearly define it. At least not in a context that Lisa would understand.

"I don't think I understand the question," I said.

"What's not to understand?"

My phone sat idly on the coffee table. I grabbed it and unlocked the screen hoping to find a message or missed call from Kadie. Nothing. I dropped the phone on the table. It hit the wood and bounced onto the floor. I rubbed my eyes, and when I stopped, Lisa was still staring at me. I had forgotten she was even there. My back hurt. I wanted my bed back.

"I think we should get married for our child," she said.

I processed Lisa's logic and dismissed it. Lisa wasn't wife material. She was ex–wife material—a reminder of a past decision that never stopped collecting interest. I imagined she would be a horror show for an ex–wife. The thought of her taking half of everything provoked my own question: "Why did you lose your job?" I asked.

It had never occurred to me before to ask her this. A year ago I went to Lisa's work. She met me at the front door to let me in because I didn't have "security access." She seemed happy to see me. We took the elevator three floors to her department. It was a hermetically–sealed maze of cubicles and carpeted walls. We traversed the maze, stopping at various cubes to be introduced to people I would never remember. Then we arrived at Lisa's. Tacked to one of her walls was a picture of a disgruntled kitten tangled in a mess of yarn. The caption at the bottom read: "Just One of Those Days." Beneath that was a poster board collage of shirtless male models and actors, along with expensive sport cars and extravagant houses. It was Lisa's vision board. She had made it a month earlier. I recalled her sitting at my kitchen table mutilating magazines looking for the right photos to plaster to the board. She believed if she willed it hard enough, the fantasy displayed on the poster would materialize in real life. Vision boards worked, she argued. She had read about them in a book.

I looked at the other cubes, scanning the maze from my vantage point. Most of the workers sat at their desks reading emails or playing solitaire. Each one had a picture tacked to their wall with an animal caught in a precarious position. Each picture had a caption meant to encapsulate the drudgery that comes with working for a business that offered Applebee's gift cards, or other similar insulting rewards, for a job well done. The whole scene depressed me. I hadn't been back since.

I never asked about Lisa's job because I was indifferent to it. Sometimes she offered workplace anecdotes, but I always tuned out right around the time she started criticizing a fellow employee or used buzzwords like "synergy" or "blogosphere." It dawned on me, as I stared blankly into Lisa's hollow eyes, that I hadn't been a very good boyfriend. I should have been more present. I should have asked questions instead of just mindlessly nodding whenever a momentary lull occurred in her tales. I should have…cared or…ended things. But I didn't. I wasn't proactive about anything regarding Lisa. I was always lost in some alternate reality that would serve as the setting for one of my books. I had known

Lisa for two years, but I knew very little about her. I'd known Kadie for three days, and I could tell you her childhood crush (John Stamos), her biggest fear (amnesia), and the first thing on her bucket list (waterboarding Dick Cheney).

"They needed to make cutbacks," Lisa said. It took a moment for her answer to register because I had forgotten what I had asked.

"So, what are you going to do?" I asked.

"I don't know."

"Do you have any prospects?"

"No."

"Why?"

It took her way too long to answer. When she finally did, she said: "I didn't leave under the best circumstances."

"What does that mean?"

"I'm not sure I'd get a good recommendation from my boss."

"Why?"

"My leaving wasn't...amicable."

"'Amicable'? Where did you learn that word?"

"It's in the employee handbook."

"Why wasn't it amicable?"

"Jeez, Paul. Enough with the interrogation."

I yawned. I was so tired. "You can't keep staying here, Lisa."

"I don't have anywhere else to go."

"You broke up with me."

"That was a mistake."

"No, actually, it wasn't. You did us both a favor."

"What about our baby?"

"I'll provide for our child. I'll be at every doctor's appointment. I'll cover any medical bills. I'll do everything I can to get him...er...her into the best schools. I'll give our child the best possible life. I will be the best parent I can, but you and I...we're done. Getting pregnant doesn't change what we are...or aren't."

Lisa started to cry. "I have no one, Paul. I'm all alone."

I thought to put a consoling arm around her, and I even lifted my limb to do so, but I dropped it limply back at my side. I didn't want to give Lisa false hope. I stood and looked down at her.

"You can stay here until you find another job, but you need to start looking for one. And a place."

She stopped crying and nodded weakly.

"When is your next doctor's appointment?"

"Two weeks."

"Okay," I said. I picked up my phone and habitually checked the screen. No missed calls, no texts. "I'll be back for the doctor's appointment," I said. I started down the hall toward my bedroom.

"Where are you going?"

"Chicago."

***

"Hey, it's me again," I said into my phone. I was standing at the entrance of an airport bookstore. In front of me were various stacks of books. One stack was my book. I picked one up, weighed it in my hand. "I'm at the airport. I'm about to board a flight for Chicago. I know you're mad. I know you're hurt, but I want to see you, and I want to explain. If you want to see me, I'll be at the place we had dinner the first night. I'll stay until ten. If you don't come, then I'll never bother you again." I paused and studied the cover of my book. "Kadie, please be there. I lo…I'm sorry, Kadie, but I want to make this right. I hope you'll meet me."

I took the book to the register, paid for it and asked the cashier for a pen. I opened the front cover and wrote:

Kadie, I am Kurt McCarthy. Sorry my writing has lost its edge, but it may be because I didn't find my muse until I came to Chicago. I love you.
Paul/K. McCarthy

***

I said I'd wait till ten; I waited until one. The place was empty. Even the piano player had gone home an hour earlier, emptying his tip jar and stuffing the wrinkled bills into the pockets of his skinny jeans. For the last thirty minutes, it was just the bartender and me. He stood under the glow of the mounted TV watching sports' highlights. The station cut to commercial, and the bartender told me that it was last call.

I finished my drink and approached the bar. "Do you remember me?" I asked the bartender. He was washing glasses. He paused and looked at me for a moment, and then resumed his washing.

"Can't say I do."

"I was in here a couple weeks ago."

"Was I working?"

"I don't remember. It was a Friday night."

"I work Fridays."

"I was in here with a woman."

"That narrows it down."

"Gorgeous woman," I said, recalling Kadie's delicate features. "Dark hair, dark skin. Hypnotic eyes."

The bartender shook his head. "Sorry."

"Her name's Kadie."

The bartender finished washing a glass and stood up straight. "Kadie Park?"

My heart leapt. "Yeah, that's her."

"Yeah, I know Kadie. She comes in all the time."

"She was supposed to meet me here."

The bartender shrugged. "I haven't seen her."

"Has she been in at all recently?"

"I'm not going to answer that."

"I'm not a stalker or anything."

"No?"

"No."

"Do you have her number?"

"Yeah."

"Give her a call."

"I have," I said. "Several. She won't answer." The bartender laughed. "What's so funny?" I asked.

"Take the hint, man," he said. "She never planned on meeting you here."

"Yeah…I guess not."

"Look, I need to close up. Can I get you anything else?"

"No, but you can you do me a favor," I said, pulling the copy of *Trainride* from my jacket. "If she comes in, will you give her this?"

The bartender took the book, studied the cover. "I've heard of this. It any good?"

"It's average." I took a hundred-dollar bill from my wallet and put it on the bar. "If you see her, make sure she gets it."

"You got it," he said, pocketing the bill.

***

The in-flight movie on the way home was a horrible romantic comedy. I forgot the title, but it had all the prerequisite romantic comedy clichés one wants in a cheesy love story. The overly attractive couple meet under unusual circumstances. They despise each other initially, both using childish tactics to display their disdain for the other. They both have best friends that serve as voices of reason, showing the main characters the one thing that has been present the entire time: their love for the person they thought they hated. The girl flees; the guy chases, and he catches her right before she's about to get on a flight to exit his life forever. He professes his love in front of various onlookers, reciting a speech that is too perfect to ever be believed in real life. Proverbial emotional walls are torn down, and through tear-stained cheeks, they share an epic kiss under the applause of all onlookers. The movie was horrible. I bawled through the entire thing.

Before I returned to the airport, I went to Kadie's house. I couldn't go home without knowing that I tried everything to explain things. I rang the doorbell; no one answered. I tried the knob. It was unlocked—another thing we had in common. I pushed it open slowly. I made my way to the darkened kitchen and turned on the light. I crept down the hall toward her bedroom. I entered her room and turned on the light. Her bed was made. The twenty decorative pillows that cluttered it were strategically in place. I scanned the bedroom. Everything was where it belonged. She must have listened to my message, assumed I'd go there when she wasn't at the pub, and found somewhere to hide for the night.

I came to the harsh reality that maybe Kadie felt differently about me than I did for her. If she felt what I did, she wouldn't have given up on me without a fight. She demanded space in the time that we'd been apart. She asked me not to contact her; she didn't want to see me. Had she decided we were finished before we even had a chance to get started? This seemed the most likely. But then why did she break her own rule and ask me to come to Vegas? Why did she assume my refusal meant I was done with her? Why wouldn't she give me the chance to explain? Was she so guarded, so afraid that I'd hurt her, that she dismissed me almost as quickly as she had accepted me? I needed a chance to explain. I needed her to hear me.

Or maybe I needed to hear her.

What was she saying by not meeting me tonight? She printed the writing on the wall very clearly. I wasn't what she wanted. She had let me in for three days and that was all I was worth. Maybe that was more than what most men got. She wanted me out of her life. I saw that now; it was just too unbearable to accept. I loved Kadie. I wanted to give her what she wanted. She wanted me to leave her alone, so I'd honor her wishes. I'd give her the one thing I didn't want to offer: my absence.

I was going to be a father. That's where my focus had to shift. Unadulterated love with Kadie wasn't in my cards, but fatherhood was.

When I returned to Arizona, Lisa was sleeping soundly in my bed. I watched her sleep for a moment. Watched her unblemished face resting serenely on my pillow. She was a beautiful woman. A lot of guys would be lucky to have her. At that moment, I resolved to make things work with her. The child that grew inside her would bridge the gap that was growing between us. The baby would serve as a resurrection, an awakening to help me understand the things I couldn't quite grasp. It would all be made clear when the baby came. Often in love stories, it's the person right in front of you that you eventually realize you've loved all along. Maybe Kadie was just blocking what should have been so obvious: I was supposed to be with Lisa. She was the mother of my child. I could love her. I would love her. I *had* to.

I lifted the comforter and slid into bed next to Lisa. She turned toward me. I opened my arms and she fell into me. I kissed the top of her head and whispered that I wanted her to stay. She held me tighter and said she loved me. I said it back, and no matter how hard I tried to pretend my repeated words were true, I couldn't ignore how heavy they felt in my mouth.

Chapter 13

Working for Cheryl was everything I dreamt of when I was a starry-eyed college student. I traveled the world: New York, California, Paris, Amsterdam, Rome, Costa Rica, and smaller towns in between. I took to my new responsibilities with great fervor. After six months of proving myself, Cheryl deemed me a "valuable asset" to the company. She gave me a better-sounding job title—Vice President of Design—along with more autonomy and authority. I now *told* people what to do. *And* I had an assistant! My very own assistant! Betty.

Betty annoyed the hell out of me. But she was still *my* assistant. Some mornings, things seemed so surreal that I had to literally pinch myself to prove I wasn't dreaming. It was all real. The career that I'd chased was now my reality. I should have been exhilarated. I was exhilarated! Mostly.

Then, unremittingly, the harsh reality that I had a profound void in my life reared its ugly head. That incessant pain that I carried daily would also wake, stretch, and take a deep, rejuvenating breath. And then I'd remember, yes, this is all real, and I'm nearly complete, yet something was still missing. I was still alone, but even worse, I was lonely.

***

"What's up, Denise?" I answered my phone while I scurried through the airport. I had just come from redecorating a conference hall for a five-star hotel in Baltimore. The hotel manager had been a supreme pain in my ass from day one. He was not happy with the idea that his hotel needed any type of renovations. I suppose he was under the impression that *I* decided that his pride and joy needed some updating, and that *I* was out to prove him an incompetent hotel manager. I didn't care about him or his hotel management abilities. Yes, he *was* about 400 years old and needed to be replaced by someone with more modern ideas for running hotels, but I was only working because Cheryl had deployed me to transform his outdated interior into something more contemporary. But since I was the one giving orders and approving all the renovations, it was me he hated. Needless to say, I was glad to be home.

"Kadie! Where have you been?" Denise's excited voice demanded.

"I was in Baltimore, remember?"

"Oh, yeah. I forgot. Anyway, guess who I ran into? You might not be super-happy about this, but hear me out first…" she paused. I stood with the phone to my ear waiting for more. Was I supposed to respond now? "Hello? Kadie?"

"I'm here." *Just waiting for you to get it all out,* I wanted to add. Evidently, she wanted me to play the "guess who?" game. Why did people always want template answers to rhetorical questions? I succumbed. "Who did you run into, Denise?"

"Brock!"

My mouth dropped.

"Brock? What do you mean you 'ran into Brock'?"

"Exactly what I said. I was getting groceries at the Corner Shop and *literally* ran into him. We both turned the corner at the same time and our carts hit. Haha! It was hilarious!"

I kept the phone pressed to my ear, but I gave no reaction to her story. Did bumping into my ex warrant a reaction?

"Kadie?" I sensed she was disappointed with my lack of reciprocated enthusiasm.

"Yeah, I'm here," I said flatly. "So…how's he doing?" I imagined him having one or two kids hanging onto him, begging for Animal Crackers or Ring Pops as he shushed them and attempted in vain to carry on some form of superficial adult conversation with Denise. Admittedly, that image panged my heart a bit.

"Well, that's the thing. It's totally crazy. We got to talking and I guess he's divorced now and living back in his old apartment. Ha! Who'd have thought…" she trailed off.

Well, considering that most marriages end in divorce nowadays, and with how fast he jumped into the marriage, his divorce wasn't that surprising. So, I guess *many* people *would have thought.* But I didn't say this.

"Anyway," she continued when she realized that I had nothing to add. I was distracted by a small child carrying a sticky sucker that was standing a bit too close to me as we rode the escalator. "I told him that you have a new job that you're loving! He seemed happy for you."

"Did he?"

"Yeah," she said.

The child held his sucker up to me. An offering. I shook my head.

"Is that it?" I asked.

"Well, no. There's one more thing."

"Hmm."

"Well, he asked for your number," she said. After Brock and I separated, I changed my number. I didn't do it to be malicious. We were on the same cell plan, and I decided to go with a different provider. When I was asked if I wanted the same number, I said no. I figured a new number was emblematic of a new beginning.

"Did you give it to him?" I asked, enunciating each syllable.

"Well..."

There was my answer. "Denise!"

"I know. I'm meddling. I'm sorry! Kind of." I pictured her stomping her foot with folded arms, face set stubbornly in her 'just hear me out' look. "Look, he just wants to catch up. He's such a great guy. Such a great *catch*! I honestly don't know why you let him go! I *know* you cared about him. And you've just been in such a...funk. Maybe this is what you need right now. Why not just meet up with him? Catch up. See if any feelings are still lingering."

"Aaauugh! Denise!" she was so adept at putting me in precarious situations. I hated and loved her for it. "So awkward!" I whined. My body cringed at the thought of the clumsy conversation I was now destined to have with Brock.

"It won't be awkward. He's still the same old Brock. He's so easygoing and...likable." My family loved Brock—everybody loved Brock. They were pretty upset when the relationship ended. They took it much harder than me, and they had required an extensive recovery period.

"You saying it won't doesn't change the fact that it will," I argued.

"Arrgh! C'mon, Kadie! *Please* talk to him. If not for yourself, then for me."

"For you? What do you care?"

"I care because you're my sister. I want you to be happy."

"You think getting back with Brock will make me happy?"

"I'm not saying get back with him."

"Then what are you saying?"

"Just talk with him. Get a coffee and catch up. I don't know what will make you happy, Kadie. All I know is what you're doing isn't working."

I had no argument to that. I wasn't unhappy, but I'd be lying if I claimed my current life left me happy and fulfilled. I was just...there. But even more than that, I *was* genuinely curious about Brock. Surprisingly, I found myself interested in reconnecting with him. I wasn't entirely sure what the motivation was behind the desire. Selfishly perhaps, just the thought of being with Brock held more temptation than it should.

"Fine," I said. "I'll grab a coffee with him and catch up."

"Yes!"

"So, you gave him my number? He's going to call me?"

"Yes. I told him he should definitely call you!"

"Okay. Look, I'm at the airport, and I can't remember where I parked my car. I'll talk to you later. Believe me, you haven't heard the last of this. You drive me up a wall, you know that, right?"

"I know. But it's only because I love you so much!" she clarified. "You'd be lost without me, and you know it."

"Yeah, yeah..." As I got off the phone, my mind wandered to Brock, and then Paul, then back to Brock. Dependable, loving, handsome, kind, stable Brock. Why couldn't I just love him? Maybe now I could.

***

"I'm glad you agreed to dinner," Brock said with his easy grin. "I have to admit that I was surprised."

I smiled. "I'm glad, too," I said, feeling that I meant it. From the moment I saw him enter the restaurant, my body relaxed, practically sighing with relief. It was like getting into bed after a long and grueling day.

"You look beautiful, as always," he said. He'd always had a way with words. "Even more so, if it's possible."

"Thank you. Time has been kind to you too," I said and then smiled. Was I flirting? I dismissed the voice inside my head warning me to be careful, and I wondered what game I was playing. "So, what happened, Brock? With

Isabelle?"

"Wow, okay. Well, you always did get straight to the point." He signaled the waiter and ordered a bottle of wine, a damn expensive bottle of wine. I think he ordered it because of the price. "You know exactly what happened, Kadie." He studied me for a moment, waiting for me to add something. I stared at him warmly. "But you want me to say it, don't you?"

Yes, I suppose I did. I don't know why. Childish triumph.

"Fine," he said. "I'll say it. I jumped in too fast. I wasn't ready." His eyes softened. "A woman whom I loved dearly had just broken my heart, and I thought that jumping into a marriage might heal it." He looked away. "That method doesn't work, just for future reference."

I forced a smile and lowered my eyes, feeling guilty and uncomfortable with his candor. Though I asked for it and respected it.

"Isabelle is great," he continued. "She's a wonderful woman. But my relationship with her was just a distraction, a Band-Aid. I was just trying to get over you, Kadie."

"I'm sorry, Brock. I know that those words sound empty and pointless. But they are genuine. I mean them when I say them."

"I know you do."

"I wanted to love you, Brock. I did love you, just not…" I trailed off. I wasn't sure what prompted my outburst. I guess I needed to defend myself.

"Let's not rehash the past. What's done is done. I believe you. I know who you are, Kadie. I know the type of person you are underneath that tough exterior." He paused for a moment. "No one knows you like I do."

I let that sink in. He was right. What did I know about love and happiness anyway? My life—my choices—were proving that I knew very little. Maybe those two ideas, love and happiness, aren't meant to be intertwined on the level that we are made to believe. Maybe you get to have a little bit of one, or a little bit of the other. Perhaps love doesn't always lead to happiness, and vice versa— you don't always achieve happiness through love. At least the type of love we're taught to want. Maybe you're just lucky to get one *or* the other. I shook my head to escape my thoughts.

"You're right," I said with an air of resignation. "I was chasing something, and even now I'm not entirely sure what it was."

"Was?"

"Is…was. I don't know," I admitted.

He considered this for a moment. "How about we just not worry about that? Wipe the slate. Just be *here*. *Now*. Enjoy each other's company without any pretenses or agendas. Can we do that?"

"Yes, that sounds nice." I smiled. It felt good to smile without forcing it.

***

Things progressed easily with Brock. Well…perhaps *progressed* isn't necessarily the right term. We just fell back into our old rhythms. We were both filling an emptiness for one another, providing companionship.

It was nice.

Often I found myself questioning my motivation for continuing down the road I'd previously traveled with Brock. I did have feelings for him, but was he someone that I could be with long term? I'd certainly changed since we were last together, and so had he. Maybe the time apart was what we needed to work. Perhaps *now* I was ready to love him the way we both deserved. Maybe I could fully commit to him now. I couldn't deny that it would be a good life. I think I'd be happy. At the very least, I'd be content. That has to count for something, right? I ruminated on these thoughts so regularly that I found myself starting to believe them.

Yet, despite this, late at night while lying in bed, too often my thoughts drifted toward the torment that lurked inside me—Paul. He was in the back of my mind, subconsciously, all the time. The strangest things reminded me of him.

One evening, while working in Boston, I got stuck on an elevator with a mother and her young son. The mother was arguing with her son over whether *he* should tie his bright-orange Nike shoes or if *she* should. (He believed that she was the one better equipped to do the job, while *she* believed he should be able to accomplish said task on his own.) I smiled robotically while my heart panged with the memory of Paul's dumb, neon-green Nikes.

The next week, I was blindsided yet again while walking through a department store in Portland and "Wonderful Tonight" started playing on the background sound system. The memory of dancing with Paul by the lake sprang to life. The breath was sucked from my lungs. It happened before I was even cognizant of it happening. I had no control over it. It was as though a subconscious awareness of all things "Paul" resided somewhere deep within me.

Every time I passed the convention center that I fled the night of our first date, or pulled on the sweater that he had sneaked his phone number into, I thought of him.

I threw the sweater away.

And, sadly, every time Brock kissed me—I wished it were Paul's lip that were on mine. Brock's affection was a constant reminder of all that was lacking.

***

"I know that you know I'm still in love with you," Brock said casually one night while we were watching television at his place. I wasn't sure how to respond, and I was exhausted, so opted for straightforward.

"Yeah... I know." A shameful admission.

"I've never stopped loving you."

"I... know."

"I also know that you love me, too," he said with an eyebrow cocked and a lazy grin. He was still looking at the television.

"Oh?"

"Sure." He shrugged casually. "You can't deny the familiarity, the comfort, here. You care about me. We have a connection. I know you've had your...hesitations with what's happening between us. But *I* know that this feels right. We're good together, and you love me. You'll figure it out soon. Until then, I'll just wait you out. I'm a patient man."

"Brock," I groaned and shoved him playfully. He chuckled.

Then silence.

Unsure of what to say next, we both feigned interest in whatever was on the television. The silence became deafening. I needed to say something. His admission needed to be challenged.

"Listen," I cleared my throat. "You're right. I do love you."

His head bounced up in surprise.

"I just need to figure out if this is the right kind of love to...I don't know...commit to someone for a lifetime. Not just for my sake, but for yours, too."

He looked away. I was unsure what he was thinking and how he was processing what I said.

"You deserve to be loved wholeheartedly," I continued. "For the woman you're with to be so in love with you that she wants to know what you ate for lunch, and if you had a good workout that morning, and…*really care* about the regularity of your bowel movements."

"What?"

"I don't know. I just mean you should love someone so much that you want to know everything about her."

"You don't care about my bowel movements?" he inquired, I think only half joking.

I laughed. "I…don't know yet, to be honest. I *want* to care about your bowel movements, and I'm starting to think that I maybe *could* one day. I'm just not sure if I'm there quite yet."

He looked at me for a moment, both of us feeling an even mixture of tenderness and sadness. He leaned forward and kissed me gently.

"Then I'll wait for you to get there."

"But, why?" His patience perplexed me.

"Because I love you, Kadie," he said. He said this with so much sincerity that it was impossible not to believe him. "And I care greatly about *your* bowel movements," he added smiling.

I returned his smile. My eyes watered, my heart-wrenching. Why was it so difficult to love Brock? Life would be so much easier if I could figure out a way to love him. He wiped my tear and pulled me into him.

I couldn't deny that I sometimes enjoyed when he held me. Sometimes comfort, no matter who's providing it, is all a person needs. I rested my head on his check and drifted off in the warmth of his arms…and dreamt of Paul.

***

Six weeks later, while eating at an upscale Chicago restaurant, Brock pulled my old engagement ring from his breast pocket and held it out to me. I wasn't sure what I was supposed to do with it. I wasn't sure what *he* expected me to do with it? Was he proposing? Doesn't a proper proposal entail a question? I waited for him to ask it, but he just held the ring over the lit candles and waited for me to react.

I hadn't seen the ring in six years. It looked bigger. Two thoughts shot through my head at that moment. The first: I wondered how much a pawn shop would pay for it. And the second: Why couldn't he have waited until I finished my dinner? I wasn't even halfway through my salmon. Could I ask him to return the ring to his pocket until I finished my meal? Probably not. Society has rules. I needed to acknowledge what was happening. I would go to bed hungry.

I put down my fork. "Brock…" I didn't know what to say. I thought that we were on the same page as far as taking things *slow*. I wasn't sure I could even define what we were at that point! Sure, we were dating, but were we an official couple? Did we have the freedom to see other people? *Good Lord!* What was the rush anyway? We'd only been dating for a couple months. A wave of annoyance swept over me. I tried to hide my disdain and failed miserably. Brock sensed my unease.

"Look, hear me out," he said. He continued holding out the ring with his left hand while gesticulating with his right. The whole scene probably looked quite confusing—or maybe hilarious—to an onlooker. "I know you want to take things slow. I know that you have your doubts about us. But I don't. I have enough faith for the both of us."

"Brock, it doesn't work that way. You know that."

"Do you love me?"

"What?"

"Do you love me?"

"I…of course I do. I just don't know…"

"Stop. Anything else you have to say doesn't matter. We have the essential ingredient. The rest will fall into place. You'll see."

"I just don't know why you feel the need to rush this," I said impatiently. "You said that you would wait until I was ready to move forward."

"I am waiting, Kadie. But in the meantime, who says you can't wear this?"

I rolled my eyes. "C'mon, Brock. You know why. That's not some innocuous mood ring. That's a symbol of commitment. That's…" I pointed accusingly at the ring, "that's a *big* deal!"

He looked down, obviously hurt. "I know it's a big deal, Kadie." He—finally—lowered his outstretched arm and returned the ring to his breast pocket. *Would it be insensitive of me to pick up my fork and finish my salmon?*

"I guess I'm just a hopeless romantic," he said softly.

I wasn't sure how to respond; my head was spinning, either from malnourishment or from the gravity of the situation.

"Evidently, an impatient hopeless romantic," he added, forcing a smile that failed to mask his pain.

"Brock…"

"Please," he said waving me off, "you don't have to say anything else. I shouldn't have put you in this position. It was a mistake. I knew that you weren't ready. I had just… I don't know. I suppose I had just hoped…" he trailed off, fumbling over the words that he hoped allowed him to retain some level of dignity. I had hurt him…again. His face screwed up in mild agony. I was hit with an urge to hug him. Squeeze him until his hurt was gone. Tell him that I *did* love and care for him. I was so dog-tired. Tired of being alone and angry and bitter for all the things I needed to take responsibility for. I looked at Brock; he was a wonderful, normal, competent, handsome man that loved me. Wanted me! What more did I need? Maybe *I* was the problem. I didn't want to be the problem anymore.

"Let me see it," I said, holding my hand out.

"What?"

"The ring. Let me see it."

He pulled the ring from his pocket and leaned across the table and placed it in my outstretched hand. I examined it. It was as beautiful as I remembered, yet it just wasn't *me*. It didn't fit my personality or my style. It was big and flashy. I'm found of more simple styles. The thought crossed my mind that yet again— a regular occurrence in our relationship years before—it reflected more accurately who Brock *wished* I was more than who I was.

In the past, Brock was always taking me (well, more accurately dragging me) to social events that made me uncomfortable. He was always buying me flashy, slinky, uncomfortable dresses that I rarely wore—usually for the previously mentioned social wingdings. He had always tried to push his friends, or rather his friends' wives, on me. Hoping, I'm sure, for a lifelong connection that helped to make my assimilation into his society more smooth and painless.

I thought about this as I stared at the ring. I imagined myself becoming attached to it. A two-carat halo diamond, set in vintage white gold, and custom-sized for my finger, of course.

"Wow...I forgot how beautiful it was." It was beautiful, even if it wasn't my kind of beautiful.

"I'm glad you like it. It *is* yours," he said.

As if in a trance, I slid the ring on my finger and then held my hand up for Brock to see. "I have to admit, it looks good."

"How about I give it a trial run? See how it feels for a while." I looked up at him sheepishly. I didn't know what I was doing, or agreeing to, even as the words escaped my mouth. All I knew was that I was tired of being sad all the time. On the days that I wasn't sad, I was numb. If marrying Brock changed that, then that's what I wanted. I was feeling selfish and reckless. To hell with it. What did I have to lose that I hadn't already lost?

Chapter 14

I volunteered to go on a field trip with Holden. His parents had to work, and the school needed at least five adults to accompany the class. Holden asked me because he needed an ally, and he was fearful of being alone. Sure, he had friends in his class, but kids are fickle. Childhood friendships can begin and end without warning. I was his safety net.

I secretly decided to go the moment he asked me, but I made him beg because that's what uncles do. It gave me some kind of unexplainable joy to see a seven-year-old want something from me. I would make a great father.

I agreed because I love my nephew, but more importantly, since I was on the threshold of fatherhood, I figured it would be good for me to spend a day with children. I was wrong.

Children are the worst.

They're little monsters who are more self-centered than celebrities. They cry if they don't get their way, and they can't eat without getting food all over their faces. They're loud and messy and expensive, and after running you through the ringer all day, they'll ask if you will stop on the way home for ice cream just so they can spill in your car and make everything sticky. They're a horror show. So why do parents put up with them? Because they're cute and they don't know any better—like puppies. If children were ugly and self-aware, we'd stop reproducing. Some children *are* ugly, but their parents are too blinded by their own creation to see the hideousness manifested in their offspring.

The field trip was to the Discovery Museum. The Discovery Museum is a hundred thousand square foot funhouse made up of different science games and activities. It lets kids play and learn and be kids. Everything is bubbled-wrapped and reinforced, and the liability waivers are ten pages and riddled with fine print which recuses the museum of any accidents or deaths. Seriously, it said "DEATH" on the form. It was the only word in all caps. It stood out in the cluster of words the way a dwarf wouldn't in a cluster of people.

The waivers were signed, and the kids were released, like captive animals being set free in their natural habitat for the first time. One kid got a bloody nose from running into a Plexiglas wall. Another vomited on a Paper-Mache rhino. A third vomited from the vomit, a fourth kid lost his right shoe, while another lost the left lens from his eyeglasses. It was bedlam. There wasn't enough hand sanitizer to go around.

The journey to the museum was a ninety-minute bus ride that lacked sufficient air conditioning for the Arizona sun. The bus reeked of feet and stale farts and the constant chatter of 40 first graders. Everyone was talking, and nobody was listening; it was like an episode of *The View*.

Holden sat with his friends while I was sandwiched between two single moms who took turns ridiculing their ex-husbands and the sluts that they were now sleeping with. Both parents wore sweatpants with their hair tied back into messy ponytails. They looked tired. They were tired. The mother to my left had made this trek on four previous occasions with her other children. She would be back in two years when her youngest entered the first grade. Six kids in ten years, she told me. She wasn't even religious. "They just happened," she said. "Mistakes...er...accidents...er...surprises," she said laughing at her own gaffe. I hoped, for her benefit, the discovery museum had an exhibit on how babies are made. The last thing she needed was another mistake/accident/surprise. She didn't work. Never had. She got married the day after she graduated high school and was pregnant before the end of the summer. Her ex pays her four thousand dollars a month for child support on top of alimony. She would have a great life if she didn't have her life.

The mom to my right was younger but just as defeated. Thirty going on sixty. She had a tomato sauce stain on her Duck Dynasty t-shirt, and the strap on her rubber flip-flop snapped just as she loaded the bus. She removed the dilapidated shoe and scrutinized it. She blamed shoddy craftsmanship; I blamed physics. A rubber flip-flop is no match for a bunion-riddled hoof. She spent the afternoon shuffling between the food court and restroom, intermittingly screaming for her kid to stop pulling his underwear out from his ass crack. She hated everything except Mountain Dew and run-on sentences.

Two other parents attended. A man and a woman. They sat together on the bus, whispering things to each other that only they heard. She giggled every so often at one of his secrets. He smiled, drunk on her perfume fumes and the fantasies taking shape in his head. Her son sat at the back of the bus, alone, watching them, staring daggers at the man courting his mother. The man's daughter sat near the front, earbuds shoved into her canals and singing off key with her best friend to downloaded Katy Perry songs. She didn't care that her dad was propositioning a fellow student's mom on a bus full of first graders. She was blissfully ignorant; most Katy Perry fans are.

The couple disappeared once we got to the museum. They reappeared thirty minutes before we were scheduled to return to the bus. The woman looked flushed and embarrassed; the man looked accomplished. She was no longer giggling, but his smile had grown exponentially. He was just waiting for someone to give him a high-five or a chest bump. Holden's teacher chastised them for their field trip behavior, hurling verbal jabs at them and the example they were setting for the children. The lady lowered her head in shame. The man beamed, and the teacher's disdain fell on deaf ears. It was difficult to determine who was more exhausting: the adults or the children.

This was what I was signing up for. Field trips and permission forms. Mingling with other parents so my child can mingle with other kids. My life gets put on hold so my son or daughter can live theirs. This wasn't a complaint, just an observation. Fatherhood's ominous cloud was closing in.

I never gave much thought to the prospect of having children. It was something I had decided to let play out organically. I had no strong feelings either way. People often told me, especially once I entered my thirties (and even more so once I passed thirty-five), that I needed to have children. I politely listened to their rationale, smiled accordingly, and then found a way to move the conversation onto more interesting topics. Children are never interesting conversation topics. Parents love to talk about their children (which is understandable) and yet have never told a stranger an interesting story about their children (which is more understandable). No stranger has ever been engaged in a conversation about someone else's child and thought it interesting. No one cares that Bobby scored the game-winning goal or which Disney princess little Sarah is dressing as for Halloween. Those details need to be reserved for grandparents and Facebook friends.

But now that I found myself on the cusp of my own paternal chaos, I caught myself committing the same social atrocities as those parents I often ridiculed behind their backs. I even took photos of Lisa's latest ultrasound to William and

Gabby's house when I picked Holden up for the field trip. I handed the photos to my brother and waited for him to offer the appropriate response to the glob of life printed on the ultrasound paper. He feigned interest convincingly, even going so far as to call the unrecognizable child "cute," before passing the photos to his wife who matched his artificial interest with her own. Society has established how to act in these situations, and my brother and sister-in-law performed admirably. Gabby even offered a congratulatory hug, which I accepted gladly. (I hadn't hugged Gabby since her wedding.) I was accepted into the bosom of the blissfully ignorant parent that pretended to care for my soon-to-be child as much as I did.

Gabby handed back the ultrasound pictures, and I pocketed them carefully. (I would even show them to Holden's teacher in about three hours. She too pretended to be interested.) It was then that Gabby asked the question that most people wanted to know: when was I going to marry Lisa?

I answered Gabby the same way I answered Lisa the latest time she asked if I wanted to get married. "I don't know." Gabby, like Lisa, stood and stared at me dumbly waiting for me to elaborate. I matched each dumb stare with my own. I answered truthfully, so why did they expect me to explain more? Sometimes the truth is never enough.

And that was the truth. I didn't know if I would marry Lisa. I'd thought about it. I'd even tried to talk myself into it (and succeeded for almost an entire day), but I knew enough about marriage, and myself, to know that I probably wouldn't be good at it. Husbands needed to be domesticated—trained—and I wasn't. I seemed to be constantly aloof to the hidden signals females use as entrapment devices for their husbands. I was always dumb enough to think if a woman said everything was "fine," then everything must be fine. If I was told nothing was wrong, then I assumed nothing was wrong. I've since learned that "fine" never means fine, and something is almost always wrong—and it's often something I did. The games exhausted me, and for better or worse, I wanted to avoid signing up for a lifetime commitment to play them.

Once it was evident I had nothing more to say about marrying Lisa, Gabby forced a smile, shook her head, and shot William a knowing look. William spied his wife, who appeared to be gloating. He scoffed and turned away. I think Gabby had just won a bet.

"What is it with men and commitment?" Gabby asked. I wasn't sure if her question was directed at me or her husband.

"Oh, here we go," William mumbled.

"Well?" Gabby asked.

"Don't start in on Paul," William said. "He doesn't need a lecture on relationships."

"It's not just Paul," Gabby said. "All men are afraid of commitment."

"I'm not afraid of commitment," I said.

"Then marry Lisa," Gabby said.

"I don't want to. But just because I don't want to marry someone doesn't mean I'm afraid of commitment. It just means I don't want to get married."

"Aren't they one and the same?" Gabby asked.

"No," William and I answered together.

"Then you're exceptional," Gabby said, looking at me, "because I've never known a man that's not afraid of commitment."

"Don't put Paul in your stereotypical man-box," William said. I laughed hoping to ease some tension. My reluctance to wed had unearthed some deep-seated argument between my brother and his wife. What I was witnessing was reason enough to stay single. William continued: "This isn't some romantic comedy where things all work out in the end. Life is messy. Marriage is hard. He's being cautious. Prudent." Even at forty, William still played the role of the protective older brother.

"Bullshit," Gabby said.

"What?" William asked.

Gabby turned to me. "Do you love her?" she asked

"I..." I paused and swallowed, "...yeah," I said. I think I was telling the truth.

"Then marry her," Gabby said.

"Why?"

"Because it's the right thing to do," she said.

"How do you figure?" I asked.

"It just is."

I stared at Gabby, not sure what else to say, and not sure if I was even required to say anything else. She stared back waiting for my answer. I wasn't even sure if she had officially asked a question. When being sold on something as serious as marriage, when asked why it's the right thing to do, I believed my question warranted a better defense than "It just is." Shouldn't marriage enhance a relationship instead of solving the problems of it? I wasn't going to do something just because an outsider believed she knew what was best for me and my relationship. I was perplexed, and a little angry, that my life choices needed validation by Gabby and her nonsensical approach to decision-making. If she were to ask me at that moment if everything was all right, I'd have answered, "Yes, everything is *fine*" and hope that her intuition would let her know how everything was *not* fine and how annoyed I was with her line of questioning.

Luckily, Holden came bouncing into the room, unaware of the confrontation his presence abruptly defused. His eyes routinely fell to my sneakers to make certain I was wearing the proper attire. I was. He beamed and gave me a hug. I looked at my wrist (I wasn't wearing a watch) and said we'd better leave, or we might be late. Gabby narrowed her eyes at me, but I knew she wasn't mad. Or at least she wasn't *that* mad. She was just a woman looking out for a fellow female. That is her job; it's in her DNA. William slapped me on the back and opened the door to help me escape. I spent the drive to Holden's school ruminating on whether I should marry Lisa. Gabby's words left an impression. Maybe I did have a fear of commitment.

Things between Lisa and me were as good as they'd ever been. I'd been making more of an effort to be more present with her. She got a new job, in a new cubicle, in a new building that had the exact same layout as the one she left. I visited her and feigned interest in her job description and nodded appropriately when she enumerated all the office politics that were nonsensical or unfair. I even took a congratulatory plant for her desk. She thanked me and put it in front of her vision board.

When she came home at night, I asked how her day was. She'd tell me about forms that were lost, co-workers who were on the cusp of being more than coworkers, data that explained something relevant to her job, and new company strategies she hoped to propose in an attempt to impress her boss. I listened—or tried as best I could. When her feet hurt, I rubbed them. When her back hurt, I retrieved additional pillows. When her feelings hurt, I listened while she vented about all the people at work who were doing her wrong. Lisa hurt a lot, and tried my hardest to alleviate the burdens of being alive and employed. I was trying. I was doing all the things every bad magazine geared toward women suggested I do. I didn't feel put out by my efforts, and I even got to a place where

I looked forward to seeing Lisa at the end of the day. But something was still…lacking. I wasn't sure what. I couldn't pinpoint it—probably because it was lacking. How do you pinpoint something that isn't present? All I knew was I still had enough hopeless romantic in me to believe that marriages should last forever. Marriage was a life-long commitment, and one I wasn't ready to make. Not because I wanted to sleep with random women or pursue other carnal desires that commonly plague men, but something just didn't feel right about closing off the possibility of meeting someone that wasn't lacking whatever Lisa was. Someone like Kadie.

I knew the door had closed on Kadie, but maybe it could still open with someone *like* her. Was that even possible? Probably not, but I wasn't sure. I just knew I couldn't kill that possibility yet. A life with Lisa would be content; a life with Kadie would have been bliss. Oh, what might have been. It's painful to be plagued with the prospect of a life I came so close to living. I had become a country song.

Did I fear commitment? No, because had Kadie called me at that moment and asked me to move to Chicago, I'd have been on the next flight. I checked my phone to make sure I hadn't missed a call. I hadn't. The only thing my phone revealed in its darkened screen was my own defeated reflection.

***

Lisa and I converted my writing room into a baby room. I bought and assembled a crib, had a rocking chair delivered, and took down my Daniel Plainview poster with his milkshake speech printed at the bottom. In its place, I hung some cartoon bears. They had just the right mix of masculinity (they were bears, after all) and femininity (they were adorable). If the desire to write ever struck me, I could go on the deck. I often retreated there with my laptop and morning coffee, but I never did much more than watch the sunrise and then stare at the horizon for hours, lost in thoughts that never took on any coherency or significance.

If I stayed on my deck long enough, eventually and unintentionally, my thoughts always drifted to Kadie. Yes, I still thought of her, but she no longer controlled my thoughts. Now she just periodically visited them. Popping in and out of my mind whenever I thought of something that would make her laugh, or woke with a start because she still had a way of infiltrating my dreams. I guess if I *had* to categorize her, she was, by definition, just a weekend fling. A lost opportunity that gave me a glimpse of what my life could have been if I made better decisions. I tried to push her deeper into the recesses of my mind. Bury her under other baggage that needed to stay buried. I put her under years' worth of suppressed bad first date memories and equally horrific childhood atrocities. But she still had a tendency of bubbling to the surface every now and then. I just needed to put more time between her and the life I was creating without her. She was part of my past. I needed to leave her there and focus on my future. I was going to be a father. I owed it to my child to be present, to live in the moment instead of longing for the past. Kadie would be the story I'd tell my kid in twenty years when he/she needed relationship advice. I'd tell them the worst thing in the world is to wonder what might have been with someone you never fully got to know. It's a fate worse than dying. Well, maybe that's a bit hyperbolic, but it sure does suck.

***

The doctor pointed to the monitor and asked if we could see the absence of a penis. (How could I see the absence of something?) "Sure," I lied. I had no idea what I was looking for, or *not* looking for. I rarely knew what I was seeing during the doctor's visits until it was pointed out to me. I could hear the baby's heartbeat, and as the transducer traversed Lisa's belly, vague shapes would take form that resembled a child. However, I often wondered if I were told to see a different shape in the screen, how easy it would be to trick my mind into seeing something different. With each new appointment, however, the child did take on more semblance of a human. I could usually make out the head now on my own. The tiny body, hands, and feet would gradually materialize the longer I stared at the screen. Parts were taking shape, features were forming—all except a penis. We were having a girl.

I didn't have a preference. I know parents say that publicly, but privately they seldom mean it. I think most guys want boys and most women want girls. Fathers want boys because they want another version of themselves, someone to carry-on their surname so their underwhelming existence can be canonized in the annals of all that never mattered. Mothers want girls because women want an entourage, and they'll both need a sympathetic shoulder down the road when all of life's shit, inevitably, hits the fan. Parents will smile and rejoice regardless of sex, but inside a father with a daughter and a mother with a son are a little disappointed they've been robbed of living vicariously through their children. Most couples remedy this by having more children than they can handle. Keep trying till God gets it right.

I didn't care, though. That was the truth. I will say, however, without reservation, that I feared having an ugly child. Yes, ugly babies exist. I've seen them. Their parents are either ignorant or in denial regarding their mutant offspring. No one will ever tell them the truth either. A grotesque animal is a wonder; a hideous human is a tragedy. I've tried my entire life not to be superficial, but that doesn't stop me from being so. Every human is. Sure, you can judge someone by the content of their character after a time, but when you initially meet someone, you're appraising them solely on their appearance. Humans are horrible. And I was about to have one and be responsible for her. God help me…and her.

I was worried Lisa would want to name our daughter something unique. That seemed to be the trend. Have a baby, name it something stupid, and then in some discontinued font, get the child's name tattooed someone on your body. Lisa had a friend who had a baby and named it October Scorpio Lancaster. The baby was born in December. A Sagittarius. The explanation for the child's name was, "I think it sounds cool." There was no father. Well, the father was somewhere, she just didn't know where. Probably somewhere exotic like Patagonia or South Dakota. The mother worked at Jamba Juice and always found herself on the bottom of every pyramid scheme. She was always one Nigerian Prince away from being a millionaire. She complained the stars were aligned against her. She was a Pisces. A Pisces who gave birth to a Sagittarius and named him October Scorpio. She had the name tattooed on her shoulder. The font: Calypso Freehand.

I refused to relegate my daughter to a lifetime of explaining why she was named Divinity or Crunch Berry. Have you ever watched a stranger try and retain their dignity when a parent tells them their child's name is Omnipotence? It's an exercise in futility. I didn't want to test strangers' poker faces. I wanted a daughter who could stand on her merits, not her lack of name uniformity.

Lisa had narrowed it down to three names: Marlee, Maizy and Jaden. They weren't horrible choices, but I wasn't thrilled about any of them either. I said they sounded made up, like hybrids that came into existence by accident. Lisa started crying. I tried defending my rationale, and she retrieved an obscure child's name book and showed me that each name was indexed, thus proving the names weren't as far-fetched as I claimed. I closed the book and scrutinized the cover. The book was compiled and edited by a woman named Lasso Jennings. Lasso. A verb now forced to pose as a proper noun. Lisa was taking name recommendations from Lasso. In the end, I caved and told Lisa that Jaden wasn't terrible. Lisa smiled and said that was her favorite of the three. We hugged and went home and had passionless sex.

Jaden was seven pounds and twenty-one inches, and I don't think it's just my parental bias talking when I say she wasn't ugly. She was perfect. A perfect child born to imperfect parents. God has a hell of a sense of humor.

Chapter 15

My bedroom ceiling's texture has a pattern that—with a little imagination—resembles a river flowing through a dense forest. I know this because of the countless nights I'd lie awake staring at the moonlit pattern positioned directly above my bed. The right side, to be specific—my side.

Some nights I would stare, transfixed, at this image for hours. I'd imagine the river, serene and crystal clear, flowing smoothly and constantly. I could even hear it. The sound that the water made as it grazed the riverbanks, caressing the rocks and jutted-out tree roots. Fertile, dark-green pine trees, so dark they almost appeared black, enfolded the river. They lined its edges and became thicker and darker the further I tried to peer into the forest. I loved this place.

I suppose I created my fictional forest because I needed it. I didn't know that I needed it at the time I created it; I just knew that I was lost and confused and in need of some kind of reprieve. However, I couldn't put a finger on how to obtain some form of…amnesty. My head was foggy and entangled with conflicting emotions, wants, needs, and desires. Nothing made sense. At least nothing regarding me and Brock.

I loved Brock—well, for the most part—but he was so smothering. Our relationship, and with it my future, had been taken out of my hands, it seemed. It had spiraled out of my control after I recklessly agreed to marry him. I felt ambushed and trapped and very alone. His family, which I adored from a distance but overwhelmed me when in their presence, had swooped in and taken over all the wedding plans. They were so happy. So happy.…

Brock's mother found us the perfect caterer. My future mother-in-law called me often to pow-wow about the Big Day. "*Did we want to have a seafood option for the dinner? And if so, mahi-mahi or salmon? Or maybe we should just stick with the chicken or steak options? No, no—we can't do that, the proper thing is to offer a seafood option, of course. What about dessert? Should we offer a few choices, or shall we just serve the caramel mousse parfait?*

Yes—we'll do that since cake will also be served." Papers shuffled in the background. She probably had a cataloged binder she was organizing as we "talked." *"You still want the chocolate-raspberry cake, right? Of course you do. It's phenomenal. We'll just stick with the three tiers, any more than that is overkill if you ask me."* She fired questions at me, or made senseless observations, faster than I could process them. Often, she'd answer the questions herself before I could formulate a response. Our "pow-pows" were just Barbara talking aloud to herself, while I sat on the other end wondering what my role was supposed to be and why she even bothered to include me.

His sister, Tanya, found for me the "perfect dress." It needed to be special ordered from Australia, and she needed my measurements *ASAP! "We need to place the order now!"* She was practically shaking with excitement. *"It will take them three months to make! And then we'll need it to be delivered at least two months before the wedding, you know, to make sure that it fits and everything is perfect!"* she clasped her hands together energetically, and explained all this to me one afternoon in my kitchen. She had a picture of "my dress" on her laptop. It was beautiful, but, like everything else that had encumbered my life lately, it just wasn't me. It was so...white? So wedding-dressy-ish. Strapless and requiring a corset of some sort. It was everything young girls dream about. It was covered in lace, with a flowing full skirt adorned with a hand-sewn, beaded garnish. It was the essence of the princess bride. Tanya assured me I would be beautiful; she would see to it! *And happy!* She added as an afterthought, as if my happiness was, and should, play second fiddle to my wedding's opulence.

So why the hell wasn't I happy? It was, after all, *my* wedding! I was downright apathetic about the whole thing. I sat numbly looking at the dress thinking, *Why does the dress even matter? They're all the same.* I felt a palpable disconnect about my potential wedding, or that I was even getting married, for that matter. I figured it was all just a dream that I would wake from before I actually had to go through with it.

Things were happening all around me, while I sat in the center of the planning frenzy that involved activities and events that I was forced to participate in. It all had to do with me, while at the same time, none of it had anything to do with me. I was just an entity, a physical being, sitting in the center of it all— providing for them a reason to get excited, while I became numb and contributed nothing. I was a spectator to my own life. It was all just...happening.

Then one night, as I was lying in my bed wide-awake, yet again, staring at the ceiling and listening to Brock's gentle snore, I spotted this impression in the texture of the ceiling. My eyes narrowed, and as I studied it, a beautiful utopia gradually formed and began to suck me in. After my first visit to this enchanted place that I knew wasn't real, but also very real, it started to beckon me night after night.

It became my escape.

I developed a routine. Every night, after preparing for bed and reading until I felt sleep creeping in—Brock long since having dozed off—I'd close my book, settle into my pillow, find the familiar ceiling pattern, and then allow myself to be taken away. I'd imagine my body drifting toward the ceiling, to my place. Once I arrived, I would sit along the river, listening to the trickling stream and the breeze pushing through the trees, feeling the fresh air tingling my skin, while I basked in the rich scent of pine and…freedom. Somewhere, deep down, I was always aware that it wasn't real, and even questioned how healthy this behavior was, but ultimately, I came to crave my escape.

The peace.

The freedom.

It was intoxicating.

***

Brock and I were walking together through Neiman Marcus searching for the chinaware set that would perfectly define us as a couple. Evidently, this was an enormously important decision, according to Brock. The china needed to properly represent our societal status. It must endure—to be loved and appreciated by the many generations to come. Mine and Brock's children and their children and all the future generations that sprang from our love must cherish the chinaware that Brock and I were about to choose. Brock had worked himself into a slight frenzy as we perused the various designer (of course) dinnerware sets locked behind the store's glass cases.

I was indifferent to all of it.

They all looked the same to me. They were all ugly. I hated china. (Chinaware, that is. I have nothing against the country. They're the best at making Trump neckties.)

But the whole picking-out-dishes-game, and what it all represented, was so ridiculous to me. What the hell was I going to do with a $1500, four-piece chinaware set? Brock had his eye on a cream-colored set with blue lattice along the edges. I scrutinized the pattern, feigning interest like a pro, as if I were imagining all the dinner parties and holidays in which these plates would be taken out, dusted off, and carefully eaten off of. Afterward, they would be washed carefully and strategically placed back into the display cupboard for all to see, a subtle reminder of our status. *We have expensive chinaware; you should want our life.*

Nope.

I couldn't do it. Once again, a repeat of six years ago, I pictured every dinner party, every social event, every morning and every evening, for the next 50 years. I knew just what my life with Brock was going to be—the stereotypical 'American Dream.' White picket fence, Sundays at the country club, weekday luncheons with friends. Kissing Brock every night before rolling over and setting my alarm, just to get up and do it all again in seven hours. Some might find this predictability comforting, stable, and safe. Not me.

I wanted life to be uncertain and exciting; future forks in the road needed to be mysterious. THAT was comfort to me. After all was said and done, I was still me. The Kadie who years ago couldn't commit to the life that being with Brock entailed. I needed the unpredictability. The not knowing—the possibilities that opened from the unknown—was what gave me energy and motivation. Thinking about a life with Brock, and the boredom it entailed, just drained me.

I wasn't falling in love with him the way that I should, or picturing a life with him wouldn't seem so dreary to me…right? I watched him scrutinizing the china. He was so handsome. He was such a catch. I closed my eyes. *Just not my catch.*

Our relationship was high on status and low on romance. I wanted to love him so much that I had convinced myself that I did, or that I could. But I didn't, and I couldn't. Our stars would never align. I was making a big mistake.

Shit. Shit. Shit.

"Where are you?" Brock nudged me gently.

"Oh…ah…sorry," I sputtered, snapping out of my epiphany.

His mouth was tight and angled downward. "It's okay."

"I got distracted for a minute. So, what do you think?" I asked, feigning interest in the plate he was holding.

He stared at me. Mouth still tight. He knew something was wrong. My back started to sweat.

"The china." I pointed to the plate. "Is it the one?"

He stared at me a moment longer, then seemed to make a decision. "You've been *distracted* a lot, Kadie. Not just right now," he said deliberately, as if testing murky waters. "You've been…disconnected from everything. Well, everything that has to do with planning our wedding."

Apparently I wasn't faking interest as well as I thought.

"Brock, I'm just tired. I haven't been sleeping well. You know that." Lame excuse, I know.

I'm tired. Isn't that the universal excuse for getting out of anything? Sex? 'Awe, babe, sounds wonderful…I'm just so tired tonight.' Dinner at the in-laws? 'Love having dinner with your family, sweetie, you know that. I'm just so dog-tired tonight. Mind if I skip?' Lunch date with your BFF's from high school? 'Shoot! Y'all know I wanna see your sweet faces! I'm just so sleep deprived because of a huge project at work. So *tired*! Next time!'

"Yeah, I know." He wasn't buying the tired excuse this time. "I guess," he murmured through his concerned expression. "It just seems…I don't know…there's more to it than that."

"I'm not sure what you want me to say, Brock," I said annoyed. I was about to lose it, I sensed everything coming to the surface, and I wasn't going to stop it. "How do you want me to act?" I said. "I have no say in anything. Your mom has chosen the cake *and* the caterer, along with the menu. Your sister has chosen my dress. The three of you have picked the venue. And now you've picked our chinaware, that I really couldn't even give two-shits about." I gestured to the smorgasbord of chinaware surrounding us. "My *being present* hasn't even been necessary, has it? But then I get in trouble for *not* being present?" Okay, my voice was maybe an octave, or two, too high. Even as it was happening, I knew I was unjustly unleashing my frustrations on Brock. Frustrations that weren't necessarily his fault. But, god, it felt good to get them out. "What do you want from me, Brock? I have nothing left to give."

Well, it felt good *until* I looked at Brock. I stood staring at him with my arms out—you know, showing him that I indeed had nothing left to give—and

I suddenly felt like a complete asshole.

"Do you really feel that way, Kadie?" He was completely thrown off.

I shook my head and lowered my arms.

"No. Well...yes. Well...god, Brock, I don't even know what I'm saying right now," I sighed. Then I stared at the ground like an ashamed child. "No, I don't," I relented. I wasn't sure what I was feeling or how to even begin to articulate it to him. "I'm sorry, Brock, I'm just exhausted and crabby," I explained once again hoping it would pacify him. "I'm going to the bathroom. Pick the dishes you want and let's go eat. I think I'm just hungry." I smiled weakly and then started toward the bathrooms. I needed to get away from that stupid chinaware, and I needed to figure out how I was going to call off my wedding...again.

***

How was it that I was in the exact same position I fought so hard to escape five years before? I knew I wasn't going to marry Brock. My department store meltdown helped me see that. It also helped me to see that I was destined to hurt him. Again. That reality brought back the heaviness in my heart that I thought I had escaped five years ago. God, I was awful.

Just awful and selfish!

I needed to tell him. I needed to say it and get it over with.

Brock and I were sitting silently and waiting for our food. We were at a high-end restaurant "celebrating" having picked out and registered for the perfect chinaware set. I didn't even know which one he chose. He was waiting for me when I exited the department store bathroom. I smiled and asked which one he chose. He said, "It's a surprise." I think he wanted me to be more interested. I couldn't fake it though. I was already faking too much.

We were *also* both pretending that my mini-meltdown two hours prior never happened.

I avoided looking at Brock; I looked everywhere but at him: my glass of wine—red, not my favorite; the embroidered tablecloth—ooh, the pattern on this tablecloth would mesh quite nicely with our new china, I bet; I rolled my eyes, turning then to observe the couple behind Brock. They were arguing about something, straining to keep their voices lowered. I craned my head to listen.

Ahh… she wants a baby, and he doesn't. Dammit. That's a tough one. Good luck to you!

"Kadie?"

Jolted out of my reverie, I looked at Brock. He was looking at me with an unfamiliar expression. "Oh…sorry. I was…what's up?" I asked and offered a quick apologetic smile.

"What are you thinking about?"

"Nothing, really. Just…nothing."

"Are we gonna talk about what happened earlier?"

"What do you mean?"

"You know what I mean."

I had no response, so I stayed silent. Brock wanted more than I was offering. The wheels in his head were turning. *Brace for impact, Kadie.* I readied myself. I sat up straight and was about to tell Brock we needed to talk when he beat me to it.

"Kadie, we need to talk."

What? Wasn't that my line?

"Look, Kadie, I'm not stupid. Or blind." He had a distinct look of resignation. "You're not happy. I can see that now. You're not…in this." He paused and looked to be fighting back tears. "Funny thing is, I don't even think you're aware of it. Of how unhappy you are." He looked down. He seemed to be fighting something or having some internal conflict.

"Brock…."

"No. I need to do this. Please, just let me…" he paused, still deliberating, it seemed. Then after a moment, he looked up resolutely and said, "I don't think we should get married."

I stared at him, speechless. He was using all my lines.

His mouth was set firmly, his eyes unreadable. His walls were up. "I know you still don't feel for me the same way I feel for you. I thought I'd be okay with that. I thought that I could love you enough for the both of us. I thought that just *having* you would be enough." He exhaled, his whole demeanor visibly deflating. "Truth is, I was so sure that you'd realize how perfect we are together and fall desperately in love with me."

"Oh, Brock—"

"Please just let me finish. This isn't easy, Kadie. But it needs to be said." His voice was stern. Then after another brief pause, he continued, "When I came to understand that perhaps that wasn't going to happen," he choked on the last word and paused again to collect himself, his eyes were wet. "I decided that…that my…surplus of love for you was enough fill the gaps." He forced a laugh and shook his head. He was looking down, attempting to hide his emotions. "I'm an idiot," he muttered more to himself than to me.

"Brock…no… I'm the idiot. I don't know why…"

"Stop." He looked at me, his face once again firm and unreadable. "Don't patronize me with anything you're about to say. I don't want to hear about how this is actually *your* loss, or that *I* deserve better. That I'm a great catch and any woman would be lucky to have me. Take those hollow reassurances and…" he stopped himself, seeking to keep control. His eyes were giving him away. They were so full of pain that my heart ached. I felt so ugly, so monstrous. "Those words don't help, Kadie. They don't take away the pain of loving someone so desperately, and that person *not* loving you back. That should be the definition of hell, because nothing is more painful, more unbearable. Nothing."

His words sat heavy around me. The silence was too much to bear.

"I…agree," was all I could summon. I wanted to scream at him that *I fucking know!* All those feelings he expressed had made an indelible home in my soul! Those feelings—that desperation, that heartache, that hopelessness—were my constant and relentless companions!

But how could I explain that to him? Explain that I would never be able to love him the way he wanted to be loved and the way I wanted to love.

He stared at the table for a while, refusing to make eye contact. I don't know how much time passed (enough time for the waitress to check on us twice, the second time Brock told her to box our dinners).

He looked up at me with a new resolution.

"I cannot love you enough for both of us, can I." This was a statement, not a question. It was his answer to his own struggle. "Love has to be there, from both parties, doesn't it? Anything can be overcome as long as love is present. But without love…nothing matters enough to be overcome, because without love, all we're left with is…nothing."

I sat still, unable to move. I wanted to hug him. Not to comfort *him*, but because *I* wanted comfort. I wanted someone to hold me and tell me everything was going to be okay. That life wasn't always going to hurt this much. That one day I was going to be happy. One day I was going to find such a blissful, intoxicating happiness that I would not even remember that I had ever experienced such pain before. I wanted someone to tell me that one day I was going to be washed clean of this relentless sadness.

"I'm…so sorry, Brock. I shouldn't have agreed to marry you," I said.

"Well, that's the thing, Kadie. You didn't. I pressured you. I barely gave you the option of saying no. I share some of the blame. I disregarded your feelings and told myself what I wanted to believe."

"You're too good for me."

"Stop!" he shouted, and then embarrassed, he lowered his voice and his head. "I told you I don't want to hear any platitudes. Really. It's patronizing." He sighed and said, "You're an amazing woman. You deserve anything and everything you want. I just wish that included me."

I slid the ring off my finger and put it on the table between us.

"Here. This was never mine."

He picked it up and examined it. "You're right. It's not you, is it? This ring." He almost looked embarrassed. "I don't know what I was thinking. I'm sorry, Kadie."

"No, Brock. You have nothing to be sorry about," I replied with utter astonishment.

"Of course I do. I wanted you so badly that I left your feelings out of the whole thing. I turned a blind eye to a huge problem that was sitting right in front of me. You haven't been happy. But I didn't care—or rather, refused to see it— because I *was* happy. I was being selfish."

"No…"

"Yes," he said, determined that our conversation end. "Now let's get out of here," he said, standing up. He dropped the ring in his pocket and started pulling on his suit jacket. It was as if now that he had accepted the reality of the situation, he couldn't get away from me fast enough. I couldn't blame him.

He made no attempt, or offer, to walk me to my door when we arrived at my house. He put the car in park and, staring straight ahead, said, "If you pack up my things, I'll come by Wednesday to pick them up."

"Sure…" I sat looking at him, wondering if I should just get out. What did I want from him at this point? Closure? I think that was something that he needed more than me, but…was I supposed to say, or do, something else? After a few more awkward minutes, I decided no, and started to open my door.

"Kadie…" his voice broke. I turned and looked at him. "You…take care. Okay?"

"Of course. You do the same." Then I got out, shut the door, and watched him drive away.

Life is a holy godforsaken mess sometimes. Yet, mess or not, it just keeps on going, doesn't it? I knew that regardless of how hopeless or discouraged I felt, I was still going to walk into my house, wash my face, change into my pajamas, brush my teeth, go to bed, and then wake up tomorrow to face another day. That's just how it works. All I needed to do now was walk through my front door and let life continue to happen, but…

No. I couldn't walk in and go through that familiar scenario. At least not right now. The thought depressed me too much. So, I turned and started walking down the street. I had no idea where I was heading. No set destination. I just walked and allowed my feet to take me wherever they wanted to go.

Thirty minutes later, I found myself at the Bar on the Corner. I hadn't been back since the night I went with Paul. I loved the place. The bartender, Ray, and I had a strong rapport, and I missed our conversations. I just hadn't been ready to revisit the place where I had fallen for Paul. I guess tonight was the night. Another step in the right direction, I told myself.

When I stepped into the dark, warm entryway, it was like an old friend welcoming me home. I took in the cozy atmosphere and inhaled the mouth-watering smell of deep-dish pizza. I meandered over to the bar and sneaked onto a stool. Even though I was always welcomed here, I knew a brusque reprimand from Ray was headed my way.

"Holy hell! Look who it is."

"Hi, Ray." I looked at him and smiled sheepishly.

"Kadie Park has come back to grace us with her presence," he mused as he dried a cocktail glass. Even though his mouth displayed a disapproving frown, his eyes were twinkling.

I obliged him with a small bow, the best I could manage while sitting at the bar anyway.

"It's good to see," he said.

"It's good to be seen."

"What can I get you, sweetie?" he asked, smiling. Apparently, I was forgiven. My heart warmed. That's why people love bartenders. Why couldn't all relationships be that easy?

"Surprise me," I said lightheartedly.

He raised his eyebrows, impressed with my blasé mood. I suppose I'm not usually so unconcerned about what I drink—that is, however, a prudent rule when it comes to letting men decide what drinks to serve me—but I did need to chill out about some things. Even bartenders noticed my neurotic tendencies.

"'Surprise' you, huh? All right. I think I have something you'd enjoy."

Moments later he returned with a honey-wheat hefeweizen. After I took my first long pull, I theatrically smacked my lips. "Perfect, Ray. Thank you."

"Anytime," he answered. "That one's on the house," he said, dunking a couple dirty glasses into his soapy dishwater.

"Why?"

"It's an incentive to make you come back. It's been too long."

I laughed, raised my glass to him, and took another drink.

"Hey!" He looked at me as if he just remembered something important. "I think I have something for you...."

"You have something for me?" I asked.

"Yeah. Some guy brought it by a while ago."

"What is it?"

"It's a book."

"A book?"

"Yeah. Some guy came in and...where did I put it..." he trailed off as he started looking around. He stood up and dried his hands, trying to recall a foggy memory. He started looking under the bar but came away empty-handed. He was on a mission, moving things around, lifting things, shuffling stray papers and all sorts of random paraphernalia that got shoved under the bar. He stood up straight. "Ah, I remember now." He snapped and pointed his forefinger at me. "I put it in the back, so it wouldn't get ruined. Sit tight. I'll be right back."

"Okay," I said.

He disappeared into the back. While I waited for Ray, I sipped my beer and casually let my eyes wander around the pub. They found their way to the table where Paul and I sat our first night together. My response was immediate, and far more painful than I'd imagined. My pulse quickened, and tears stung my eyes. I shouldn't have come here after all. I wasn't ready. I was still too vulnerable, and the wound I had inflicted by calling off my wedding to Brock an hour earlier was still fresh. What was I thinking revisiting this place?

I took another sip from my beer. It was tasteless. My heart was pounding. *Breathe, Kadie.* I told myself. *It will pass. You can do this.*

I took a few deep breaths, willing my pulse to slow. I looked back at the table. Paul's face flashed through my mind. I pictured him smiling his quirky sideways smile. The one that was both mocking and affectionate. The one that sent my heart on a roller-coaster.

Nope.

I sat my drink down and fished through my purse for a twenty. I dropped the bill on the bar and muttered an apology to Ray.

I was gone before he came back with the book.

***

"I need you in Maine," Cheryl said. I rolled over and looked at my bedside clock. It was exactly 5:00 AM. Did Cheryl ever sleep? "We're renovating hotels in areas outside of our usual scene," she explained. " *You're* going to head it up. The whole project."

"Maine?" I sat up. "Maine is a pretty different scene from our usual clientele." Most of our hotels were in highly-developed cities that boasted heavy tourist traffic and an active nightlife. Maine was out of the norm. It sounded perfect for me.

"We're partnering with some owners looking to expand. I've been keeping my eye on this area for a while. It has a lot of potential. I found a hotel that's struggling to stay afloat; a little family-owned B&B that's about to go under." I pictured a Cruella De Vil-esque Cheryl seated in her massive office, elbows resting on her massive desk, strumming her fingers together cunningly, devising a plan. "I offered to help dig them out in return for a partnership. It's perfect."

"Sounds great," I said. Cheryl was an acquired taste. If I didn't know her so well, I wouldn't like her. Throughout her career, she'd made a lot of enemies; she viewed this as a badge of honor. Yet, each of those "enemies" would do business with her again in a heartbeat if the situation arose. She's that good. Like a hound dog with a scent, she could smell potential, and once she sniffed it out, she worked her ass off to ensure success. I envied her. I appreciated her talents and lack of fear.

"The whole place needs to be renovated—updated, modernized. This is your specialty. It must scream luxury and status. We're going to change the coastline."

"I'm up for it." Cheryl's self-assurance was contagious. "This is perfect timing. When do I start?"

"Next week. The project is extensive. It will take a while. You'll have a better idea when you arrive and assess how much work it needs. I can't imagine this taking you less than a couple months. You'll need to pack a few bags, dear."

"I can do that." *Oh, thank you, Jesus.* "Not a problem at all!"

Chapter 16

Zoe flew in from New York without telling me. She arrived at my front door carrying a basket filled with different baby paraphernalia. A congratulatory gift from the agency, she said. I was surprised to see her since she had flown in seven months earlier when Jaden was born.

After her birth, Jaden took to Zoe immediately, as if she were the mother and Lisa a surrogate. Neither Lisa nor I could ever seem to soothe Jaden when she'd burst into a crying fit. We'd cradle her, sing her lullabies, rock her, take her for a ride, and anything else we thought might alleviate her distress. Nothing worked. On our first day home from the hospital, Jaden began wailing. In a bit of hysteria, I handed her off to Zoe, so I could search for a pacifier. As if on command, her crying stopped. I located the pacifier and took Jaden back from Zoe. Her crying resumed. I handed her back and the crying ceased. She turned off like a switch, closing her eyes and drifting back into some dreamless sleep that only Zoe's touch could induce. Zoe was a lifesaver. The next afternoon while Zoe was bathing Jaden, I ran to the store and bought the most expensive air mattress and set it up in Jaden's room. Zoe studied it suspiciously, but she understood my intentions.

"Is that for me?" she asked.

"Yes."

She sat on the mattress's edge, testing its buoyancy and comfort. She was pleasantly surprised. "It'll do," she said.

Zoe only intended on staying a few days, but Lisa and I begged her to stay longer. She must have seen the desperation in our eyes, so she agreed to stay until the end of the week. At the end of the week, I convinced her to stay through the end of the month. She acted put out, but it was all for show. She wanted to stay just as much as we needed her to. Often, I woke wake in the middle of the night to find Zoe rocking Jaden. She'd sing her obscure songs by obscure artists whose work was never meant to be adapted to lullabies. I would stand in the doorway and watch. It brought me immense joy.

During her stay, Zoe never missed an opportunity to remind me that I still owed her and my publisher a public appearance. My disappearing act in Chicago did increase book sales, but fans, especially ones who had paid to see me read, were still upset. I said I understood, but I still wasn't ready to do a public reading.

"What about something smaller? A book signing or something?" she asked. I wasn't ready for that either. Zoe looked to Lisa for support—a confidant to help grease the rails. Lisa would smile and explain how she tried for years to get me to cash in on my fame. In a world where every innocuous task is uploaded to the internet for public approval, my desire to stay hidden confounded them. Zoe asked if I would at least start a Twitter account. I laughed, and when I realized her suggestion wasn't a joke, I laughed harder.

The day she was scheduled to leave, before stepping out of my car and into the chaos of the airport, she turned to me with a serious glint in her eye. "Look, I know you don't want to do a public reading, but you did agree to one in your contract." I opened my mouth to offer a counter-argument, but she cut me off before I could say anything. "I know you were tricked into it, but you still signed it. It was a shady move, but understand that I'm the one fielding the telephone calls and getting the threats that the publisher may sue if you don't follow through. You have a huge fan base, Paul. You don't need to be cold to the people that are letting you live your dream. Think of how you'd feel if you got stood up by one of the author's you admire. Stop being so stubborn."

She waited for me to speak, to offer some lame rebuttal, but I had nothing to say. Whenever I'm put in my place, I've always considered the necessary response is to just stay silent, so that's what I did.

"Take a few months and raise your child but know that the mess you caused in Chicago isn't going away," Zoe said. "I'll keep the sharks at bay for a while, but sooner or later, you have to give them what you promised."

I nodded.

"I love you," Zoe said. "I love your baby, too. I'll definitely miss her more than you." Zoe said. She meant it as a joke, but it was still the truth.

"You have no idea how much you're going to be missed," I said.

"You'll hear from me soon," she said.

But I didn't. Zoe left me alone for the next six months until she unexpectedly returned brandishing the overstuff basket of baby goods. When I opened the door, she brushed past me and placed the basket on the kitchen table. I asked what she was doing in Arizona, and she said she had something important she needed to talk to me about.

"Okay," I said. "How about I buy you a cup of coffee?"

"Sure," she said, "but I want to see Jaden first."

***

I handed Zoe her coffee and took the empty chair across from her. "I have a favor to ask," Zoe said. I sensed what was coming. She had given me six peaceful months, and now it was time to talk business. I readied myself.

"What's that?"

"Charlie and I want a child."

I stared at her for a moment, puzzled. "Ah…good for you," I said. I had no idea who Charlie was.

"We've discussed our options, and we were wondering if…you'd be willing…"

"Yeah?"

"We need a donor."

"For…what?"

Zoe looked at me as if I was missing something. Evidently I was. "Are you serious?" she asked. Her crooked eyebrows were more crooked than usual. Her discerning eyes looked at me critically.

"What?" I asked.

"We want you as our donor."

"Who does?"

"We do."

"You and…"

"Charlie."

"Charlie…right." I was confused but pretended otherwise. I tried putting the pieces together, but I couldn't get them to fit. Zoe sensed I was lost.

"Charlie is my partner, Paul," she explained. I was still lost. "She's a woman," she said, frustrated that I wasn't privy to this pertinent information.

"Charlie is a woman?" I asked.

"Yeah."

"You're a…"

"Lesbian? Yeah."

"Huh," I mumbled. I had no idea. I wasn't surprised Zoe was gay; I was surprised with my ignorance of it. I should have known. I was realizing lately that I didn't pay much attention to other people. Lisa often told me I needed to be more present. I was working on it.

"You're a shit, you know that?" Zoe said.

"What?" I said, but I knew I was in the wrong.

"You met her last year at my birthday party."

"Yeah, I…I remember," I lied.

Zoe shook her head. "Do you ever think about anything outside of yourself?"

I lowered my head. "No."

"Do the hamsters in there," she tapped my forehead, "ever slow down long enough for you to remember something outside of your own messed-up mind?"

"I'm sorry."

"How did you not know I'm gay?"

"I…knew," I lied. Zoe sensed my lie and rolled her eyes. She wasn't hurt or offended, just tired of having to put up with my constant aloofness.

"So…will you donate?" she asked.

"I don't know."

"Come on," Zoe said. "You owe me."

"I owe you?"

"Yeah."

"How do you figure?" I asked.

"I discovered you, you dumb shit."

"Please," I scoffed.

"What? I did."

"So because you liked my book, I have to give you my sperm?"

"Yeah," Zoe said. She acted as if my question was a stupid one.

"Come on, Zoe," I said incredulously. "You benefit from my success as much as I do."

"What's the big deal, Paul? Just let us use your sperm."

"Why me?"

"You're fit, not entirely retarded, and you still have your hair," she said matter-of-factly. I pictured her and Charlie at home in bed, filtering through all possible sperm candidates before settling on me because I still had hair.

"You've set the bar high, haven't you?"

Zoe reached across the table and took my hand. "The truth is you're handsome and brilliant. And I love Jaden. She's perfect, and even though you suck at parenting, you're loving, kind, patient...you're all the things I would want in a man if I liked men. I'm hoping you can pass those traits on to our baby."

"I don't suck at parenting."

Zoe smiled. "You're adequate, but you're not as good as me."

I thought to protest, but I knew she was right. I looked at Zoe. She was unorthodox in all walks of life. Her unorthodoxy is what inspired her to take a chance on me so many years ago. She read something in my writing that so many other agents ignored. She was authentic and honest. She never judged me for giving Lisa a second chance. She accepted me for who I was despite my faults and pain-in-the-ass idiosyncrasies. Zoe was one of the best people I knew. She was right: I did owe her. I owed her just for letting me call her my friend.

"I'd be honored to give you my sperm, Zoe," I said. It seemed a lot less painful than doing a public reading, which is what I thought she was going to ask.

***

I met a doctor at a party once that told me whenever he has bad news for a patient, he always calls the patient by their last name. "I'm sorry, Mrs. Ferguson, but it appears you have cancer." "It appears your boyfriend gave you herpes, Mrs. Howard." "The shampoo bottle is lodged up there too far, Mr. Naylor."

If the doctor comes bearing good news, he always uses the patient's first name. "Congratulations, Bob, the tests came back negative." "No. Those are *not* genital warts, Stacey." "Robert, I believe I can retrieve the shampoo bottle without needing surgery."

It was while driving home that I realized the sperm doctor hadn't called me by my first name. He entered the sterile white room and closed the door behind him without looking at me. He stood awkwardly, shifting his weight from one foot to the next.

"I'm sorry to tell you, Mr. Stevens, but you have a very low sperm count."

I remained silent. The words didn't make sense. After a beat, I told him he must be mistaken, that I just had a child a year ago. He chuckled and expressed his disbelief. I told him it was true. He asked me if I was certain the child was mine. I jumped off the exam table, and I would have given him an open-hand chop to the Adam's apple had I not slipped and fallen forward into a diagram of a penis. My head hit the concrete floor and I blacked out. When I came to, the doctor stood over me, looking down at me quizzically. Something warm crawled down my forehead.

"You've cut yourself," the doctor said.

I touched the wound and drew my hand back to survey the blood. "You may have a lawsuit on your hands," I said. I was joking, but the doctor looked worried. He offered to dress the wound.

As he cleaned and stitched my cut, he explained that normal sperm densities range from 15 million to greater than 200 million sperm per milliliter of semen. A man with a low sperm count has fewer than 15 million sperm per milliliter or less than 39 million sperm total per ejaculate. When I asked how many sperm I had, he laughed and said he'd seen men with vasectomies with more baby batter. Yes, he said "baby batter." Ignorant prick.

"How is it that I had a kid a few months ago then?" I asked.

"Maybe you should ask your wife."

"I'm not married."

"Well," he paused, "that's fortunate."

"Why?"

"Divorces are expensive."

He turned and walked out of the room.

Lisa and Jaden were sleeping when I got home. I took Jaden from her crib and cradled her to my chest. She was soft, smelled fresh, and cooed in my arms. She was perfect, but the doctor's searing words were mocking me. I appreciated science. It had kept me away from a life of nonsense, liberating me of any sense of faith that asked me to abandon logic for stories that defied it. I came in a cup, and the sperm sample showed my progeny was an anomaly. That was science. So, I was either the father of a miracle, or I wasn't a father at all. My heart and brain were at war—like an educated republican. I held Jaden at arms' length and studied her innocent features. She stared back at me dumbly, ignorant that she was being scrutinized. I always thought she somewhat resembled me. Did she, or had I just convinced myself she did?

"What are you doing?"

I turned. Lisa stood in the doorway. She yawned, still fighting some of her nap's residual fatigue. I looked at her for a long moment, scrutinizing *her* features, and then back to Jaden. I definitely saw Lisa in her. They both had the same nose and delicate forehead, the same mysterious eyes. It was evident Jaden had some of Lisa's features.

Lisa came into the room, rested her head on my shoulder, and looked down at Jaden. I enjoyed holding Jaden and having Lisa by my side, resting her head on me in such a familiar way. It would have been a nice family moment, had I not been doubting my place in the family at the moment. I handed Jaden off to Lisa and retreated to the opposite end of the room.

"Where did you go this morning?" Lisa asked.

I stared out the window. It looked hot outside. Across the street some neighborhood kids were running through the sprinklers. They looked happy, like kids who've never had to wonder who their father is.

"Have you ever been with someone else?" I asked.

"Someone else?"

"Yeah." I turned from the window and faced her.

"What are you talking about?"

"Just what I asked. Have you ever been with someone else?"

"You mean since we've been together?"

"Yeah."

She scoffed. She didn't answer; she *scoffed.* Words were reserved for people without anything to hide. Jaden started fussing, and Lisa, thankful for the diversion, asked her if she was hungry. Jaden did not answer because she is a baby.

"Zoe asked me for my sperm," I said. Lisa looked at me.

"What?"

"She and Charlie want to have a child. Charlie is a woman, and Zoe is a lesbian."

"I know who Charlie is," Lisa said.

"Well, did you know Zoe is a lesbian?" I asked.

"Yeah. She introduced us to Charlie last year at her birthday party." I hated that Lisa paid better attention to things.

"Well, they want my sperm," I said.

Lisa stared at me for a moment trying to sense if I was joking. "I'm not so sure that's a good idea," she said.

"It doesn't matter because my sperm count is too low."

"What?"

"I don't have any baby batter," I said, and then closed my eyes, angry that the asinine doctor's lexicon somehow found a way to seep into mine.

"Baby batter?"

I opened my eyes and leveled them on Lisa. "Have you ever cheated on me?"

"How could you ask me that?"

"That's the second time I've asked you, and it's the second time you haven't answered me."

"Because it's a stupid question." She started for the door.

"The doctor says Jaden can't be mine," I called after Lisa. She stopped and turned back to me.

"You really don't think she's yours?" She turned and faced Jaden toward me. "Look at her, Paul. How can you think she could be anyone else's?" Jaden smiled at me, and my heart broke. She was perfect, which gave me more reason to suspect she may not be mine. I was incapable of perfection. I was wretched, like Frankenstein's monster or Nicolas Cage.

"The doctor…" I tried to explain.

"Doctors are wrong sometimes," Lisa interjected.

"And they're right the other times."

"Paul, look at the time frame. We had sex nine months before Jaden was born. We came home from the party, made love, and I got pregnant."

I went back to the party in my mind. I remembered the proctologist and still wished I'd let him finish his story before letting Lisa pull me away. She was in a sudden hurry to leave that night. She was distraught, bothered about something. She was having fun, laughing a little too hard with the guy she was speaking with. Then the other woman approached. She ignored Lisa and went right up to the man. She whispered something, and his expression changed. He gave Lisa a confused look and then followed the mysterious woman from the room. The man left with the strange woman and Lisa came to me. She kissed me hard on the mouth and then asked if I was ready to leave. It was all so abrupt.

"Who was the man you were talking with at that party?" I asked.

Lisa spied me for a minute, and then swallowed hard and acted as if she wasn't sure who I was talking about. "What party?" she asked. "What guy?"

"The party the night we had sex. Who was the guy you were talking to?"

"What guy, Pa—"

"The guy you were with. At the party. You know who I'm talking about."

"I wasn't talking to a guy. I was with you."

"No. You spent most of the night talking with a guy."

"I don't—"

"Damn it, Lisa!" I yelled. Jaden started to cry. "Who was he?"

"I don't know who you're talking about," she said, raising her voice to match mine. Jaden cried harder; Lisa rocked her, but her crying only increased. "I have to feed her," Lisa said and then started to leave the room.

"A test will prove if she's mine."

Lisa paused again, turned to me. She looked scared. I'd never seen her scared before. "Why are you doing this?" she asked.

"Who was he?"

"He was…" she started but struggled to find the words. "He was my boss," she said, fighting back tears. As if sensing something was wrong, Jaden's crying subsided. She looked from me to Lisa curiously, as if she wanted to hear Lisa's answers as much as I did.

"Your boss?" I repeated.

"Yeah," she said. Her voice cracked. "I was talking with my boss."

"Talking or flirting?"

"Fuck you."

Lisa's curse hung in the air, floated there, as it played back in my head. She had never sworn at me before. She was either genuinely insulted or trying to hide the truth through poorly constructed language.

"Why did you get fired?" I asked evenly.

"What?"

"You heard me."

"I told you. Cutbacks."

"Who was the woman that came up to you at the party?"

"What woman?"

"Was that his wife?" I asked, ignoring her question.

"I don't know who you're talking about," Lisa said. She reached up and tucked a strand of hair behind her ears. It was her tell; I'd often caught her tucking her hair that way when she was lying. I first noticed it when I asked if she enjoyed my first book. She said yes and tucked her hair. Later I learned she hadn't even read it.

"Wow, Lisa," I said. I began to see things clearly.

"What?"

My mind raced, trying to put the puzzle together. The overzealous attention she paid him before being accosted by his wife. Lisa, suddenly jilted, approached me, kissed me, and wanted to go home. The look of horror on the man's face from across the room when he saw Lisa leaving with me. We went home and had sex. Me, because I'm a stupid man with carnal instincts, and Lisa, because she was subconsciously getting back at him. Getting at him for what, though? Then I understood.

"Were you sleeping with your boss?" I asked, but I already knew the answer.

"What? Of course not."

"That's why you got fired?"

"I never got fired, Paul. I quit."

"Why did you quit?"

"I'm not doing this," Lisa said. She turned and left the room, and Jaden started crying again.

**

Jaden wasn't mine. The paternity test confirmed what I had suspected. I read the results three times. I was sitting on my deck with my laptop opened. A blank word document sat before me, tempting me to write. I put my fingers on the keyboard and typed: "Jaden is not my daughter." I looked at the simple five-word sentence. I read it repeatedly, hammering the words into my head until they became real. I was exhausted. I closed my laptop and stared at the horizon.

I thought of Kadie. I wondered what she was doing. Was she still cynical and beautiful, or did she learn optimism and turn ugly? I wondered if she ever thought of me. Did she despise me, or was I just a distant memory that never stopped her in her tracks the way her memory still stopped me? I lost her because I thought I was going to be a father. Had I known the truth, that Lisa was just using me as a means to an end, how different things might have been. I couldn't be certain, but I was confident that had I known the truth about Lisa's pregnancy, I'd very likely be in Chicago at that moment watching a different horizon.

Lisa and I were at a crossroads. Ever since our conversation when I asked if she slept with her boss, we only spoke to each other about Jaden. ("Can you give Jaden her bath?" "Will you fix a bottle?" "Is Jaden napping?") The eggshells we walked on were cutting both our feet.

Most mornings Lisa got up before me and ran a five-mile loop. She was gone when I woke, and she returned without me hearing her. It was by chance that I looked inside the house and spotted her, water bottle and in hand, staring back at me. Our eyes locked for a moment, both lost in the expression of the other. I turned away first. I was close to breaking, and I didn't want her to see when it happened. She came outside and sat down across from me. The paternity test lay on the table between us. She looked at it, looked at me, and then snatched up the test and read. Her eyes scanned the results, moving left to right at a fervent pace. She gasped and dropped the test results back on the table.

"Was it the man at the party?" I asked.

"Yes."

"Does his wife know you were sleeping together?"

"Yes."

"Is that why you quit?"

"Yes."

"Are you still sleeping with him?"

"No. I haven't spoken to him or seen him in over a year," she said.

"Is he why you broke up with me last year?"

"Paul...don't do this."

"Is he why you broke up with me last year?" I repeated.

"Yes."

"So why did you come back?"

Lisa began to cry. "He wouldn't leave his wife."

"Do you love him?"

"No."

"Did you love him?"

"I—it was a long time ago."

"So, you did love him?"

"I love you, Paul."

Her words were hollow, like they were said out of some unfounded relationship necessity instead of unadulterated sincerity. "I met someone in Chicago," I said. "Someone I was falling for hard. I…I lost her because I thought…Jaden was mine."

"I didn't know Jaden wasn't yours. I knew it was a possibility, but…well, I hoped…" she trailed off.

"You hoped she was mine because you were unemployed and pregnant and recently dumped. You used me because I had money."

"That's not true," Lisa said.

"Yeah, Lisa, it is," I said, tired and defeated. Lisa wanted to explain further, hoping to say something to soften the blow, but she knew I had already figured out everything. Her lie was uncovered. She knew it wouldn't benefit either of us to cover one lie with another, so she said the one thing everyone says in those situations: sorry.

"You know the worst part?" I said. I struggled to keep my composure. "I love Jaden so much." My voice failed me, and I blinked away the tears. "Had Zoe never asked for my sperm, I never would have even suspected Jaden wasn't mine. I'd have raised her and loved her as if…as if she were mine."

"You can still be in her life," Lisa said. "Nothing needs to change." I laughed at the absurdity of her comment. I gathered my laptop and stood up.

"I'll get a hotel till the end of the week," I said. "When I come back on Monday, I want you gone." Lisa nodded. A soft breeze tickled the edges of the paternity test. "You can show that to the father," I said. Lisa looked at the paper. The breeze picked up, and the test slid to the edge of the table. I thought Lisa would reach for it, but she made no reaction. Another gust blew the test to the ground. She let it fall without making a move for it. I went inside to say goodbye to Jaden.

Jaden was sleeping. I watched her for a moment. Soon she'd take her first step and say her first word. I'd miss both. I wasn't her father, but that didn't stop me from thinking that her life (and mine) was better with each other in it. I loved her like a daughter because that was what I thought she was to me. I loved her still. She was innocent of her mother's indiscretions and my ignorance. If she had no one, I would have taken her. But she had Lisa, so she couldn't have me. I leaned down and kissed her forehead.

I didn't think it possible to ever feel worse than I did the night Kadie never showed up at the bar when I returned to Chicago to find her. Turned out I was wrong. Losing the love of your life is hard; losing a child is goddamn torture.

***

"Jaden is not my daughter." The words stared back at me. The cursor blinked, beckoning me to write more, but every time I placed my hands on the keyboard, my faculties failed me. It was now official: I was suffering from writer's block. I knew I had a story to tell, but I lacked the words to tell it. My limited lexicon confined me, so I'd spend hours staring, often becoming hypnotized, by the blinking cursor that mocked my inability to write.

I stayed at a Holiday Inn Express. (The commercials lie; you won't feel smarter.) I checked in five days ago. My phone died in the middle of the first night, and I let it stay dead. I didn't want to be reached, nor did I want to be found. I cleaned out the mini bar by the second day. I ate room service and watched whatever was on TV. The "Please Do Not Disturb" tag was a permanent fixture on my door since my arrival. The front desk called on the fourth day asking if I needed more towels. "No," I said and then hung up the phone. I hadn't showered since I'd checked in.

I spent my days at the small corner desk with my laptop opened. I wanted to write, but I couldn't. The story wouldn't materialize; my mind wandered.

I'd be forty by the end of the year. Half my life was gone. Shouldn't I have figured it out by forty? Instead, I was sitting in a Holiday Inn reading the same sentence over and over again: "Jaden is not my daughter." I read and reread it. I tried to refuse the revelation entwined in the simple sentence, but I knew it was correct. My life was broken, and I had no idea how to pick up the pieces.

Zoe found me on the sixth day. I heard a room card slide into the door's lock, and a moment later, she stood in the entryway looking at me. (The Arizona State student working the front desk offered up my room card after Zoe teased him with the prospect of sex. Go Sun Devils!) We stared at each other for a moment. I was the caged animal and she the intruder, both fearful of how the other may react if things weren't handled appropriately. She sidestepped the discarded liquor bottles and room service trays and sat on the edge of the bed. She stared at me and refused to break the silence. Her demeanor told me that she would wait until I was ready. After a moment, I said the first thing that seemed appropriate: "I have bad sperm." I said this as a way of explaining and apologizing. Then, without any forewarning, I began to sob. Zoe came to me, took me into her arms, and held me until I fell asleep.

I woke a few hours later. I was on the bed, and Zoe sat at the desk in the corner looking at my lone sentence on the white computer screen. "I see you're writing again," she said.

"I'm trying," I said, "but…"

"What can I do for you, Paul?"

"Do you know why I'm here?" I asked.

"Yes, I talked to Lisa," Zoe said. I sat up. I felt hungover, but I knew that wasn't possible; I finished the last of the liquor three days ago. "Do you want to talk about it?" Zoe asked.

"No," I said.

She pointed to my laptop. "Is this the first line of your next book?"

"I…don't…know," I said. "I typed it six days ago. Every time I read it, I feel a little more…numb."

She nodded sympathetically.

I wished I could fall back to sleep and never wake up. "I've been happy three times in my life," I said. "When my first novel was published, that weekend in Chicago with Kadie, and when Jaden was born. It's funny how they're all connected."

"What do you mean?"

"The reason I went to Chicago and met Kadie was because of my writing— because you got me published. Lisa tricked me into thinking I was Jaden's father because I have money—from my writing. My happiest moments are connected to my saddest. Yin and yang, you know?"

I sensed Zoe wanted to say something comforting and profound, but she was drawing blanks. She listened and nodded understandingly instead. I appreciated that she didn't try and placate me with platitudes. She let me vent and simply listened. Zoe was a true friend.

"You've been good to me, Zoe," I said. "I shouldn't have walked out on that reading. I need you to know that I feel bad about that."

"I know you do, Paul. Don't worry. I'm over it."

"You are? Why?"

"Because I know if you had to do it over again, you wouldn't change what you did. I can't ever fault a person for doing what they feel is right. Even if it screws me over in the process," she added, smiling.

I thought for a moment. "You're right." And she was. I wouldn't change a thing if I could go back to that night. It was one of the few perfect nights of my life.

"What ever happened with that woman anyway?" Zoe asked. "The one from Chicago? Kadie."

"She…I…I thought I was going to be a father, so…" I couldn't continue. I didn't need to; Zoe was able to fill in the missing pieces.

"Well…that sounds like your next book," Zoe said.

"What?"

"The last year and a half. Chicago, Kadie, Lisa, Jaden, all of it. It should be your next book. It will help you…purge the pain you're feeling." She pointed to the laptop. "You've already written your first line."

I smiled weakly. "Yeah, maybe you're right."

"I know I am."

Zoe's words made sense. Writing had always been a catharsis for me. It was a healthier remedy than alcohol and more fulfilling than random sex. I needed to write. A fire had been lit. "I need to get out of here," I said.

"So go home. Lisa is gone."

"No. I'm not ready for that yet. Jaden's room…is there. The last six months are still there. It's all too fresh still."

Zoe looked at me for a moment. Her eyes grew wide, on the edge of a breakthrough. She got to her feet and took her phone from her purse. "I think I may have a solution," she said. She dialed a number and stepped out into the hall.

***

The diner had twelve tables. A high school couple sat at one sharing a milkshake, and an elderly man sat alone in another eating clams. I was the sole patron at the bar, eating pie and drinking milk. It had been my routine every evening for the past six weeks. I'd become a regular, and I was even on a first-name basis with everyone on the wait staff. Tonight Trudy worked the bar and Steven had the floor.

From my vantage point, I could see the front door, so I was able to watch her enter. She looked like a model from the Anne Taylor businesswoman catalog: mid-length skirt, white button-down top, matching jacket, high-heels. She looked mid-forty but could pass for mid-thirties. She was attractive, but frightening. She had the type of presence that could silence a room: authoritarian, sexy, sharp features that demanded respect. She gave the diner a brief overview and then made her way to the bar. She was impossible not to watch, not because of her dominating appearance, but because of the contrast her appearance had with her newfound environment. She belonged in an upscale, after-work Manhattan bar, not a mom and pop diner on the coast of Maine.

Trudy emerged from the kitchen and asked if the woman wanted something to drink. She asked for bourbon. Trudy looked confused and then called back to the kitchen and asked if they had bourbon. A minute later, Steve came through the kitchen with a dusty bottle. He showed it to the woman. She rubbed the dust from the label, scoffed at the brand, but said she'd give it try it. Steve poured her a sample. She tasted it, winced and said it was awful. Steve laughed and said not all bourbon gets better with age. She agreed and told him to fill her glass. Steve poured the drink and handed the bottle to Trudy before returning to the kitchen.

I watched her curiously. Hints of her perfume made their way to me. It smelled expensive. She looked in my direction, caught me staring and smiled. I lowered my head. She laughed. I knew it was directed at me, so I pretended not to hear her.

I finished my pie and Trudy came over and asked if I wanted another slice. "Why not?" I said. I'd had a good day. I had hit two-hundred-and-fifty pages earlier that morning in my new book. Another day or two and it would be finished. Pie seemed the appropriate celebration. Trudy brought me another piece and refilled my milk. She asked if I needed anything else. "No," I said. She winked and said, "Okay, sweetie." I would miss Maine.

"How's the pie?" someone asked. I thought the question had come from the mysterious woman, but when I looked in her direction, she had her bourbon glass to her lips. I looked around, but no one else was in the vicinity. I looked back at the woman. She put her glass on the bar and looked at me, evidently awaiting my answer. "So...?" she said. The question had come from her.

"Best apple pie in Maine," I said.

"I can't say the same about their bourbon." She lifted her newly emptied glass toward Trudy. As if on command, Trudy approached and refilled it.

"If it's so bad, why do you keep drinking it?" I asked.

"Bad bourbon is still bourbon," she said.

"Yeah. It all burns going down, right."

"Do you drink?"

"On occasion. Milk goes best with pie though." I lifted my glass to her and took a drink.

"After the day I've had, milk wouldn't cut it. No matter how good the pie."

"What do you do?"

She shook her head and took another drink. "Don't ask."

"You can't walk into a locals' diner dressed like Tess McGill and not expect me to ask what you do."

She laughed, exposing a mouthful of perfectly aligned white teeth. "Fair enough. You know the hotel about a mile down the road?"

"The one that's being renovated?"

"That's the one. Well, I'm overseeing the renovation." Trudy and Steve overheard this revelation from the other end of the bar. They gave the woman a contemptuous sneer that went unnoticed by the woman.

"You may want to keep your voice down," I said. "Not a lot of locals are happy about what you're building down there."

"Are you one of those people?"

"I'm empathetic."

"To whom?"

"The locals."

"Do you live here?"

"Nope. Just visiting. A friend of a friend owns a house on the shore. She's letting me use it for a couple months."

"That's a hell of a friend of a friend."

"It's good to know people." The friend of the friend was Ray Goldstein, the CEO of Makeshift Publishing—my publisher. Zoe told him I was having a bit of a personal crisis and a sabbatical was needed. Ray understood. He was a writer himself. He purchased the Maine oceanfront property twenty years earlier with a hefty inheritance. He wanted to pursue the romantic notion of writing for a living and believed the bungalow the ideal place to draw inspiration. He soon discovered, however, that he was better at selling other writers' books than his own. Most of the year his house sat abandoned. He romanticized the idea of an author using it to write. He told me to take all the time I needed.

"So, what are people saying about me behind my back?" the woman asked. She lowered her voice for dramatic effect, but I, as well as Trudy and Steve, knew she had no qualms if the town hated her. Money-grubbers are immune to the proletariats' contempt.

"They're pissed," I said. "This is a nice, peaceful town, and you've come in with your bulldozers and high-end retail shopping and want to change all that."

"I don't want to change it. I want to cash in on it."

"Explain the difference."

"If I make money from it, they will too. Everybody wins."

"You'll drive up the prices and force everyone out."

"And they'll leave rich," she countered.

"Not everyone is driven by money. You're upending their way of life to make room for more people like…"

"Like me?" she asked.

I smiled. I looked past the woman to Trudy and Steve. They approved of my criticism and respected that I was standing up for them. My next slice of pie would be on the house. "Yeah, like you," I said. I smiled, to offset any offense she might feel. Something told me, however, that this woman never got offended.

"Kind of hypocritical, don't you think?" the woman said. She downed her drink and then looked back at me. "You're giving me a hard time for trying to increase tourism around here when you yourself are a tourist."

"I'm not a tourist," I countered. "I'm a house guest."

"Explain the difference," she said and then offered her own smile, relishing in using my own words against me.

Steve approached and refilled the woman's glass without being asked. "The difference," Steve interjected, "is he understands this is a simple town. He's not trying to exploit that for personal gain."

"Is that right?" the woman said and Steve nodded. He looked as if he wanted to say more, but four new customers walked through the door and were waiting to be seated. He went to seat them—abandoning his idealistic debate for business. I chuckled at the irony.

She turned back to me. "So when you're not a house guest, what are you?"

"I'm a writer."

"Oh, god," she said. "I should have guessed you were the starving artist type. Did you come out here to write the next great American novel?"

"Something like that."

"Well, you are officially uninteresting to me now," she teased.

"I wasn't before?"

"No. You have a rugged masculinity. Square jaw, straight teeth. You look about the right age, too. Maybe a little young. What are you, mid to late thirties?"

"Almost forty."

"Yeah, I'm not averse to younger men," she continued. "Physically, I'd give you a shot, but a writer? Come on."

Her ridicule made me laugh. Her confidence was amusing, even if it was a little off-putting. "What's wrong with writers?" I asked.

She leveled her eyes on me. "Let me tell you something: You won't make it. Your ideas are not interesting. I know you think you have something worth saying, but you don't. The world doesn't care about what you have to say. Get a real job. Stop chasing silly dreams."

"How do you know what I have to say?"

"Because all writers say the same things, only differently."

"Ouch."

"I'll tell you what though," she finished her bourbon, placed the glass on the bar, and made her way toward me. "I do know someone you'd be perfect for." She took the stool next to me, reached onto my plate and broke off a piece of my piecrust and popped it into her mouth.

"I'm not interested," I said.

"Wait till you see her. She's gorgeous, and she makes enough to support your little writing hobby. I should know. I'm her boss, and I pay her well."

"Is she anything like you?"

"Not as much as she should be."

"Well, she has that going for her, at least," I said.

The woman smiled. She picked up my fork and took a bite of the pie. "That *is* good," she said. She went in for more, so I slid the plate in front of her so she wouldn't have to reach across me. She took the offering without reservation.

"Do you want my milk too?" I asked.

"No thanks," she said. "Not a fan. So tell me, have you published anything?"

"Yeah."

"Anything I may have heard of?"

"Do you read?" I asked.

"Not novels. The last book I read was in college. *Slaughter House*...something."

"Five," I said. "*Slaughterhouse Five.*"

"Yeah, that's it. You heard of it?"

"Yeah, I'm familiar with it."

"It was atrocious."

"You have no idea what you're talking about."

"You some kind of expert or something?"

"Something."

"So, what have you written?"

The diner, like all great diners, had its fair share of regulars. They often came in for breakfast and stayed until lunch, passing the time by reading or playing chess. Six weeks ago, the first night I came to the diner, I spotted a bookshelf in the corner. Out of habit, I gravitated toward it to see what it housed. Two of my books were stuffed neatly between a variety of others. I used to have to catch myself when I found copies of my books in random places. The shock of knowing that my words had somehow found their way to obscure locations always filled me with an unrequited surprise. That same excitement occurred when I spotted two of my books in that small Maine diner. It pleased me to know that someone possibly read something of mine in a place as idyllic as this. In some unexplainable way, it made me feel accepted.

"You'll find two of my books on that bookshelf," I told the woman, hoisting my thumb toward the corner bookshelf.

"Is that right?" she asked. She almost sounded impressed.

I smiled. "Yep."

She got up from the stool and walked to the bookcase. "Which ones are yours?" she asked.

"*Boarded Window* and *Rearview Mirror,*" I answered. Normally, I wouldn't reveal my work to a stranger. Anonymity was one of the reasons I opted for a pen name. But I was at a new place in my life. I was as much Kurt McCarthy as I was Paul Stevens, the two separate beings were merging into one, and I no longer cared to keep up the facade.

The woman spotted *Boarded Window* on the bookcase and pulled it out. She looked at the cover and read my name aloud: "Kurt McCarthy." She turned the book over to see if it had a picture to confirm it was me. It didn't. She scrutinized the cover a moment longer and then shelved the book before returning to her stool.

"The cover said, '*New York Times* Bestseller'," she said.

"Yeah."

"So you're kind of a big deal?"

"Authors aren't ever a big deal."

"Not really, no." she said.

"Yeah. People don't read much. The thinking process is too hard." I looked at her and smiled. She shook her head, unimpressed with my dig.

"You need to meet my friend," the woman said. "She loves to read. She's probably even read some of your stuff if you're a bestselling author."

"I'm not interested."

"I have a sixth sense for these things. She even prefers hole-in-the-wall joints like this to high class places with good bourbon. You two are perfect for each other."

"I'm not interested."

"She's stubborn, too. Another thing you have in common."

"She more stubborn than you?" I asked.

"I'll bring her by tomorrow," she said, ignoring my question. "What time will you be here?"

"I don't want to meet your friend."

"Are you married?"

I shook my head.

"Do you have a girlfriend?"

"I just got out of a serious relationship. I'm not looking to start another one just yet."

"She just got out of one too. Another thing you have in common."

"How many times do I have to tell you I'm not interested before you hear me?"

"I don't listen to people when I know they're lying."

"I'm not lying."

"Just a drink. I'll come with her. I'll drink bourbon, you can eat pie, and she'll have a milkshake or something." She paused for a moment, but I knew she wasn't done speaking. "Come on. Do it for me. She's one of the best people I know, and she's had the worst luck with guys. I know you two will hit it off."

I reached across her and pulled my pie plate back in front of me and took the final bite. She looked peeved that I had the audacity to finish my own pie. I took a twenty from my wallet and placed it on the bar.

"That's not going to cover my bourbon," she said, smiling. I reached back into my wallet and retrieved another twenty and dropped it on the bar next to the first one.

"I usually come in here for dinner around five," I said. "You can stop by tomorrow with your friend. I may be here, I may not. I won't promise anything."

"Five? Good Lord! Is the early bird rate *that* great?"

"I start my days early and my nights too."

"This town…," she trailed off. "What am I doing here?"

"If you can't answer that, maybe you should leave."

"That hurts my feelings," she said, flashing her perfect teeth.

I stood. I took my jacket from my seat and put it on. "What's your name?" I asked.

"Cheryl," she said, extending her hand.

"Nice to meet you, Cheryl." Her hand was soft and sharp and cold. "I'm—"

"Kurt," she said. "Your name is on your book."

"Right," I said, "Kurt." I smiled and then walked out the door.

Chapter 17

I was walking on the beach as the sun rose. This had become my habit during my stay in Maine. On my second day, while getting groceries at the market, the cashier had gushed about the beautiful sunrises—specifically when viewed from the quiet, damp beach. So the next day I set my alarm for an early run and to verify if the grocer was correct or hyperbolic. He was correct.

Every morning I got up at four o'clock, laced up my sneakers, and ran six miles (a different path every day, to help me familiarize myself with the town) that always ended on the beach. I then slipped off my shoes and let the wet sand massage my toes while I watched the sunrise.

I could live in Maine. I found myself envisioning it often. I loved its quietness. I enjoyed the friendly, small-town atmosphere (that I hoped I wasn't spoiling with the hotel renovation), the easy life, the beaches, and...the lobster! God the lobster!

Sunrises and lobster.

I'd learned to appreciate life's small pleasures.

One evening, while I was getting ready to eat my routine lobster dinner, Cheryl called. I prayed for a short conversation. I did not want to eat cold lobster.

"Hey, Cheryl,"

"Kadie, where are you?" she said in her typical, right-down-to-business, fashion.

"At a restaurant. Eating dinner. Why?"

"I just got into town. I need to decompress, and I need a drink." She paused for half a second and then said, "Good Lord! It's six o'clock. Why in the hell are you eating dinner so *early?*" Her words were drenched in distaste.

My confusion kept me silent. I had no idea she was even coming to Maine. I shook off the frustration. It was typical of Cheryl to show up unannounced. As much as I appreciated her, her tendency to do what she wanted and let others in on the plan when it suited her was often discombobulating.

And she thought eating dinner before eight o'clock was immoral.

That was my bedtime, not dinnertime.

"Oh, I'm sorry…I can wait…if you'd like." *Please Jesus, don't let her ask me to wait.* "I had no idea you were flying in today."

She dismissed the passive-aggressive hint of my annoyance. "Don't wait," she said. "I'll go to the hotel and check-in. We'll meet up for coffee in the morning. I'll be in touch. Rest up." Then the line was dead. I sighed. I'd get back to my hotel by a decent hour, put on my pajamas, and read myself to sleep after all. Ahhh…that sounded nice. As the relief swept over me, I dug into my lobster. I moaned with the first bite.

***

Cheryl and I spent most of the following day meeting with the hotel contractors. Cheryl scrutinized the work we'd done, touring the hotel grounds with a discerning eye. As was her custom, she rarely offered praise and was quick to point out any mistakes or improvements that needed to be made. Without saying as much, Cheryl was pleased with the work I had done. She was even more pleased that I was, as usual, ahead of schedule.

"Well," she said as we finished going over the budget changes that needed her approval. "This is coming along quite nicely. You're under budget *and* two weeks ahead of schedule. You never disappoint, dear. And this town, the people; it's all very…cute." She looked at her watch. "We're going to Alexander's tonight for drinks and dinner. Five o'clock."

"Alexander's?"

"Yes," she answered indifferently as she slipped into her suit jacket. "You've heard of the place, I'm sure. It's right by my hotel. I had a drink there last night. It's adequate."

"Yeah, I know where it is. I went once. It was…fine," I said, recalling the single time I went. The people were friendly, but the lobster was average. I hadn't been back since.

"Good. I'm going to my hotel to freshen up. I have a car. I'll pick you up. That way you don't have to wear those." She frowned at my flats.

"Five? Since when do you eat at five?"

"I don't, but I know you do."

My knees nearly gave out. Since when did Cheryl acquiesce anything that she wouldn't benefit from? Although my interest was piqued, I didn't investigate. If she wanted to accommodate my early-bird dinner proclivities, who was I to complain?

"Okay, Cheryl. Dinner at Alexander's. At five o'clock. You're picking me up because I am not to wear my flats."

"Perfect." She grinned and then pivoted and clicked off down the street, strutting in her three-inch heels.

***

Cheryl sipped her bourbon while I stared at the one sitting in front of me that she had ordered on my behalf. I disliked bourbon. I'd told her this too many times to count. Either she kept forgetting (unlikely), or she figured if she continued to ignore my distaste for it, I'd get over the silly aversion (likely). I reluctantly picked up the glass and touched it to my lips. Yuck.

"It's great that you came to Maine," I said, meaning it. "I can show you the town tomorrow. I've gotten familiar with the area. It's so quaint. I love it here."

"It suits you." She finished her bourbon and signaled for another. I think her diet consisted mostly of salmon, Melba toast, and bourbon. I rarely saw her eat anything else. Maybe that's the secret diet for longevity.

"I may have to keep a room on retainer once we finish," I said.

She smirked.

"What?"

"You're a perfect match," she said.

"What are you talking about?"

"I found someone for you," she answered nonchalantly, taking a sip of her newly refilled bourbon.

"What?"

"I met someone here yesterday," Cheryl said. "A man."

"You *met* someone here? You haven't even been here for twenty-four hours! When do you sleep?" Confusion and trepidation swept over me. I looked around, and understanding dawned on me. I was being set up! What a sneaky little....

"He was here last night," she explained. "I came in for a nightcap. We ate pie."

I was stumped stupid. "You ate pie? *You* eat pie?"

"Occasionally," she replied, completely unconcerned about my bewilderment. Then she looked at me with a conspiratorial expression. "He's very handsome," she said.

"Cheryl, I don't want to be set up with someone right now. I just got out of a serious relationship. Besides, I'm here for work!"

"And work needs to remain your focus, but I don't mind if you have other hobbies on the side."

"I'm not interested."

"You're young and talented and beautiful. You need to stop being so *boring*."

I looked at her quizzically. Can she say that? Should I take offense? I sat with my mouth opened, trying to decide if she had just complimented or offended me.

"Anyway, he's meeting us here tonight," she said, glancing at the door. "Maybe."

"Maybe? What does that mean? And why didn't you tell me? I mean *ask* me?" A hot flash came on. "I hate being set up." I had a sudden urge to pee. That was my nervous tick: an indelible need to pee.

"Kadie," she smiled, waving me off. "You look beautiful. You're fine. And you wore your heels!" She beamed at my feet. "Good girl."

"Cheryl, it's not about how I look. I don't want to be in this situation. It's too awkward."

"If he's not for you, signal me, and I'll get rid of him. No pressure."

"Why don't you date him?"

"Initially, I wanted to, but we aren't compatible." Did she expect me to be grateful she deferred him to me? Was I some game show contestant runner–up receiving a set of steak knives. "He's a writer. In fact, some of his books are over there." She pointed toward the back of the restaurant where a bookshelf sat.

I drained my bourbon and signaled for another. Suddenly, the taste wasn't too bad.

"He writes," she continued, "he eats dinner with the senior citizens, and just like you, he likes boring necropolises like this place."

I stared at her, speechless. "I have to pee," was all I managed to say. I slid off my barstool and headed for the bathroom.

I splashed water on my face, mindful not to ruin my makeup. Cheryl would have a fit if I returned with my mascara smeared. In fact, the more I thought about it, the more tempting it was to dunk my whole head under the faucet. If I returned and the mystery man was sitting at our table, and I looked ridiculous, it would reflect poorly on Cheryl more than me. The idea of mortifying her was appealing.

I studied my reflection and thought about the series of events that had brought me to that moment. I was in a bathroom in Maine, with my beautiful and brilliant boss awaiting my return, and a stranger on his way to meet me. I wondered if he knew about me. I wouldn't put it past Cheryl to keep him in the dark as well. How humiliating.

My thoughts wandered to Paul. I wondered what he was doing at that moment. Was he staring at himself in a mirror, too? Contemplating his life's decisions? Probably not. He was probably with his ex. Or girlfriend. The one he left me for. Maybe she was his wife now. The thought made my stomach turn.

I lowered my eyes. I guess I wasn't as healed from Paul as I had thought I was. Why did wounds take so long to close? I thought about him less than I used to. The incessant melancholy was gone, aside from a random bout of it here and there. But the feeling of a great loss? The empty spot? The 'what could've been'? It still lingered, clinging to the fringes. I feared it may last forever.

The desire to date, to meet people—men people—it just wasn't present yet. Brock had just been conveniently available at the right, or perhaps wrong, time. He wasn't sought after. He had just shown up, and I had accepted him into my life because...because...well, just because.

I dried my hands and went back to our table. I was relieved when, upon my return, Cheryl was still sitting alone.

"Cheryl, can we just get out of here," I said.

"Finish your drink. I ordered you another one. If he's not here by the time you're done, we'll go."

I picked up my drink and downed it in one gulp. It felt like someone lit a match and dropped it down my throat. I slammed the glass on the table and exited the diner. Cheryl came out a minute later.

"You may be the only person I know more stubborn than me," she said.

"I don't need a man, Cheryl."

"You're right. You don't. No woman *needs* a man."

"Then why are you trying to find one for me?"

"Needing and wanting are two very different things."

"I don't want a man either," I said.

Cheryl laughed. "That's a lie."

"No, it's not."

Cheryl stepped toward me, her eyes level with mine. "Why did you almost marry Brock?"

Her question threw me. Never before had Cheryl ever asked me anything about Brock. On the rare occasions when I mentioned him in her presence, she appeared indifferent or bored.

"I...I don't...know," I stammered.

"Yes, you do," Cheryl said, keeping her eyes drilled into mine. "You almost married him because you *want* someone. It's human nature, Kadie, I get it. Brock's problem is he's a dial tone. You faked it as long as you could, but ultimately, you knew not to settle for someone so...vanilla."

I opened my mouth to argue, to offer a scathing rebuttal in a vain attempt to retain some dignity, but I couldn't. Cheryl's critique stung, but it was accurate.

"Well, what about you, Cheryl? Why don't you have a man?"

"For the same reason you don't," she answered, and for a brief moment, I sensed a shred of vulnerability within Cheryl. She looked away for a beat and blinked hard as if trying to suppress some tears, but I think I may have imagined it. I don't believe Cheryl capable of emotion. "But don't fret about me," she said. "I have ways of fulfilling my needs."

"Yeah? Like what?"

Cheryl smiled. Any vulnerability she showed a moment ago had vanished. "Let's not get too personal," she said.

"Too personal?" I scoffed. "You just tried setting me up."

"Yeah. I tried setting you up with someone who is the opposite of Brock. You're welcome."

"Opposite of Brock, huh? You barely know this guy."

"I barely knew you when I gave you this job. I'm an excellent judge of character." Cheryl offered one last all-knowing smile and then started down the road.

"So now what?" I called after her.

"Let's go get lobster."

***

"What are you doing next Sunday evening?" Denise's asked. I hadn't even meant to answer my phone. I picked it up to see who was calling and accidentally hit the answer button.

"I'm going to bed early. I'm heading to Maui on Monday, remember?"

"Oh, that's right! You poor thing," she replied, her voice soaked in sarcasm.

"I wasn't complaining. Also, don't be jealous. It makes you look fat," I quipped.

Really though, I wasn't as excited as I should have been. When Cheryl told me last month that she needed me overseeing a Maui resort renovation, I was more or less apathetic. I had been back from Maine for less than three months, and was just getting back into a routine, when Cheryl told me about the Maui project. I didn't mind the traveling my work required, but for some reason, I wasn't impressed or affected by the prospect of working in Maui for the next few months. It was going to be, in Cheryl's words, an "extensive project." It seemed that all projects lately were extensive.

"Blaugh! It doesn't take much to make me look fat nowadays," Denise whined. "And I still think I should come with you."

"You're welcome to come."

"You know I can't," she said. She didn't have to explain why, and I knew she was rubbing her eight-month pregnant belly.

"You can always come after," I said. "This project will take the rest of the year."

"I'm planning on it. Let me get this thing delivered, and then give me a month or two to lose some baby weight, and I'm on the first flight out."

I smiled, but silently I wondered how much Denise is too much Denise on vacation? We'd definitely need separate rooms.

"So, about next Sunday," she continued. "Do you remember that Kurt McCarthy reading a couple years back?"

"Yeah, I remember," I said. "I wish I could forget."

"Right...sorry. Of course you remember."

"What about it?" I was anxious to get off the phone now, feeling reluctant to find out where this was going.

"Well, if you remember McCarthy never showed."

"Yeah, I recall your disappointment," I replied.

"Well, he's coming back for another reading. He's going to read from his new book."

"He wrote another book?"

"It hasn't even been released yet. It's all very mysterious and exciting!" Her infatuation with McCarthy hadn't waned since he stood her, and the rest of Chicago, up. The people who receive one's loyalty always baffled me.

"Well, good for you, Denise. Maybe you'll finally get your chance with him!" I teased. "However, that big bump that you're sporting may get in the way of your love-at-first-sight fantasy."

"Shoot! Do you think he'll notice?" Denise asked.

"Not if you wear that dark green, low-cut blouse you wore last week. Trust me, he won't be looking at your belly!"

"Oh no! Are they that big?" She was pretending to be mortified, but I knew she was enjoying her new and improved chest, as I'm sure Clay was as well.

"Yes. They are."

"The perks of being pregnant, huh?"

"Well, let me know if it's true love. Or if he even shows this time," I said in a vain attempt at ending the call before she got to what I feared she was getting to.

"You're not off the hook. You're coming with me."

And there it was. The invite I was fearing. "Why?"

"Because you're my sister, and I love you. And it's your duty, remember?"

"Take Bridge and Sam. I don't think I'm up for it."

"They're coming, too. We're all going. McCarthy is giving a free ticket to everyone who was at the last reading." She was so smitten. "You know, to make it right. It's very generous, don't you think?"

"Yes. What chivalry."

She ignored my sarcasm. "So you're coming."

"Denise...do I have to? Kurt McCarthy reminds me of Paul, and I don't want to spend the evening thinking of Paul."

Denise took a dramatic beat before answering: "Okay, I understand."

I groaned. "Denise..."

"Kadie, I understand. It's not a big deal."

Yup. She was pouting. I'm sure she did sympathize with my pain on some level, but right now, she was pouting.

"It's just..." she hesitated. Here we go. "You'll never move on if you're still hung up on the past. How can you ever find peace in the present, or happiness in your future, if you're still dwelling on something that will never happen? You're never going to find happiness because you're not even trying. You won't allow yourself to because you're still holding on to things that you need to release."

"Ouch."

"Well, it's true, Kadie. You know it is."

She was right. I knew I needed to let go of Paul, but...how? Why in the hell was he still a part of me after all this time? When you take into consideration the brief amount of time we spent together, it made absolutely no sense. Yet— it made perfect sense.

"Come with me, pleeeease? You shouldn't let him, or anyone, have this much control over you. Own your own life."

"I do own my life," was my weak rebuttal. I knew how lame it sounded as I was saying it, but I had no other argument. She was right. I was lame. "You're right. I know I need to move on."

"Come this weekend. It's a small step in the right direction."

"What? Doing something I don't want to do?" I replied, sounding a bit more irritated than I meant to.

"No," she sounded hurt. "Doing something that is going to force you to push back at your fears and make you stronger. Doing something you're scared of—even something this small. It's a step away from those shackles you've bound yourself to." The hurt that was in her voice was turning into anger. "I mean, God, Kadie, you're barely living! It's like you've become a...a...a robot."

I was stunned. She switched tones fast. Pregnant women can sure keep you on your toes. Despite myself, I started crying. A healthy dose of reality can do that to a person. I covered my mouth to stifle my sobs. Her sudden and intense veracity caught me off guard. I was so stupid and lost. Denise was right. I think somewhere along the way I'd given up on living and just settled on existing.

Denise heard my muffled sobs through the line. "Oh, Kadie. I'm so sorry. I shouldn't be so harsh. I just…care about you so much. I'm sick of seeing you so absent. So despondent. I guess I just want you back," her voice faltered.

After taking a few moments to regain my composure, for some insane reason, I suddenly found this whole scene very funny. Hilarious, actually. I started giggling, quietly at first, then harder. Life was such a silly, goddamn circus!

"What in the ever-loving hell?" Denise blurted. "Is this it? Have you officially lost your mind? Do we need to have an intervention?"

"Isn't that what this is?"

"Is it working?"

"Yeah, I think it is."

"So…I'll pick you up at six?"

"Sure."

"Wear that black dress that shows off your legs. Clay says it's a winner. Oh—and wear your heels!"

"It's a *book* reading Denise, and *eww!* *Clay says it's a winner?* What the hell?

"Yeah, yeah. But you never know. Heels! Don't forget!" I could see her pointing her finger at me through the phone.

Jesus! What did people have against my flats? They're sensible!

Chapter 18

I was seven floors up, staring out the window of Zoe's office at a building across the street. Most office views in New York consist of seeing other buildings with views of other buildings. Everyone tries to get higher to see past the glass and metal of their neighbors, but only so many offices can fit at the top. Zoe had another thirty stories to go until she reached the apex. On the street below, pedestrians hustled along the crowded sidewalks. Everyone was always in a hurry in New York, getting to places they did not want to be. I missed Maine.

"This is the best thing you have ever written, Paul. This will be your comeback."

I turned and looked at Zoe. She had my manuscript opened and resting on her legs. Her feet were ostensibly propped up on her desk, while she chewed on the end of an overpriced cigar. I had never been to her office before. She was trying to appear serious and dignified, a Manhattan woman who played by her own rules. She was failing miserably. The entire act was for my benefit. Zoe took her job seriously, but I'd wager she'd never had her feet on her desk before this moment. She borrowed the cigar from her boss. It was all for dramatic effect, a parody of the type of people neither of us liked. Of all the agents in New York, I was glad Zoe was mine. I looked at her for a moment, evaluated her performance, and shook my head. She laughed and dropped her feet to the floor and tossed the cigar in the trash.

"Comeback from where?" I asked.

"Come on, Paul. You and I both know *Trainride* was a train wreck." Zoe smirked at her joke.

"It was my best-selling work."

"It was a fluff piece. It pleased everybody."

"Not the—"

"—except the critics," she said, dropping my manuscript on her desk. I turned back to the window. I noticed a man sitting on a bench across the street.

He watched everyone hurry past him with a bemused smile, baffled as to where everyone was going and why they needed to get there in such a hurry. His countenance contained an unspoken joy, which I envied. What wasn't to envy about the man who can sit on a bench in the heart of New York without any place to go? If he was still on the bench when I left, I'd ask to sit next to him and offer to buy him lunch.

"I know you don't want to talk about it," Zoe said, "but I have to bring it up."

"I know what you're going to ask," I said. And I did. She wanted me to do a reading. "And I agree. Reschedule Chicago," I told her. "Give everyone who attended last time a ticket. Free of charge."

"Are you serious?" Zoe asked surprised.

"Yeah, I'm serious. I owe it to my fans to explain what happened that night. To explain where I've been for the last two years. This book will do that."

"Yeah, it will. That's a brilliant idea, actually."

I smiled and shook my head, dismissing the compliment but still touched that she offered it. "You don't need to kiss my ass, Zoe. I already agreed to do the reading."

Zoe laughed. "I appreciate you not fighting me on this," she said. "But we can't give away the tickets for free. All the people that had tickets for the first reading were reimbursed."

"I know."

"So, we don't need to give them a free one. The whole point of doing the reading is to sell tickets. That is how we make money. That, and book sales. We'll have a kiosk at the reading where people can buy a copy."

"Everyone who had a ticket for Chicago gets another ticket," I said evenly and then added: "*and* a free copy of the book."

"What? No, that can't happen."

"It has to."

"Why?"

"Because it's the right thing to do."

"Paul…"

"This is how I'm going to make things right," I said. Zoe wanted to protest, but I cut her off. "You do this for me, and I'll do a nationwide tour. I'll do signings. Interviews. Whatever you want. I will submit to whatever prostitution gigs you get me."

I looked at Zoe's reflection in the office building's glass. She stared at the back of my head, putting the pieces together. She was on the verge of a breakthrough. The knowledge seeped in. She had it. Ta-da! She shook her head and smiled. She got out from behind her desk and came to my side. "You think if she has to buy a ticket, she won't come," Zoe said. "Is that it?"

"That may have something to do with it," I said. "She walked out of my first reading, remember?"

"She thinks you've lost your edge."

"Have I?"

"You did, but this book brought it back."

"Her sister is a fan. She'll likely have to talk Kadie into coming."

"If she does come, how do you think she'll react?"

"I don't know. But I never got a chance to explain. This is my chance."

We were silent for a moment, then Zoe asked, "So why Elizabeth?"

"What?"

"In your book. Kadie is Elizabeth, right? You changed her name from Kadie to Elizabeth."

"Yeah."

"So why Elizabeth?"

"Her favorite book is *Pride and Prejudice*."

"Interesting."

"Is it?"

"Yeah. She hates clichés, but her favorite book is riddled with them."

I smiled. "She recognizes her own irony."

"I'm surprised you didn't choose something…closer to home."

"Like what?"

"I don't know," Zoe thought for a moment. "Daisy."

"Daisy?"

"Yeah. From *The Great Gatsby.*"

"Things didn't end well for Gatsby."

"Yeah, and they may not end well for you either, but Gatsby is about a man trying to reclaim his past. It's more fitting, don't you think?"

"Yeah. Maybe," I said.

Zoe opened her mouth to say something else, thought better of it, and closed it. She was biting her tongue for my benefit. She never bit her tongue for anyone. "What?" I asked.

"Nothing."

"Don't do that. If you have something to say, say it."

"It's just…I guess I don't understand."

"What don't you understand?"

"It was just three days, Paul. Why is it so hard for you to let go of someone you only knew for seventy-two hours?"

I understood Zoe's confusion. The more I thought of Kadie and the hold she still had over me, the more embarrassed I became of myself. Perhaps I'd romanticized the whole thing. If I bumped into her on the street, chances are she wouldn't even recognize me. I'd have to explain to her who I was and the weekend we shared two years ago. She'd slowly start to remember, but the memory would remain hazy and distant. I was just another guy in a long line of guys who tried and failed to make an impression on her. That was the most probable reality, and I was in complete resistance to it. What did I need to do to compartmentalize her the same way I assumed she did me?

"Do you remember after *Rearview Mirror* sold a million copies we went to Six Flags?" I asked.

"Sure."

"What ride was your favorite?"

"The blue roller coaster. The one you called the 'penis tickler.'"

"Of course," I said, smiling at the memory. "We rode it at least ten times. Why was that your favorite ride?"

"The drop at the very first. You climb above the entire park and then it just…drops you." Zoe emulated the movement with her hand and even punctuated it with a *whoooooossshhh!* as she brought her arm down.

"That ride is fifty-five seconds, and the drop is two-and-a-half," I said.

"How do you know that?"

"I looked it up."

"Why?"

"I'm not sure. But that's not the point."

"What is the point?"

"We spent ten hours at that park riding different rides, yet only two and a half seconds of them made an impression," I explained. I'm sure Zoe already caught the metaphor, but I still had the urge to clarify it. "I've been alive for almost forty years doing all the meaningless tasks that come with being alive. Forty years, Zoe, but those three days are the only days that I felt alive. She's my two-and-a-half second drop."

Zoe considered my logic and nodded. We stood silently for a minute before Zoe spoke again. "Can I ask you something else?"

"Sure."

"Why didn't you go back to the diner that last night in Maine? The night you were supposed to meet that woman and her friend?"

The final chapter in my book tells of the encounter I had with Cheryl—the hotel renovator that hijacked my pie. After I left her at the diner, I went back to the beach house and spent the rest of the night finishing my novel. My book claims I never returned to the diner the next evening because I knew that the entire enterprise would be futile. In fact, that is how I ended the book. The last line reads: "I didn't return to the diner because I knew that a life without Elizabeth was futile."

The ending was only ninety-nine percent true though. I *did* return to the diner the next night. My book was finished, and I felt good about it. It served as a catharsis. A purging. A cleansing of Kadie and Lisa that would allow me to put my past in my past. Or so I thought. I knew it was time for me to reassemble my life's pieces, so I resolved to meet Cheryl and her friend.

I was about thirty minutes late (I couldn't find the right outfit, and yes, I know how that sounds), but I figured they would still be there. I got to the diner, put my hand on the door, and froze. I tried for over a minute to summon the strength to push myself through, but I couldn't do it. The restaurant's tinted windows shielded my view to the inside. It occurred to me Cheryl or her friend may spot me stalling outside and believe something was wrong with the door, forcing one of them to rise and come to my aid. I turned and quickly walked away. When I arrived back at the beach house, I packed my bag, and left the following morning on the earliest flight.

"I did go back...somewhat," I said. "I got as far as the front door, but I never went inside."

"Why?"

"Too afraid, I guess. Between Kadie and Lisa, these last two years have scarred me."

"Scarred skin is stronger than unblemished skin," Zoe said.

"That a proverb?"

"No. That's just me," Zoe said.

"Wise."

"Remember it. You can put it in your next book."

I laughed.

"I love you, Paul, but I want you to promise that if this reading doesn't reunite you with Kadie, the next time you get the chance, you'll go through the door."

After a pause, I managed to give her the promise.

Zoe and I stared out the window for another minute. Neither of us spoke because neither of us needed to. Zoe put her head on my shoulder. "You're a good man, Paul Stevens Kurt McCarthy."

I turned and kissed the top of Zoe's head. "I never apologized for having bad sperm. I'm sorry. I wanted to give you and Charlie a baby."

"That's okay. Your bad sperm led to your greatest work."

"I've never looked at it that way."

"That's what I'm for. I help you see the silver linings."

Chapter 19

I stood in front of my full-length mirror appraising my appearance. I was okay with it. I was more than okay with it. I felt alive. I felt...beautiful.

I was wearing a standard, yet versatile, black dress—appropriate for almost any occasion. It was just short enough to elicit a second (maybe even a third) glance, but long enough to leave plenty to the imagination. My skin had a healthy nutmeg glow, and my freckles popped, creating a youthful sparkle. My brown eyes looked bright and alive. No longer dark caverns of nothingness. In fact, they looked almost optimistic, ready for whatever may come.

Outside, Denise impatiently honked. The optimism I experienced excluded the actual evening I was about to have. Truthfully, I had zero hope for tonight being anything more than an enjoyable (one can only hope) night with my sister and friends. But my countenance now carried a newborn confidence that something good, and nourishing, may be on the horizon.

Since my conversation with Denise, I had been working on adopting a new and improved outlook on life. I had shifted my focus to things that had a positive effect on me. You know, all the things those self-help books say to do.

I took one last look at the woman in the mirror. I smiled, almost shyly, at her.

"Holy Hotness!" Denise whistled her approval as I jumped in the car. "You've got some nice-ass legs on you, girlie. I've always been jealous of them."

"Oh, please. What do you have to complain about?" Denise was all legs. It ran in the family.

"Yours are...shapely. Way more shapely than mine." She put the car in gear.

"Your legs are perfect." I waved her off. "I've never seen such an adorable pregnant woman, who, I might add..." I pointed at her feet. "...still wears three-inch heels."

"Comfort is overrated. I *will* be beautiful!" she announced dramatically. I laughed and rolled my eyes. "Speaking of heels…" she auspiciously eyed my feet, "good job."

I looked at the heels I had slipped on before heading out the door. "Did I have any other choice?"

"No, but you could've fought it, causing us both a bit of grief, and you chose not to. So good job. You look beautiful."

I smiled, and Denise pulled away from the curb with a lovelorn haze plastered on her face.

Chapter 20

The hall was crowded, but it was evident many were not coming. My exodus two years earlier may have added to my enigmatic persona and helped sell books, but in the process, I lost some fans. They felt slighted and indignant. Even a free ticket was not enough to garner their forgiveness. If online comments were any indication, then most questioned the manufactured pneumonia story Zoe used to explain why I walked out of the reading. They were wise not to believe it, and they would soon learn my abandonment was impulsive, not methodical. They would then have to decide if I still deserved their loyalty.

Zoe was in the lobby looking for the right place to set up an autograph desk along with the fifteen hundred newly printed books promised to everyone at the end of the night. She tried convincing me to pose for a life-sized cardboard display of me holding my book; I shot the idea down almost as quickly as she had proposed it. I think she knew I'd never agree, but she wanted to test the limits of my newfound generosity.

From backstage, I scavenged the audience looking for Kadie. I struggled to formulate a mental image of her appearance. A foggy, vague picture seeped into my consciousness, but the finer things about her that made her unique would not fully materialize. It had only been two years, but I wasn't sure what to look for amongst the crowd. Maybe she had changed her hairstyle. Maybe she gained or lost weight. Or maybe she decided a Kurt McCarthy reading just wasn't worth her time, and I was searching for a ghost. That was my greatest fear, and it seemed the most probable. Zoe was able to offer a free ticket to everyone who had originally purchased one, but she had no control over the seating. Kadie wasn't in the seat she had been in two years ago. Neither was Denise. An elderly couple was occupying their seats.

I checked my watch. The reading was scheduled for seven. I had six minutes…or maybe longer? Did book readings start on time? Concerts never did. Part of the rock star persona was not caring about schedules. Were authors expected to follow the same protocol? If I started at seven and people expected me to start later, would they be annoyed with my punctuality? If I delayed the reading, would people be put-off by my tardiness?

My head was spinning.

I couldn't find Kadie.

My shirt itched.

My tie was too tight.

My pants were bunching.

I wanted to flee again. I turned and ran smack into Zoe.

"Whoa," Zoe said. "Where are you off to?"

"I can't do this," I said.

"Oh shit."

"I don't think she's coming."

"Breathe, Paul. Breathe."

I breathed. I didn't feel better.

Zoe took me by the shoulders. "This isn't just about Kadie," Zoe said. "This is about your book. This is about your fans. Kadie may not be out there, but a thousand other people are."

"I…I…" I couldn't speak.

"Settle down, Paul," Zoe said. "Close your eyes and take a deep breath." I did as instructed. I felt a little better. I opened my eyes and looked at Zoe. "You okay?" she asked.

"Yeah…I guess."

"Are you ready to do this?"

"No."

"Well…what do you need?"

"I…don't…know."

"You're going on stage in two minutes."

"So, I'm not a rock star?"

"What?"

"Nothing."

"I need to know that you're okay."

I took another slow, deep breath. "I am," I resolved. I could do this.

"Say it."

"Say what?"

"Say you're okay."

I said it. Zoe studied me and nodded. "Okay, I'm going out there now. I'll introduce you, and then you're on. If I turn around and you're not standing here, I'll...I'll..."

"What?"

"I'm thinking."

"Kill me?"

"Worse."

"What's worse than that?"

"I'll sign you up for Dancing with the Stars."

"Jesus."

"I mean it, Paul. Don't mess with me tonight."

I smiled weakly and nodded.

Zoe straightened my tie and brushed my shoulders clean. She gave me a hug, another brief overview, and then stepped out onto the stage.

The lights dimmed, and scattered applause greeted her. A spotlight shone down on the podium. Zoe arrived at center stage, stood behind the podium and spoke into the microphone: "Good evening." She paused, expecting the hall to erupt into anticipatory applause, but no one stirred. She cleared her throat, stole a quick glance in my direction, and continued: "Thank you all for being here tonight, and I can assure you Kurt has not left the building." A few people laughed, but it was evident Zoe expected a warmer reception. If the cold reaction unnerved her, she hid it well. She continued: "My name is Zoe Salinger. I'm Kurt's agent. Kurt has written a new novel. It is loosely autobiographical, and it is, in my estimation, his best work to date. He will be reading from it tonight, and as a sign of appreciation, everyone in attendance will receive a complimentary copy of the novel." She paused so everyone could process her generosity. A few people clapped; most sat still. "You can claim your copy at one of the three kiosks located in the lobby. Also of note, following the reading, Kurt will hold a signing on the north side of the lobby." Zoe glanced again in my direction to make certain I hadn't fled. She smiled and then said: "Ladies and gentlemen, please welcome to the stage, for his first public appearance, Kurt McCarthy."

A modest applause greeted me as I stepped onto the stage. The spotlight followed my trek to the podium, blinding me from identifying anyone in the audience. Intermingled with the routine cheering, were some scattered boos. Evidently, some fans had returned mainly to express their distaste for my earlier premature departure. Zoe waited for me at the podium. When I arrived, she gave my arm a comforting squeeze and then exited to stage right. The applause dissipated, and in the momentary silence, a few more boos filled the hall.

"I deserve that," I said into the microphone. A few people laughed, and then a few more. Gradually, a crescendo of laughter filled the hall. The tension was broken.

My book and a bottled water were placed beneath the podium. I removed the cap from the water and took a quick drink. I wanted more but resisted for fear that it may cause an uncomfortable need to urinate. I put the book on the podium and opened it. My words stared back at me. I cleared my voice and said, "This should have happened two years ago, and I apologize that it didn't. This book explains why. My hope is that you'll understand, and maybe you'll be willing to forgive me." I paused and then looked down at my book and read: "*Three Days* by Kurt McCarthy. Chapter One: Jaden is not my daughter. The paternity test…"

Chapter 21

My mind raced as I tried to grasp what was happening. Just as it did in my car on that haunting day in Las Vegas, my body numbed—starting from the extremities and working toward my core. As if Paul (or Kurt) pushed the rewind button on an old VCR player, the memories of the last two years played before me. Were my ears deceiving me? My eyes too? Was I dreaming? Everything was foggy. My heart pounded, and my stomach was in knots. My palms were sweating and my hands shaking. Denise kept asking me questions, poking me and shaking my arm, trying to snap me back into the world. My mouth was moving. I was trying to respond, but no sound emerged. The fog closed in around me; like the light at the end of a tunnel, all I saw was Kurt...er...Paul on the stage, reading. Reading his book that was telling our story.

Everything else around me, us, was just darkness. Nothingness. I listened intently to every word he spoke. Then he stopped. He closed his book and reached down and retrieved a water bottle. He unscrewed the cap and took a drink. The hall erupted into applause. I returned to my surroundings. People, some with tears streaking down their cheeks, were getting to their feet. They were crying from my story, *our* story. I was touched and angry. I felt betrayed yet...honored. My breath was sucked from my lungs. I turned to Denise. She was talking to me, but the applause drowned out her words. I grabbed her purse from off the floor and dug through the contents looking for her keys. I found them. Then I fled.

Chapter 22

"...I didn't return to the diner because I knew that a life without Elizabeth was futile."

I closed my book, ran my fingers over the cover and looked up. I had been so absorbed in the reading that I had momentarily forgotten where I was. The spotlight still shielded the audience from me. Their silence was suffocating. For a moment I thought maybe they had all sneaked out during the reading as some sort of synchronized payback. I had nothing else to say, so I said nothing. I glanced backstage, looking to Zoe for assistance. She smiled and wiped her eyes. I turned back to the hall, not sure how to proceed when, unbidden, the audience erupted into applause. Relieved, I retrieved the water beneath the podium and downed the bottle. I stepped out from the podium and bowed. The crowd cheered louder. A few spectators got to their feet.

With the spotlight no longer obstructing my view, I could see the crowd more clearly. Toward the back, I thought I saw Kadie. She wore a perplexed expression. Her hands rested in her lap, ostensibly not applauding. I squinted and stepped to the edge of the stage to better put her in sight. Before she could materialize, the people in front of her stood and obstructed my view. The entire hall got to its feet. I kept my eyes locked on the area where I thought I saw Kadie. I noticed an obvious gap in the sea of people in the area where she sat. I stood on tiptoes and craned my head, but it was no use.

I turned and glanced backstage. Zoe was making her way toward me; her makeup was smeared, but she looked happy. I turned back just in time to see the mysterious woman that may have been Kadie, slip out the back entrance and out the hall.

Chapter 23

I broke countless driving laws as I sped haphazardly away from the conference hall. Tears stung my eyes and ruined my mascara. My hands shook uncontrollably. My ears rang, thinking of the words he'd written to document the last two years. I was on a roller coaster. All my physical abilities and sensible thinking skills were temporarily impeded and not to be trusted—I gave all my focus to my breathing.

Get oxygen in. Body needs oxygen.

My cell buzzed. I ignored it. I knew it was Denise.

It rang again. And then again. I finally answered.

"Kadie!" Denise's voice fired at me from the other end. "Are you okay? Where did you go? Holy shit! Holy… SHIT! Where *are* you?"

"I'm…" I looked around, trying to get an idea of where I was, but nothing looked familiar. "Denise. I don't know where the hell I am!" The irony that that was true on so many levels was not lost on me.

"Pull over, sweetie. Take some deep breaths and get ahold of yourself," she instructed, her voice softening. I did. Again, breaking about five more laws as I pulled off the road.

I sat silently for a moment and tried to reclaim my self-control. When I attempted to finally talk, all I muttered was, "Paul…he's Kurt…he's …*Paul.*"

Denise exhaled deeply. "Yeah…I mean. Wow. This is one hell of a doozy. You're the main character in a Kurt McCarthy novel, Kadie. It's a beautiful love story. And it's real! It's…a fairytale."

"Yeah…" I shook my head. *I'm such a cliché,* I thought to myself. I remembered the very first conversation that I had with Paul about clichés. I remembered voicing my distaste for them. I scoffed at the irony.

Denise's voice snapped me out of my reverie.

"Wow, Kadie," she paused for a moment, "or should I say…*Elizabeth?*" she teased. She had obviously picked up on my "fictional" pseudonym.

"I can't believe…" I shook my head. "He wrote a *book* about me, Denise."

"I know, sweetie. An amazing book."

"Should I feel honored or betrayed?"

"I…I don't…I don't know. Both?"

I laughed, not because anything was funny, but because of the absurdity of life. "Where the hell do I go from here?"

"Literally or metaphorically?" Denise asked. It was a valid question.

"Both, I guess."

"I think you know."

I did, but I wasn't sure I wanted to. "I'm not ready to face him yet."

"I get that. But you can't just let this go. For two years everything was working to keep you two apart. It seems the stars have aligned for you, Kadie."

"This is unreal."

"It isn't. You just have to allow yourself to feel what you're experiencing. You don't need to rush back here now. Take your time and collect yourself. Come back when you're ready."

When I'm ready? I was ready for two years. Then, once I take the first step to unready myself, here comes Paul. He comes steamrolling back into my life with a book starring me. I dropped my phone and screamed into the night. I clutched the steering wheel and started laugh-sobbing. Denise's voice rose from the floor asking if I was okay. I picked up my phone.

"Hey."

"Hey," she said. "Are you okay?"

"No. But I will be."

"Yeah, you will."

Neither of us spoke for a minute; My own thoughts racked me, and Denise knew I needed her to stay on the line even though I wanted her to stay silent. After a beat, I spoke into the phone: "Thank you, Denise," I said. "You're…you're amazing. Your baby is one lucky kiddo."

"Shut it. No gushy stuff," she said trying to sound severe, but the huskiness in her voice gave her away. "Go find your happy, Kadie. You deserve it."

"I love you."

"I love you, too," she sniffled. Then she cleared her throat in an attempt to brush aside her brief emotional display. "In the meantime," she said, "I have to get in line, and that is going to require some running. And I don't run very well right now, so I'm going to hang up."

Chapter 24

I don't know how she managed it, but Denise was first in line. I emerged from backstage and our eyes locked immediately. I smiled nervously; she leveled me with her eyes and shook her head. I looked away, scanning the line of people behind her. No sign of Kadie. I started toward the desk and looked back at Denise. She still wore her ambivalent expression. I started shuffling through the different routes our conversation may take, and then I paused. Upon first seeing her, Denise's face looked fuller and more vibrant. Now that she was within twenty feet, I understood why. She was pregnant. I took in her protruding belly and smiled. I stepped around the desk and opened my arms. She dropped her façade and accepted my embrace.

"Congratulations," I said in her ear.

"Thanks," she said and then stepped back and punched me in the arm. A few pedestrians gasped. "You're an asshole," she said.

"I know," I nodded and massaged my arm.

"It never crossed your mind to tell us who you were while we were discussing your book?"

"I was afraid she wouldn't want to see me again if she knew who I was."

Denise scrutinized me. "That's fair, I guess. She wasn't your biggest fan."

"Did she come tonight?"

"Yes."

I scanned the line again, thinking I must have overlooked her.

"She's not here, Paul…or…Kurt…what do I call you?"

"Call me Paul," I said. "She left?"

"She had to."

I was deflated. "Why?"

"Tonight was a lot to take in, Paul," she said. "Kadie spent two years getting over you, and then you came crashing back into her life. And as a character in one of your books. I mean…wow!"

"I tried to explain," I said hopelessly. "I came back here to explain."

"Yeah. I think she noticed."

"Does she hate me?" I asked. My voice broke under the weight of the question.

Denise considered my question before answering. "No, she doesn't hate you. She loves you."

"What should I do?"

Denise shook her head, bothered that I needed to ask something that was apparently clear to her but eclipsed me. "I don't know where the truth ends and the fiction begins in your book, but if you love her half as much as your book claims, then you know what you need to do."

Her words rattled around in my head, ricocheting here and there and waking me to the obvious. I was overcome with the notion to once again flee. To escape the signing and scour the city searching for Kadie. I was done settling for safe. I wanted the three days I'd spent in Chicago with Kadie to be the rest of my life. I wouldn't leave the city until Kadie, face-to-face, either told me she'd give me a change or to go to hell. Anything in between wouldn't suffice.

"I think this line is getting anxious," Denise said, bringing me back to the moment. My eyes followed the line of people and saw that it extended out the door. I didn't want to keep people waiting, and the sooner I got through the signing, the sooner I could chase Kadie.

I went around the desk and sat down. To my right was a stack of books. I took the top book, opened the front cover, wrote a brief note, and signed my name. I handed the book over to Denise. She read my inscription and nodded approval.

"Make one out to Kadie too," she said.

I paused for a moment, not sure what inscription would be appropriate. I was struck with an idea. I took another book from the stack. I opened it and wrote:

Kadie, "Our scars help us know that our past was for real."
– Paul

I closed the book and handed it to Denise. "No," she said, refusing to take it. "You give it to her when you see her." She turned and started for the door, but then stopped and turned back to me. "By the way, this may be your best work," she said. I smiled and looked away for a moment, and when I turned back, Denise was lost in the crowd.

***

The bar had twelve customers who were being served by a lone bartender. Kadie wasn't there. I stood in the entry holding the signed copy of my book and surveyed everyone twice. This was my first stop. Next, I would try her house, then Denise's. If she wasn't there, I'd enlist Denise for a list of other destinations Kadie frequented. I was preparing for a long night. I turned to leave when the bartender, watching me stand in the entry, asked if I needed help with something.

"No, I'm just looking for someone."

"I know you, don't I?"

I gave the bartender another overview and recognized him as the same one that was working two years ago. "I was in here about two years ago," I said. "I think you were here."

"You left a book, right?" he said.

"Yeah. For Kadie Park."

"Yeah," he said. "She came in a few months ago."

I stepped to the bar. "She did?"

"Yeah."

"Did you give her the book?"

"I tried. I went in the kitchen to grab it for her, but when I came back out, she had already left."

"So, she never saw what I wrote?"

"Wrote?"

"On the inside cover," I explained. "I wrote her a message. She never saw it?"

"No, man. Like I said, I went to the kitchen to grab it, and when I came back, she was gone."

My body ached with the knowledge of how close Kadie had come to discovering the truth. "She never came back?" I asked.

"No."

"Do you still have the book?"

"Yeah, it's in the kitchen," he said. "Do you want it?"

"Please."

He entered the kitchen and returned a moment later carrying the book. He set the book on the bar in front of me. I opened the front cover and found my inscription. I closed the cover and placed my other book on top of it.

"Every time you come in here you're carrying books," the bartender quipped. "Can I get you a drink?"

"No, I can't stay. I'm on a…quest of sorts."

"Suit yourself," he said.

"When she was in here, did she…say anything?"

"What do you mean?"

"I don't know. I'm trying to find her. I feel like I'm so close, and I'm just missing the clues, you know?"

"Well, last I seen her was a few months ago. She came in, ordered a drink, and then left in a hurry. She didn't even say goodbye."

"That was it?"

"Yeah."

"Okay. Thanks." I picked up my books to leave, but then put them back on the bar. I needed to use the bathroom. I determined my books would be safe unattended for a minute or two and made my way toward the glowing restroom sign in the rear of the bar.

Chapter 25

I parked Denise's car in her driveway and went inside. She was waiting by the front door.

"You owe me $47 for my Uber," she said.

I fished in my wallet and pulled out three twenties. I handed them to her and told her to keep the change. She studied me for a moment before reaching up and removing a strand of hair from my face.

"Do you know where he is?" she asked.

"I think so."

"Do you know what you're going to say?"

"No."

"Then don't say anything. Don't ruin the moment with words."

I nodded. "Did you see him?"

"Yeah. He signed my book."

"What did he say?"

"He loves you."

"He said that?"

"He didn't have to."

"What if he doesn't."

"He does. You heard what he wrote."

My chin quivered. I swallowed hard and fought the tears. "It's a beautiful story, isn't it?"

"Yeah," Denise said, her own voice breaking. "It really is."

"I should go," I said.

"Yeah. You should."

I turned to leave. Denise placed her hand on my shoulder. I turned back to her and she wrapped her arms around me. "Go get my man."

I shook my head and laughed. What kind of world was it where the man of my sister's dreams was in love with me?

***

The familiar smell of pizza and beer greeted me as I walked through the door. I searched the bar. Paul wasn't there, but Ray was.

He stood at his post behind the counter looking back at me with an unreadable expression. This was not what I had expected. I'd expected the fabricated gruffness I'd received the last time I visited, showing his disapproval of my long absence, or a friendly welcome. But instead, his expression was more...shock and confusion.

"Hey, Kadie," he said.

I meandered over to him. "Hey, Ray." I forced a smile. "How's it going?"

"It's...going," he said. "Interesting that you came in here tonight," he said.

"Why's that?"

"This guy was in here looking for you." Ray gave the bar an overview, searching. "He's been here a couple times hoping to find you."

My heart leapt. "How long ago was he here?"

"Two minutes, maybe."

"Did he leave a message?" I was frantic.

"No, just a book."

"A book? What book?"

"Look, I tried to give it to you last time, remember? When you came in a while back? I said I had something for you and then you were gone when I came back."

My mind was racing. Holy shit. Whatever Ray was going to get was from Paul. "He left me a book?"

"Yeah, then he brought in another one when he came in tonight. This guy has a thing for books, I guess," he snorted.

"Yeah. Listen, you don't know where he went, do you?"

"There!" He pointed to the end of the bar. "There they are. Those are the books. Looks like he left them both."

My eyes followed Ray's outstretched finger where I spotted two books sitting at the end of the bar.

"Those are for you, I think."

In a trance, I floated to the books, horrified and excited at what I might find. How long ago had he left? Could I still catch him? I looked back at Ray for answers. But he was talking with another customer. I picked up the first book. With a trembling hand, I opened the front cover and noticed an inscription.

Chapter 26

I was washing my hands when I heard the music in the bar change. It seemed abrupt, as if someone went to the jukebox and decided something better needed to fill the bar instead of what had been playing. But I knew this wasn't the case because the bar didn't have a jukebox. It did have the decrepit piano in the corner, but it sat vacant when I'd entered the bathroom less than a minute ago. This was a moot point however, because the new music wasn't a piano melody. It was something familiar. Something that made me shut off the faucet while I tried to place where I had previously heard the tune. The recognition seeped in. It was the Eric Clapton song Kadie and I had danced to two years ago on the restaurant's patio. I craned my head and spotted a small speaker mounted in the corner of the bathroom. An employee must have switched the satellite radio station. I dried my hands and exited the bathroom.

She stood at the bar with my books opened in front of her. Her hair covered her face, but I knew it was her. I stood frozen to the ground and watched her. She brought her hand up and tucked her hair behind her ear. With her hair no longer obstructing my view, I recognized her delicate features as unmistakably her. My heart sank. A lone tear escaped her eye, got caught on the tip of her nose, and then fell to the page where she read my latest inscription to her.

She stood up straight, turned, and looked right at me. We stared at each other for a moment, both unable to process and understand that we were there, feet apart, looking into the eyes of the other. I approached her slowly, never losing sight of her for fear that if I looked away even for a moment, she may vanish. I reached her and took her hand in mine. Her hands were soft and familiar and reminded me of how she felt two years ago. I led her away from the counter and into the center of the empty bar.

Neither of us spoke; neither of us could. I took her in my arms, and she rested her head on my chest and pulled me closer to her. We held each other closely and swayed with the music until the song ended. We both stopped moving, but we refused to let the other go. She took her head from my chest and turned her tear-stained eyes to me. I opened my mouth to speak, but she shook her head, fearful I may ruin the moment by talking. I closed my mouth, and she put her head back on my chest.

From the corner of the bar, the piano player took his position and began playing a slow melody that entranced us both. I began to move to the music; she tightened her grip on me. When the song ended, another began. We danced to that one too, and every one that came after until the bar announced last call. It was then that Kadie looked up at me, her eyes warm and inviting and said, "I fly to Maui in the morning."

"Okay," I said. "Can I come?"

"Yeah, I think you'd better."

About the Authors

Felicia Case

Felicia Case was a public school teacher and college professor. Her passions were reading and running. Michael Wojciechowski is like her, only much less remarkable.

Michael Wojciechowski

Thank you so much for reading one of our **Literary Fiction** novels.
If you enjoyed our book, please check out our recommended title for your
next great read!

The Five Wishes by Mr. Murray McBride by Joe Siple

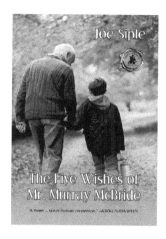

2018 Maxy Award "Book of the Year"

"A sweet...tale of human connection...will feel familiar to fans of Hallmark

movies." –*KIRKUS REVIEWS*

"An emotional story that will leave readers meditating on the life-saving
magic of kindness." –*Indie Reader*

CPSIA information can be obtained
at www.ICGtesting.com
Printed in the USA
JSHW010702271219
3202JS00003B/9